M000021461

ANYTIME,
ANYWHERE

GINA HOFFMAN

For my mom and all the women who encourage.

TABLE OF CONTENTS

NEW MEXICO SPRING, 2008
Mile marker?

"Freakin, frackin, fruck! No, not you, too. Don't let me down now. I need you to hang in there just a little longer. Please, please, please!"

Arianna's pleas fell on deaf ears as she guided her limping car to the side of the road. Her poor abused car could no more hear her than fix itself.

Giving in to despair, she thumped her head against the steering wheel. "How much more rubbish do I have to take? I've paid plenty of dues! I have a freaking degree! All I want is to earn a respectable living."

And right when she found the perfect job, she couldn't get to the interview on time. Arianna looked out on miles of blowing sand and scrubby cactus. Stuck in the middle of No-F-ingwhere, New Mexico, with a death knell to her dreams, a flat tire.

She jerked the cranky door open, yanked herself out of the car, slammed the door shut and proceeded to glare murderously at the offending piece of rubber. A car now with two flat tires because of course, her mind berated her, the spare was flat too.

After giving herself a few minutes to really hate where her life had taken her, Arianna mind grasped for what to do. First, the tire needed fixing. That meant a call to AAA. Reaching in her car for her member ID card, she remembered getting the lifetime membership on her 16th birthday from her Dad. She didn't appreciate how thoughtful the gift was until now.

"Thanks, Dad!" She placed her first two fingers on her lips, kissed them, then lifted them up toward the sky, smiling.

Crossing her fingers as she brought them back down, she looked at her phone, hoping to see that one bar of service still there. "YES!"

Dialing the number, she waited as it rang and rang, then was picked up by a harried woman. "AAA Roadside assistance. My mane is Nadine. How can I assist you?"

"Hello, Nadine. Yes, I have a flat tire and I need help."

"First, I'll need your membership number and then where the car is located."

Arianna recited the digits, then thought of all the unpleasant descriptions for her location but decided to keep it simple. "I'm halfway between Albuquerque and Santa Fe."

"Oh dear, I'm so sorry. It's going to be close to five hours before we can get to you. There's been a multiple car accident on the highway in the city."

"FIVE hours," she screeched, nearly dropping her phone.

"I'm afraid so," Nadine said, her false compassion doing nothing to comfort Arianna.

Arianna sighed, running her hand through her hair. "Okay, I'll keep my cell with me. Please call if anything changes. Yes, Okay. Bye."

Opening her contacts, she clicked on the number for the perfect job: assistant manager of a hunter-jumper stables outside Santa Fe.

She listened as the phone rang and a gruff male voice picked up on the other end. "Mr. Markus? This is Arianna. I've had some car trouble, but AAA is on the way. Is there any way we could reschedule the interview for later in the day, say 4:30 this afternoon?"

"Oh, I'm so sorry to hear that. But these things happen. Sure, we can reschedule for this afternoon, no problem."

She exhaled with relief. "I think that they will have me well on the way by then. Thanks, thanks a lot! I really appreciate this! You won't be sorry, I promise."

Disconnecting the phone, she drooped with relief against her car.

She reached up to absentmindedly twirl one of her diamond stud earrings, letting the familiar motion comfort her. A family heirloom she never took off, they were a gift from her mom and had been worn by the women in her family for many generations. Her parents had even speculated that the earrings were one of Louis-François Cartier's early creations. Cherished for their brilliance rather than size, they were cut in a rare and unique style for their time.

Arianna blew out her breath, already bored. Studying the surrounding landscape, she noticed a butte in the distance, a lone sentinel standing against the winds of the past. She slapped her hands against her thighs and pushed off her car. Hiking had always been a way to find beauty and peace in the most stressful situations. Her heart clenched. She'd started doing that a lot when her Dad was battling cancer.

When she needed a break from watching reruns of her dad's favorite National Geographic and classic movies on his hospital room TV, she'd grab the hiking pack and boots she kept in her car for these situations and go find a nearby trail. She looked down at her dress clothes, then reached for the trunk release. First she needed to change.

She glanced around the empty road and rolled her eyes at herself. Was she really worried about being seen in the buff way out here? She snorted and pulled off her shirt. After putting on a t-shirt, thin synthetic fabric cargo pants, and her hiking boots, she shivered from the crisp, cool spring morning air and reached for her jean jacket. She swept a finger across the small cupcake patch sewn on the collar point, a smile pulling up one corner of her mouth.

After Arianna had a particularly bad day, her mom had written her a note and placed it on a cupcake in the middle of the kitchen counter where she couldn't miss it.

Disappointments to a noble soul is what cold water is to burning metal, it strengthens, tempers, intensifies, but never destroys it!

It had been a nice thought but soon after, dad got sick and the continuous cash flow dwindled. She went from shopping at Bloomingdales, riding lessons at the stable and going out to dinner at nice restaurants to Wal-Mart and microwave dinners. Then Dad died, the medical bills piled up, and her mom ended up working herself into a stroke and subsequent death. Arianna's disappointments seemed to be destroying everything until she had seen this job listing.

After tying her boots, she put her purse in the trunk and grabbed her hiking backpack, checked that it had a few bottles of water and some energy bars, closed the trunk and started out.

Smiling as she walked, the possibility of being close to horses again filled her with promise of a new chapter of good in her life. Riding horses, much like hiking, grounded her. It fed her soul. Everything was always okay after she rode. Big problems didn't seem so big anymore. She didn't know how or why, but it just put things into perspective. That's why she knew the job was meant for her. It was just what she needed.

She wasn't five feet from the car when she felt an uneasiness around her. The atmosphere was complete quiescence. Maybe it's the absence of the city noise that's making her tense, but it felt more than that: there was no sound at all and it was creeping her out. If she didn't know better, she would have thought she was being watched. But the isolation of her situation made that seem impossible. Seeing only struggling dwarf trees and scrubby bushes with the occasional yucca and agave plant scattered here and there, she shook herself and checked her compass. Her thinking was ridiculous. But the path before her did seem to be kind of brighter. The absurdity of that thought had her flinging it aside.

As she scrutinized her surroundings, she discovered that what she thought earlier was ugly was in fact interesting in its own way. The yuccas were a contrast in themselves with their spiky leaves framed in curling wisps of fiber. Then unbelievably, as she continued, she glimpsed flowers. Going down to one knee to get a closer look, she felt a kind of kinship with this wooded flowering bush that could thrive in such a harsh, unforgiving, and crusted environment.

As Arianna got closer to the base of the butte, the silence that had been accompanying her was interrupted by what sounded like barking. Listening intently now, she had no doubt; a small dog was yapping somewhere close by. She circled the butte's base looking for it but couldn't get any closer to the sound. What's a little yippy dog doing out here? How could anyone abandon a lap dog in such a hopelessly remote place? It had to be up among the rocks.

The animal lover in her could not in good conscience leave a defenseless animal up there with the probability that it would be snatched up by an eagle or hawk and be eaten in no time. She had had no intention of actually climbing the butte before, but she would have to now. She sized up the challenge before her. She had the skill to scale it but without ropes she would have to be very careful. At least one side had a bit of a slope to it; otherwise the climb would be next to impossible.

At about 45 feet into the climb, she looked up and a few feet over her head was a little face peering down at her, barking. It looked impatient, like it had been waiting for her all day. She climbed the remaining distance and was about to pull up to the landing on which the dog was standing, when the shoebox-sized rock she was perched on gave way and clattered down the side of the rock face. As she started slipping, panic rolled over her. Her heart rate went through the roof. Sweat hurled out of every pore on her body. She scrambled, her arms and feet trying to find purchase. Her toes and fingers were digging into the rock face for anything to grip to stop the descent. As she did, her palm was ripped open on a particularly jagged rock that stuck out far enough for her to grab hold of but was taking a bite out of her as payment for purchase. She held tight through the scathing pain. Seconds later, she found a good toehold. She took a minute to gather her composure and take a few deep breaths. Okay, maybe a dozen.

Once she felt like she had her heart rate under control, she resumed the climb upward, her muscles shaking and stuttering the whole way. This time, she inspected each hold twice for its steadfastness.

When she got to the edge of the landing, the little dog started spinning and barking. She knew that there was no way in hell, on earth, or anyplace else that this dog should be up here. It was one of those lap dogs with long hair that required hourly grooming. She thought the dog was a Shih-Tzu. Even though she knew the correct pronunciation, in her mind, she renamed it what it sounded like, a Shit Zoo, due to its relentless caterwauling. And what's that on its head, a bow?

Perched right there on the crown of its little head was a red bow tied around a tuft of hair that made it stand straight up, defying gravity. Seeing the red bow reminded her of the one her father preferred to use after braiding Arianna's hair down her back, saying that the red color matched the Ferrari she mirrored after he was finished, racing toward the door as fast as possible to go play.

After she pulled herself successfully up onto the ledge, she stood upright and was overcome by the craziness of the situation. It made no logical sense whatsoever that a dog, much less this kind of dog, would be on a butte far from any population that would harbor such a pet.

The dog kept spinning and barking like a tiny tornado. Arianna felt she was having her very own "Lassie is trying to save Timmy!" moment. She could sense the dog was trying to convey something to her, but her hand was yelling at her louder, the cut throbbing with every heartbeat. Looking around, she found a small stool-sized rock and sat before yelling back at the dog, "I will be there in just a minute." Unbelievably, it stopped barking.

Arianna pulled her backpack off, grabbed a bottle out and squeezed the water liberally over the cut, picking out the bits of rock debris she could see. She scoured the pack for some kind of wrap to keep it covered and clean. Pushing aside a flashlight and a tube of sunscreen, she could only find Band-Aids that were too small, better suited for blisters. The wound was dripping blood, so she held her hand high above her heart in an attempt to slow the flow. She put the bottle back in her pack, slung it on to a shoulder and turned her attention back to the dog. She stood and wouldn't you know it, the darn thing started barking and spinning again.

"You are driving me crazy! If I weren't such a nice person, I would just turn around, head back down and leave your little heinie to the wolves!"

The dog just glared at her as if to say, "Are you done now?"

Annoyed, Arianna, growled as she tramped toward the contrary dog. Unbelievably, the thing started backing away from her. Okay, maybe growling and stomping wasn't the best way to communicate "safe harbor" but the dog was working on her last nerve. The landing was only about 5' by 15', where was it going to go? On one side, a vertical wall of rock continued up 30 or more feet, on the other, a lethal drop to the desert floor. Really the thing had only two choices, her or death.

Turning back toward the dog, all she saw was rock. The little hellhound had disappeared from sight. How was that even possible. A split-second later she heard an echoing bark. She stepped closer to where she last saw the little gremlin and sure enough, if she angle just right, there was a body-sized chasm in the rock face. If she took off her backpack and exhaled all of her breath, she may be able to just barely squeeze through. Which she did, dragging her backpack behind her.

Dark and still, the cave felt empty. Every hair on her body was standing straight up, lending a sense of eeriness to the silence. Heedless of the alert her subconscious was trying to send, she rummaged through the pack at her feet and grabbed the flashlight. Flicking it on, she looked around and gasped. She was in a hollowed-out horseshoe shaped space the size of a small room. In the center there was a waist-high rock pillar that appeared to have jetted out from the floor. Still keeping her injured hand elevated, she used the flashlight to methodically illuminate every inch of the space she somehow knew few if anyone had ever witnessed. Dozens of petroglyphs decorated the walls, each having a significance she was not privy to. All thoughts of the dog vanished as she inspected each one. There were drawings of stick people, spirals, suns, and handprints among other designs she didn't know the term for. There were different shapes: a step pyramid surrounded by squares, concentric circles, and circles that had a line from top to bottom and side to side with dots around it. Scattered amongst those, she recognized some animal depictions: squirrels, bighorn sheep, birds, snakes, eagles . . . so many. An ambiguous vibration seemed to radiate from each one. Oddly, fear never entered her mind as she slowly walked around, taking it all in.

She had almost completed the circuit when her attention jumped back to the dog who appeared to be staring at the petroglyphs too, not paying any attention to her. Now was her chance to snatch up the little thing. She lunged for it, but it bolted around the center stone and gave her what she was sure was a dirty look. "Unbelievable. I'm trying to save your ungrateful life!"

She moved closer to the center pillar. The top was etched with a clockwise spiral design that must have a dozen tiers to it, circling toward a carving of a hand; a right hand, to be exact. She felt something urging her to join her hand with the carved one. The pull was almost a physical thing, almost as if it were a mandate. Slowly she started to lower her hand but realizing how bloody it was, she fought against the impulse and halted the downward motion. She didn't want to desecrate the carving with blood. She was pretty sure that would be immoral. But there was a sense of urgency beating down on her. For what, she hadn't a clue. Her heart was pounding in her chest, but her skin felt clammy. And why did it feel like everything around her held its breath?

That's when the devil hound charged at her. Arianna acted on pure instinct, trying to move out of its way but in doing so, she and the dog got tangled up; the dog weaving its body through her legs. She was caught off balance and slammed both her hands down on to the baluster trying to keep from squishing the little dog. In doing so, her right hand landed directly onto the carved image doing the very thing she tried to prevent.

At that exact moment, the world seemed to shift. The feeling of complete detachment from the rest of the world came over her; it felt like what she thought outer space would feel like. She heard what sounded like rocks scraping against each other and detected a rumbling under her feet. A change in the air pressure made her ears pop. She felt woozy, dizzy -- and then nothing, as she crumpled to the floor.

~ ~ ~

Bill drove his repair truck to the coordinates on the order form for a flat-tire repair. Sure enough, there was a car pulled off to the side of the road. He looked in the car and not seeing anyone, yelled to the surrounding area but couldn't find the owner anywhere. He tried to call the phone number listed but didn't get an answer. He decided to fix the flat anyway. He didn't want to drive all the way back out here when the recall would inevitably occur. It was against AAA policy to touch a car without the owner present. But what were they going to do? Get someone else to cover this desolate road? Good luck with that. He fixed the flat and placed the paperwork under the windshield wiper.

NAVAJO LAND JANUARY, 1864

Hashké scanned the landscape, all his senses on alert for any indication of his enemies. Opportunistic warring tribes and the bilagaana (white man) cavalry, made vigilance mandatory for all Navajo still free. A breeze that shifted strands of his hair across his chest, brought with it a hint of smoke. Hashké pulled back on the reins, halting his horse.

When the faint sounds of a woman's screams carried from the direction of their camp, he kicked his horse into a dead run and bent low over its neck. He crested the last hill, smoke now smothering every breath he took in. Hashké was just able to make out the scene but still too far away to stop it. His worst fears were confirmed as four Ute warriors circled his sister, attempting to get close enough to grab her while trying to evade her blade.

His pulse raced and he clenched his jaw. They never should have left her alone. After running from the U.S. Cavalry that massacred the rest of their village months earlier, they'd foolishly thought themselves safely hidden here in this canyon. They'd failed to take into account the tenacity of their neighboring enemy tribe and its thriving slave trade.

Hashké bellowed out a war cry as he frantically raced closer. But just as he was confident he could reach her in time, his horse stumbled, and he barely avoided being thrown. Vaulting off the now limping, very lame horse, he sprinted toward his sister as she attempted to fend off the dismounted enemy warriors. But she was outnumbered. Still too far away to help, he pushed himself to sprint faster, forced to watch helplessly as she was roughly unarmed and thrown up over the withers of a horse. One of the Ute mounted behind her. As soon as he was seated, they all sped off.

Hashké cried out in anguish as they disappeared behind a cloud of dust, then searched the surrounding horizon for any sign of his two brothers, praying they'd appear. Despondent when they didn't, he jogged back to his horse, tormented to see the bowed tendon on his horse's front leg, confirming that there was no hope of catching up to his sister and her captors today.

The adrenaline that had fueled Hashké evaporated and left him bent at the waist, his hands on his knees, gulping down air as despair washed over him and reality sunk in. His only sister stolen away. His vow to protect her after the cavalry murdered their parents sat empty on the ground beside him.

He fisted his eyes; they burned as memories flooded his mind. Gifted with the name Shándíín at birth, meaning "Sunshine" in their people's language, she was aptly named. Her bold, beautiful smile brightened even the most trying day. She didn't speak until she was close to three summers old, because she didn't need to. All she had to do was point her finger at what she wanted, smile, and he'd get it for her.

Even though she was closer in age to Adika'í, his younger brother whose heart was distant toward others, Shándíín clung more closely to Hashké. She was always following him around, trying to do everything he did. She did not understand that she was too little to go where he went. The times he had to bring her back to their mother after she snuck away to follow him were as numerous as the stars in the night sky. He knew

GINA HOFFMAN

deep in his soul that her very determination would help her
stay strong until he could get her back.

Hashké led his horse slowly to the ransacked camp, his gut
churning with frustration as he refused to consider what the
Ute had planned for his sister. Forcing himself to focus on
the present moment, he applied a poultice to his horse's leg
to quicken the healing time, but the bow was severe. It would
probably take weeks to completely recover.

Later that night, Hashké choked down part of the rabbit
he'd caught for his sister and willed his brothers to return.
It was taking them too long, adding to his worries. They
should have returned hours ago. Unable to sit still, Hashké
paced around the burned-out camp most of the night, his
emotions teetering between fury and despair. Hours later, he
reluctantly gave into his body's needs and grabbed a moment
or two of sleep.

Hashké squinted through gritty eyes at the sun's first rays
as they peeked over the horizon and raked his hands through
his hair. If he lost his brothers and sister in the same day,
he would be left with nothing but his growing rage at those
responsible -- and his need for revenge.

As the sun crossed the sky, Hashké was forced to accept
that perhaps his brothers weren't coming back; he was sure
the cavalry would be to blame. He mindlessly sifted through
their belongings in the burned-up rubble of their camp as
he contemplated his predicament. He finished gathering the
mementos he managed to save, then sat staring at the leftovers
of the rabbit he had intended to share with his family, knowing
he needed the nutrients to carry out his plans.

Lost in his thoughts, he jumped to his feet when he caught
movement from the corner of his eye.

Bidzii (He Who Is Strong), his oldest brother, swept a
wide-eyed gaze around the camp. "What has happened here?
Where is Shándíín and Adika'í?"

12

"Bidzii, thank the holy people, you live," Hashké said, the knot in his stomach easing but only slightly. "Have you seen Adika'í?"

Bidzii's eyes narrowed. "No, but where's Shándíín?"

"The Ute took her." Hashké's shoulders slumped. "We never should have left her alone."

Nostrils flaring, Bidzii snatched up his horse's reins, grabbed a tuft of mane and swung his leg over, seating himself in a mere split second before Hashké could stop him and take his horse for himself.

"Stay and wait for Adika'í. The cavalry patrols have increased; avoiding them cost me many hours to return so be vigilant. I will send news as I can."

Hashké knew arguing with his oldest brother would be a waste of time but still, not being able to search for Shándíín himself was infuriating. He had half a mind to set out on foot. But he knew he couldn't leave if there was a chance Adika'í would return.

It was very late that night when Hashké passed out in sheer exhaustion. He blinked awake when the sound of his horse neighed a welcome. He jerked into a sitting position as Adika'í appeared at the edge of their camp.

"Thank the holy people you're alive."

Adika'í frowned, confusion written clearly on his face. "Where are Bidzii and Shándíín?"

"Shándíín was taken by Ute warriors. Bidzii went after her," Hashké said in a hoarse voice, his pulse jumping every time he thought of what could be happening to his sister.

Adika'í froze and his face paled. "Changing Woman, watch over her."

3

NAVAJO LAND (NEW MEXICO TERRITORY) SPRING, 1864

Arianna had no idea how long she was unconscious. She remembered grabbing onto the pillar and the flashlight hitting the floor, rolling toward the cave wall. She looked over and it was there, the beam still shining. Repeatedly opening her mouth wide to unpop her ears, she got to her feet unsteadily and went to pick it up. Turning it off, she put it into her backpack, then headed to the entrance where daylight shone in. The dog was nowhere to be found. She sat down on a rock outside, grabbed a bottle of water and began drinking, hoping that would clear her mind of the fog it was swimming in.

Maybe the local evening news would have a story on the earthquake she had experienced; come to think of it, where was the dog?

Who was she kidding, New Mexico doesn't have earthquakes, that was ... I don't know... something else maybe. That dang dog had something to do with it, she was sure of it, kind of. If she were a believer in the supernatural, she might be persuaded to think that it was . . . but she's not. She had prayed plenty when her dad was sick and never heard a peep, not one of her prayers was answered, not one.

Wondering what time it was, she looked at her watch, it read 2:12 pm, she better call AAA. If she missed them, she would be so mad at that dog.

No service read on her phone and only one bar of battery life showed. Not a problem, she could just climb down and head back to the road and try again after plugging it back into the charger cord.

"Shih Tzu is my new favorite curse word," she told herself. "Dang dog," she muttered under her breath.

Climbing down was harder than she thought given that she had to hold her right hand up the entire way. It had stopped bleeding, but she knew that if given half an excuse, it would start dripping again. She may need stitches, stitches that she could not afford.

Once she reached the bottom, she looked around. Things appeared different, not in a major way but a little greener, more plants or something, she couldn't quite put her finger on it.

Looking at her trusty compass, she headed back to her car in a southwesterly direction. As she hiked back, she enjoyed listening to the birds and insects' intricate sounds. Wait, what? She distinctly remembered the absence of sound the first time she traveled through the terrain; it had creeped her out. The sounds that accompanied her walk now comforted her.

But after over an hour and a half of walking she did not see the road anywhere. Checking the compass yet again, she confirmed that her path was indeed correct. She should have verified her orientation when she was up high on the butte. But at that time, she was more focused on how to climb down without reopening her wound, not checking direction. It didn't even enter her mind. "Shih Tzu!" She checked her phone once more for service but it was completely dead; no power, no service.

Coming to the conclusion that somehow, she remembered the direction wrong, didn't settle her as she hoped it would.

Glancing back down at her compass, she noticed her hand was trembling. Tightening her hand angrily, she headed for the butte. She could get a bird's-eye view and correct her trajectory to the road.

Actually, the trek back was not that bad and she reached the base as she was starting to get hungry. Grabbing a power bar while sitting on a rock, she munched down the not-so-delicious dinner and got ready to head back up for Climb 2.0.

She struggled up about 20 feet, looked out and saw none of the things she expected to see; no power lines, no road, no car, only flat desert terrain. So, she traversed the butte horizontally peering out each direction for signs of civilization. After her third attempt, anxiety started fountaining up. The slight trembling she noticed in her hands before had amplified. It now enveloped her entire body. Tears burned the backs of her eyes and her nasal passages swelled. Light was dwindling, nighttime insects were starting their competing melodies and she could hear a wolf howling in the distance. She was tired, couldn't find her car, and she was alone.

The tears she was trying to hold back brimmed over her lashes, cascading onto the parched rocks, where they were devoured on impact. She couldn't just hang there, she had to make a decision: up or down. More wolves joined in the communion and that settled it for her; up to the cave. At least in the cave she thought she would regain a sense of security.

On the brink of exhaustion Arianna gained the platform and ambled toward the cave. Not finding the opening immediately, she studied each rock and crevice but still found no opening. Questioning her sanity now became a recurring torment. Stepping back and looking around, she recognized the rock she had sat on to pour water on her hand so she knew she wasn't completely out of her mind. There has to be an opening. It was here.

Arianna gave up and sat with her back against the ascending wall. She drew her knees to her chest and circled her arms around them, scanning the horizon and sky. She searched for some sign of life in the form of light, any man-made light, whether from a car's headlights or a passing airplane, she wasn't picky. But instead what she witnessed splayed out before her was the majesty of the night sky without civilization's light pollution to dim the grandeur. She lay down where she sat, keeping her eyes open, looking for one of the lights to cross the sky, promising inorganic origins. She placed her pack under her head for a pillow and shortly after, slipped into sleep.

A bright light was nagging her into consciousness. She was so uncomfortable; her hip and shoulder hurt. What she was lying on was too hard. And what's up with that light? That's when her mind was flooded with yesterday's events. She shaded her eyes, opened them slowly, and sat up. Well, at least she didn't fall off the cliff last night. That's a positive. Again, she went over every inch of the rock wall in broad daylight; there was no chasm or opening of any kind. Slumping down to the floor, she sat turning things over and over again in her head. Was it just some kind of crazy dream? Did I get dehydrated and hallucinate it? She looked down at her hand. No, her hand was still messed up, reaffirming her current reality.

So, what's really going on? The dog, the red bow, the cave, none of it made any sense. She walked to the edge of the landing and looked out as far as the eye could see. No road, no car. Hunger pains interrupted her meandering thoughts and she focused them on her physical needs. She dumped out the contents of her backpack. Okay, there are five power bars, a few Band-Aids, a tube of sunscreen, a flashlight, two empty and one almost-full bottle of water. Finding water was definitely her priority, so she stood up and walked close to the cliff's edge, where she could see an increase of vegetation and even proper trees to the north. It would be a bit of a walk but what else did she have to do? She gathered up her things and started down. She was getting good at using her elbow instead of her injured hand to assist in climbing.

As she walked, she tried to remember all she had learned watching those wilderness survival shows on the Nat. Geo.

Channel. She thought she remembered that trees were plentiful if a water source was nearby and wished she could recall which plants were edible.

As she got closer to the trees, she saw more insects. They buzzed her like planes to an airport tower. She hadn't missed the annoying things in the desert. Her surroundings started to change the farther she walked from the butte. Where there was only rock and dirt, now broken tree limbs were scattered among the brush and clumps of grass became more frequent. There had to be water around here somewhere.

She reached the actual tree line by mid-afternoon and tried to listen for any trickling water sounds as she walked, but so far, nothing. What she did find was a perfect walking stick. It stood out to her, all smooth and straight, just lying across her path. An inner voice urged her to pick it up. She heard somewhere that if something grabs your attention, intrigues you, then there is a reason for it. So, she picked it up and continued on, periodically checking in with her compass to make sure she wasn't walking in circles. If she just kept going in a straight line, she should run into something eventually, right? She kept an eye out for some nuts or berries or something edible. She was down to three power bars, half a bottle of water, and needed to conserve.

Once she found a stream of some kind, she was going to follow it until she found a ranch or town. Aren't ranches located near a water source? Made sense to her.

After walking for an hour more, she thought she heard something. She stopped and strained to try to hear more clearly. Confident that she was hearing water babbling through rocks, she picked up her pace toward the sound.

Finally, great tufts of tall grass bent, heavy with moisture, into ever-flowing clear water. Vegetation battled with rocks for pole position at the stream's edge.

"Thank you, thank you, thank you," she said as she reached the edge of the stream. She put her backpack down, pulled out the empty bottles, and filled them. She sat back on her haunches and drank her fill of the sweet liquid. Finally satiated, she just sat there replete and enjoyed the small victory. A loud crack disrupted her serenity and had her whipping her head to the side. A shiver crept up her spine. Eyes darting, breath quickening, blood rushing, her body immediately sensed the danger her mind was slow to behold. Scanning the same placid scene she had just minutes ago walked through, she saw nothing new, nothing to alarm her. She had gotten used to the soothing sound of water flowing that dominated her hearing, that's all, she reassured herself. With the second snap, she bolted up trying to ready herself for what, she didn't know. Turning her back to the water, she saw them, 20-some feet away: one, two, no, four wolves, their snarling jowls was all she could focus on. With a paralyzing stare and pinned ears, they slowly, purposely crept toward her. Arianna's face paled, drained of blood that was being diverted to her extremities in the age-old response to danger. Her mind grappled for a defense strategy. All it came up with was Cesar Millan and how he said to be the pack leader. She didn't think she could be the leader of this pack in any way, shape or form, so she needed to pad her body as much as possible.

She thought she shouldn't take her eyes off the predators, so without losing eye contact, she stealthily wrapped her jean jacket around her right arm, tucking the sleeves in place to secure it. She bent one knee, felt for her pack, and slipped it onto her back. As quickly as possible, she snatched up her walking stick (now she knew why she needed it) and stood braced for the attack she knew was coming. Her plan was weak, but it was all she had, given the closest sturdy tree thick enough to climb was behind the wolves.

The leading wolf sprung forward in what she felt deep in her soul was the last few moments of her life. She was not going down without fighting back. If they were going to take a piece of her, she was going to try to take a piece of them. She lunged toward the alpha and yelled as loud and angrily as she could, brandishing the stick like a sword, trying to intimidate. She was not proud of the sound coming out of her but if it worked, she'd keep doing it.

At first, the wolves were taken aback, they actually stopped and stared. If nothing else, she was gratified by that. But it didn't last, and they resumed advancing.

Damn. They're coming. I hope I pass out. I just don't want to feel the flesh being ripped from my bones. Please, God, let me pass out! These were her thoughts as she finally acknowledged there was more to this world than just the physical.

It was at that very moment, the leader leaped for her throat, as it did, she stepped to the side and swung the walking stick and nailed him in the ribs. She heard a satisfying yelp and had a brief moment of victory, very brief moment because now she noted that she was surrounded. Dang.

A split second before they made contact in a coordinated attack, a sense of peace enveloped her as she thought, *This is going to hurt.*

4

NAVAJO LAND SPRING, 1864

For days Hashké had been following the tracks of a herd of wild horses. It was the next step he needed to accomplish for their plan to get his sister back. With his pack horse ladened with the bundle of pelts he had hunted, he could now focus on catching the horses he would need to train, then sell to the traders. His brothers were each trying to gather as much money as possible so they could purchase their sister back from the slavers.

He dismounted and examined the tracks more intently. He must be getting close to the herd, the tracks very fresh, the ridges of each hoof-print still intact, their dung still moist.

He leaped back onto his horse to continue, when a horrible noise made its way to his ears. It was a sound unlike anything he had heard before – kind of a growl, kind of … No, that was definitely a woman's scream. He dropped the lead to his packhorse and kicked his stallion into a gallop. Dodging limbs and fallen logs, he and his horse sped toward the commotion. As he reached a stream, he saw a white woman, in strange clothing, fighting a pack of wolves! And they were winning, each of her appendages clamped in a different jaw.

He brought his left leg over his horse's withers while the stallion was still galloping, not wanting to allocate precious time to slowing his mount. He slipped off into a run, all the while reaching behind his shoulder for the bow Bidzii had crafted for him. The grooves from the ceremonial carvings his brother purposely etched into the wood guided his grip toward the leather brace. He seamlessly notched the arrows with expert hands and let them fly one after another until all four wolves were dead or dying. The eagle fletching he had painstakingly searched for and used in crafting his arrows aided them in unerringly finding their mark. In a matter of a couple seconds, it was all over. The wolves' blood drained into the dirt.

As he thought about what he witnessed, he was very impressed with the fierceness of the woman; standing her ground resolutely, combatting her foes. Even though he didn't and would never tolerate bilagaana (white people), she had his respect.

As he reached her, he pulled off the wolf carcasses that had landed atop her and started to check her over. She was unconscious, with blood seeping from multiple wounds exposing ripped muscle and even bone in some places. As his examination continued up her torso, he brushed her hair from her face and caught his breath. She was beautiful. He was grateful her face was spared. Hashké shook his head to clear it, telling himself to focus. If she weren't already dead, then she soon would be if he didn't act quickly. He gently placed his hand down on her sternum to feel if she was breathing. Her chest rose and fell, but shallowly. She was still alive! He couldn't believe that he was relieved by this fact; it astonished him, actually. His hatred of bilagaana was well known by all close to him. Now, he had to decide if he would help the white woman. His mind immediately went to his sister and the horrific path her life has been forced down. He hoped that if she was hurt and a white man happened upon her, he would help her regardless of her skin color. That decided it; he must try to help this white woman.

With that in mind, his attention turned to her arms. He started with the one that looked like it had the most damage as it lay in an angle that nature never intended. Surfacely, there was some serious ripping of the flesh that needed stitching. In addition, her bone had been snapped in two by the wolf's powerful jaw. It was not compounded so it's mending should be uncomplicated. Her left hand had several punctures and cuts; it was starting to bruise and swell from impact. He would check this more thoroughly in the coming hours to see if there were any fractures. She must have been trying to hit one of the wolves attacking her. *She was not going to just surrender.* He pulled off his shirt made of woven broadcloth, ripped it into wide strips and wrapped her forearm to try to staunch the bleeding.

He then checked her torso. Pulling the remnants of her shirt up, he noticed the unusual material. There were a few cuts but none that were serious. He moved on.

Her right arm was in much better shape; she had some sort of stout, durable cloth wrapped around it and because she did, her wounds were not as deep here. But there was a gash in her palm that would require a couple of stitches.

Her legs got his attention next. They were in a terrible state. Again, he noted the material of her clothing as he carefully picked the remnants out of the wounds to get a better look; it was very different from all that he knew. She must be from back east; he had heard of such finery, but he didn't think very highly of it. The material was so thin; it wouldn't stand up to a strong bush, much less an encounter with a predator. Her boots were a different story. They were odd but substantial. As he took them off, he knew he wouldn't find anything requiring his attention there. He didn't; her feet were fine.

It was fortunate that this confrontation occurred near a stream. It would make it easier to find the herbs and plants he would need to help in healing. He had some in his medicine pouch but not enough for all of this destruction. After wrapping the most severe wounds firmly, staunching the blood flow, he dragged the wolf carcasses several feet away; they shouldn't be anywhere near her. He left to find the necessary herbs and plants and to retrieve his packhorse with his supplies.

He gathered sagebrush for an antiseptic wash, hard stem bulrush for the poultice, and moss for a dressing to cover the wounds, but most important the pulverized puffball to stop the bleeding. Upon his return, he quickly gathered wood and made a small fire. He retrieved his medicine pouch and two cooking pots from his grazing packhorse and set his largest pot full of fresh stream water over the flames to bring it to a boil. As it did, he added sagebrush and let it reduce. Once it was cool enough, he would pour it over the wounds to cleanse them.

After preparing the medicinal herbs he would need, Hashké turned his attention back to the woman. He carefully removed her pack and set it aside. But to adequately address all of her injuries, he had to unclothe her. He unsheathed his knife and easily slit through the fabric of her shirt like a finger through water. After removing it, he took a valuable second to try to understand what he saw. Her breasts were enclosed in some sort of bondage wrap. This piece of clothing was made with a delicate white lacy material, the likes of which he had never seen. Why would anyone wear such a thing? He admired it, true, but the purpose he could not understand. Not being able to stop the impulse, he slipped a finger under the edge of the fabric at the top of her breast just to feel it. It was soft but flimsy.

Removing his finger, he shook his head again and tried to refocus. Next, he had to cut away her pants to expose her leg wounds. He decided to just cut the legs off the pants about mid-thigh but leave the upper part intact, saving her modesty. His mind couldn't help noticing the lovely shape of her legs; they were toned but elegant. She was the most beautiful creature he had ever seen. He would have this vision of her in his head for the rest of his life, he was sure.

Reining in his wayward musings, he reminded himself of the amount of work that lay ahead of him but foremost, she was bilagaana, damn it. Just patch her up, get her back on her feet and be done with her. It was the Navajo way to help those in need, he would do so, but then he would walk away.

He began chanting the healing words of his people as he started to spoon the cooled sagebrush infused mixture over the wounds, then added the puffball crushings to the worst ones.

It was a good thing she remained unconscious, because now she had hours of painful stitching ahead. Hashké used what deer sinew he had on hand for the sutures of the deepest wounds, but it was soon apparent he needed more. Hunting for deer this late in the day was not an option. The only thing he could think of that would work was his hair. The strands were thick and strong. It wasn't as strong as the sinew, but he had no choice. If it didn't hold, he would hunt down a deer tomorrow and harvest more.

Placing the last suture, the grueling procedure was finally finished. He arranged moss over the wounds, then wrapped them with thin leather strapping. Lastly, he picked up some branches and snapped them into the needed lengths and placed them under her broken arm and tied them with more leather strapping. *That should keep her arm steady so it would heal straight.* His voice was roughened from the continuous chanting of the healing words. Hashké was relieved to be finished.

Even though he was exhausted, his chores were still waiting on him. He whistled for his horses that were grazing in the nearby fields. They came immediately and he bedded them down for the night in an adjacent meadow. Next, he grabbed two deer pelts from the pack and placed them on each side of the fire. He gently lifted her up in his arms and placed her on the pelt nearest to him. He then went back to the pack and got out two blankets. He covered her with one and put the other one on his pelt. He sat down for the first time in hours. He was exhausted, his arms heavy with the tension of the day's activities. Just then his stomach started to growl. That's right, it had been half a day since he last ate anything. He slowly rose to grab some jerky from his pack.

Gnawing on the dried meat, he returned to his bed. His mind was confounded. Her clothing. Her under clothing! Her beauty. "Cease," he muttered to himself. Just eat and go to bed. It's been a long day. You need to sleep. Agreeing with himself, he placed his bow and arrows along with his knife next to his pallet, took his moccasins off and. Hashké stretched out on his back, pulling his blanket up.

What a day, he thought as his eyes shut and he dropped off to sleep.

5

After a scant couple of hours of slumber, something woke Hashké. He tried to muster a clear thought through the fog his mind swam in and then it hit him -- the woman! She was thrashing about. If she rips open those stitches, *I'll kill her myself*, he thought as he jumped up and, in two angry strides, reached her. He knelt down and restrained her arms, but her legs were still kicking. She was reliving the fight and his efforts to keep her still were not working. Restraining her with ropes had merit but the soil was too loose and wouldn't hold up to any force. He needed another person to confine her legs. Knowing that there wasn't another around for miles, his mind scrambled to come up with a solution. He concluded he would have to use his whole damn body to subdue her.

He got up, grabbed his pelt, blanket, bow and arrows along with his knife and stormed back toward her. He quickly laid out the pelt alongside hers, placed his weapons within reach, and tossed the blanket up around him and inched close to her body, wrapping her up while trying not to touch any of her wounds, not an easy task. His leg lay over her thighs, his arm around her upper arms.

She immediately started to calm and unbelievably, nestled into him. *Damn, she smelled good*, was his first thought. Her hair, the color of sand, was soft and had a floral smell he was

27

unfamiliar with. It hung past her shoulders and had a slight wave to it. *Damn, she feels good,* was his next thought. *Quiet!* he rebuked his mind. She is bilagaana. She is not for you. These thoughts are bad. Her people killed your parents. Stop thinking about her. She was probably sent by the evil spirits to veer you off your path of vengeance. You must stay focused on getting Shandíín back. Do not lose your way. Clear your mind and go back to sleep.

Arianna felt pain, a tremendous amount of pain, every square inch of her was in agony. And she also felt an odd sense of warmth and comfort she could not decipher. As she slowly opened her eyes, she became aware of her surroundings. Faint heat radiated from a dying fire across from her. She was lying on some kind of fur pallet with a woven wool blanket over her body. And there was a man's heavy leg and arm on her! That thought should freak her out but oddly, all she was feeling was security. She would freak out in just a minute, as soon as she had enough of the yummy feeling of contentedness she hadn't experienced in far too long. Who could this man be? She tried to remember what happened to get her here. She remembered she was walking to the line of trees; she found the stream, then -- the wolves! Her heart rate shot up and she gasped, fear eclipsing all thought.

"Hello." The man brusquely said as he removed his remaining leg from her, allowing her to turn and.... Holy Heck! He was gorgeous! She would have thought she had died and gone to heaven and he was her reward for living through all of the trials and tribulation she had experienced, except the screaming pain said otherwise.

The Native American man she was lying next to was dream-worthy: he had a ruggedly angular countenance with a nose that was strong and masculine like the rest of his face. His mouth was perfect; his lips not too full or thin. His cheekbones were high and proud. He had straight long black hair that was held back by a leather headband. His jaw was sturdy. He had the most striking dark chocolate ganache eyes

28

thaaaat looked pissed. "Hello?" she volleyed back unsteadily. She had not one clue why she deserved such a look.

Hashké felt her stirring in his arms. His feelings of warmth and protectiveness toward his bedmate were shattered by the recollection of what she was. He yanked on the 'I don't tolerate bilalgaana' persona he proudly wore at all times; it strengthened his resolve and suited him and his purpose. While he was clearing his head of all the positive, weak thoughts toward the white woman, he was glad for the first time in his life that he learned the white man's language while trading and racing horses with them. For now, he could use it to find out why she was out here alone, unprotected.

"Where am I?" Arianna asked and followed immediately with, "And who are you?"

Hashké, following through with his thoughts of distance quickly sat up, then hopped up to a standing position as if she were a poisonous snake. He replied looking down at her, crossing his arms across his chest, in his Navajo-accented English, "I am Hashké. You are on Navajo land."

It was then that she got a full-length look at him and what he was wearing. He had the appearance of someone who just walked off a western movie set. He was bare-chested, which thankfully, allowed her to see just how muscular he was. He had strong shoulders and a trim waist. His muscles were toned like a swimmer; they were really sculpted. Her favorite spot was his stomach muscles. They were delicious ripples and bumps that led to a cloth; a breechcloth gathered between his legs, the ends of which hung over a concha belt with large silver medallions and buckle securing it in place. All kinds of yum!

Slowly, she realized she was just staring at him, well his body more specifically, when she sensed she should look up. She saw his face change to a glower. That's when it hit her, he had asked her a question and her response so far was drool. She snapped her jaw and mind back to a more appropriate place and finally answered, "I was lost." At that moment pain forced its way to the forefront of her brain, demanding immediate attention to the state of her body. "Did you do this?" she asked, lifting her splinted arm.

"Yes."

"Thank you," she said trying to smile through her agony.

Her smile lanced something within him. And her eyes, he would have never guessed that her eyes would be such a striking color. They're the green of the moss in the forest while being struck with bright sunlight, where normally, very little light reached.

"What is your name?" he asked,

"Arianna," she replied and then winced due to a particularly vicious stab of pain.

"I will give you medicine for the pain," he said and turned to get his pouch. When he returned, he said, "Here, take and chew, do not swallow." He handed her some leaves and seeds.

"What is this?" she said, wrinkling her nose.

That face she made caused him want to smile but he didn't, of course. Instead he scowled and replied, "Datura, it will help."

She hesitated until another sharp pain hit her. She chewed and chewed until he commanded, "Spit out now."

With muffled speech she said, "Okay," then rolled to her side, up on an elbow and did so. Lying back down, she said, "Thank you. Thank you for all of this. What happened? I mean, I remember the wolves attacking and then, thank God I do not remember anything else."

Hashké answered with, "I was hunting. I heard your noise."

She self-consciously laughed and said "That was my, Cesar Millon 'be the pack leader' attempt. It worked for a few seconds, then it didn't."

Her laughter was another stab to his chest. "Who is this Cesar Millon?"

"You know that guy on the National Geographic Channel? The one who trains dogs to behave."

"I know not."

"You must not have cable, then."

"I know not. Why are you here?" he asked pointedly.

"I was driving through Nowhere New Mexico on my way to interview for a job, when I got a flat tire. I called AAA, but they were going to take forever to get to me, so I went on a walk to check out the butte not too far from the road." She took a moment to suck in a breath through her clenched teeth, as another pain wave hit her and continued, "Anyway, I was close to the base of it when I heard this little dog barking. It wasn't a big dog's bark; it was a little yippy kind of bark. You know, the kind that sits on a lap, the kind whose feet never touch the ground because someone is always holding it, carrying it about. Anyway, I couldn't just walk away from it. It would have been some predator's lunch, the way it was carrying on, making all that noise. So, I climbed up and there it was on this small landing about two thirds the way up. I was just about to pull myself up when the rock that I was standing on gave way. I slipped a bit, but I caught myself. That's how I got this." She held up her right hand.

He had a feeling this was going to be a long telling, so he sat back down and crossed his legs and kept listening.

"Anyhow," she slurred slightly, "that bunch of sticks and twigs is good!" she giggled.

He started to smile back but then caught himself.

"I climbed back up and this time I made it up on to the landing and there was this prissy dog with its hair in a bow and everything. That darn dog kept barking and spinning, like we had some place to go or something."

Given the stern look on his face she tried to explain herself, "I know I'm just babbling on, but I don't know how else to explain how I got here."

She continued, "I couldn't leave it up there, so after I cleaned the cut, I tried to grab the dog. But that thing took off and slipped into a crack in the rocks. I followed it, of course, into this cave. The cave had all these carvings in it, and then the rocks moved and when I came back out, my car was nowhere to be found." Her speech was even more garbled now. "I needed water, so I walked toward the tree line to try to find a stream or something. I found this one but then the wolves found me.

"Speaking of water, I'm really thirsty, can you get my backpack?"

He got up and went to where he set it after removing it from her. He held it up and she said, "Yes, that's it." He brought it to her. She tried to pull what looked like a glass vessel out of a netted side pocket, but she couldn't quite get it out. He grabbed it out for her. The bottle flexed and gave way under his fingers but didn't break. Puzzled, he handed it to her.

"Thanks." She said and twisted off the top and drank. "Ah, much better." And smiled.

Her eyes started to droop, and she smiled some more. She slurred, "I'm getting sleepy", and then smiled again.

"Rest," he ordered.

"Okay, handsome," she said as she drifted off to sleep.

"Handsome? I am not handsome… I am a warrior… Warriors are not handsome," he grumbled to himself. While she was sleeping deeply due to the effects of the datura, he checked her wounds. He was concerned about the ones he used his hair to suture. They were holding for now, but he did not know how much longer that would be the case. He should go hunt for a deer, but he was reluctant to leave her. Plus, he had a lot of work to do right here. He needed to skin the wolves and discard the carcasses before their death odor began attracting other predators.

What was that crazy story; Cesar Millon, flat tire, dog with a bow? Maybe he gave her too much datura. I will give her less next time, he thought, as he stood and walked toward the dead wolves. He did not understand everything she said, but he thought he understood the main points. After he skinned and hung the hides to dry, he moved the carcasses far from the campsite and buried them so they wouldn't bring any more trouble. Along the way, he set a couple of traps to try to catch something for dinner.

When he got back, he checked on her. She was sleeping peacefully. He couldn't help but notice her beauty. Every time he looked at her, there was a strange, inexplicable pull inside him. Maybe she was the white man's witch and had cast a spell to get power over him, to keep him from taking back his land from the white men. Dinetah has been Navajo land since the beginning, long before white men came to the land. It was given to them by the gods. The blagáana have no right to it.

Some say that a witch is to blame for the Long Walk. That the witch, who is evil and wants to gain power, is trying to destroy the Navajo who strive to have perfect harmony with all living things. Some of his people say the witch makes the white man hate the Navajo. And that's why the white men do what they do to them, killing tens of thousands of Navajo and forcing those that remain on the Long Walk to encampments. The witch has been winning, but not for long. He and his brothers are going to see to that.

Arianna began to stir. She tried to sit up but struggled unsuccessfully. Hashké rushed to her and said, "Wait." He rolled up his pallet and blanket together, then placed the bundle beside her. He gently sat her up, using his arm behind her back. Once she was far enough off the pallet, he pulled the bundle behind her back. Then he carefully lowered her to it. At that moment, he realized how close she was and turned his head toward her. She was so very close and her lips ....

Arianna's heart quickened into thumping a hard and heavy percussion. His arm was so capable. He was so strong, so masculine, and so close. She could feel the heat ignite between them causing polarity, allying magnetic fields, pulling her to his lips. Her mouth suddenly parched, she licked her lips instinctively, and he was there, approaching. She glanced from his lips to his eyes and back. He was so gorgeous. Her eyes started to smile. Her chin buoyed up to join her lips to his and ... it was life altering!

Hashké was a captive in her eyes. As her tongue peeked out to moisten her lips, he could think of nothing else but possessing her. He wanted, he needed, he had to dance his tongue with hers. When she raised her lips to his, the fire of wanting her consumed him. He kissed her like their kiss was the only thing that mattered. When their tongues met, it was as if the sun had burst and its particles were raining down, prickling his flesh. He had never felt anything like this. It was vast and deep, so deep that he sensed there was no end to it. He did not want to stop but this could not be right. He had never felt this depth of feeling with anyone else. He kissed plenty, been with plenty. Women always found him attractive. Even the white women whores, who would never consider having sex with other Indians, would open the back door to him. That got him thinking about why this yearning might be happening. Legends told that if a man knew about the evil trying to get him, then the evil would lose its power. He jerked back and yelled, "You are a witch!"

Incensed, she drew in a deep breath and said, "What are you talking about?" She had thought that the last few moments were the best of her life and now this!

"You are different than other women. This that is between us is not like it is with other women. It does not feel like this does."

"Damn straight I'm not like other women. I have taken strides my whole life not to be like anyone else, to be my own person. But that does not mean I am a witch!"

Hashké stomped off, out of the camp.

Arianna was left reeling.

She was angry and she was hungry. Luckily her backpack was within reach. She could satisfy one of those appetites. She grabbed a power bar and angrily consumed it. *Where does he get off saying I'm a witch? I have done nothing.* None of this was her fault. She was just trying to get a stupid job and save a stupid dog, then all of this. She didn't seek it out, ask for it; it found her.

She tried to hold them back, but tears started rolling down her face. Once she started, she couldn't stop. She silently cried for her father, for her mother, and for the job she knew she wouldn't land now.

Ignoring the emotional pain, she inattentively twirled one of her earrings and thought about what she should do. Waking up in a strange place and in pain wasn't so bad when she felt him next to her. But now, with that outburst about her being a witch, not so much! *I think he really believes it too*, she thought. She could see it in his eyes. They were accusing and made her feel vulnerable; like he was going to assault her. She didn't, in truth, know him; he could be a crazy mountain man serial killer. What was she thinking, kissing him? As soon as she could, she was going to get up and leave his sorry ass. She did not know where she would go, just away from him. That jerk!

Shih Tzu. I am so out of here. However, her mind was more resolute than her body. She struggled to get up. It took her a while, but she finally did it. Man, was she weak. And looking down at herself for the first time, she realized she was almost naked. She was wearing only her bra and now, cut-off shorts. She wrapped the blanket around her and, bending to grab her backpack, nearly fell over. She knew there would be no way she could get it on her shoulders, so she tried to drag it behind her. She slowly got in a few dozen determined steps when her world started spinning; blackness shadowed her, then took over.

Hashké had stormed off, deciding to check his traps. His mind was buzzing. He knew something was not right with her. Her clothing, her pack, her shoes! More importantly, the way she made him feel, she must be a witch. There was no other explanation. She spoke oddly and of things he did not understand. What was he going to do with her? She maddened him. But then he thought of her eyes and how sweet she looked as she was telling her story. His heart ached, thinking of her. She reminded him of sunshine, not darkness. How could sunshine be evil? Even so, she did not fit into his plans. First and foremost, he must get his sister back. There is no place for a white woman in his goal.

She would have to go. As soon as she was strong enough, he would take her to her family. They could take care of her. But he remembered finding her alone. No woman travels alone, unless she has no one to care for her. If she has no family, he would just take her to a trading post, drop her off there and be done with her. One way or another, he would put her out of his life, and then get back to his agenda. But the thought of leaving her somewhere and riding away made his heart sink. Could he? He had to, that was all there was to it. His sister needed him and his brothers, right now. He really could make no other choice.

Having made up his mind, Hashké finished checking the traps and found one had a robust rabbit snared in its grasp. After killing the frantic creature, he slung it over his shoulder and headed back to the camp. When he got close, he could feel something was wrong. He looked for Arianna, but she was not on her pallet. His heart plummeted. As he looked around, he tried to think of what could have happened to her. Did a predator get her? He should have never left her alone. *His woman should never be unprotected.* His woman? Where did that outlandish thought come from? She was not his.

Ah, there, he saw her. She was crumpled in a heap on the ground, not far from camp. It looked like she had tried to flee, having dragged her pack with her. She could not leave; he just found her. She could not leave; she needed to rest and get better. She could not leave, and go off on her own, unprotected. What if something happened to her? He could not abide that thought.

He bent down and carefully gathered her in his arms where she belonged. Did he really think that? He brought her in close and nuzzled her neck. How could he feel this deeply for someone, a white woman, whom he had just met? If he were honest with himself, he really didn't even care if she were a witch. He had to have her in his life. He would figure something out. Maybe he would bring her to a medicine man and have the witch cast out of her. Indeed, that is what he would do.

He kicked away the rolled-up bundle, laid her on the pallet and covered her with the blanket. He swept her hair from her eyes and noticed how warm she was. A fever! He needed to get his medicine pouch.

He retrieved the necessary herbs for an infection fever and made a tea out of them. He sat her up with one arm and with the other tried to get her to drink.

Arianna regained consciousness with something dripping down her neck. Handsome was back and he was holding something to her lips. "Drink," he told her.

"No! Get away from me, you jerk!" she said, trying to push him away.

He didn't budge.

"Drink, you have fever."

"So. Why do you care? Why help a witch, you ass. You're not a nice person. I don't care if I do have a fever, I want you to go away and leave me alone. I would rather die than have you help me!"

Now he was getting angry again. "You do not know what you are saying. You need to drink and get better." *I cannot lose you*, he thought.

"You hate me, remember, I'm a witch?" She threw his words back at him.

"I do not hate you and if you are a witch. I will take you to the medicine man. But you have to drink and get better," he said.

"I am no witch. I may be unpleasant sometimes." Thinking of PMS, she definitely wasn't going to give him that info. "But I'm a nice person who goes to church." Occasionally, well actually rarely because she worked as much as possible and Sunday shifts were often up for grabs, but he didn't need to know that, either.

"You need to drink to get well to fight more with me." he said, interrupting her thoughts.

Wearing down with fatigue, she admitted, "I am so tired. You promise you don't hate me?"

"No, I do not hate you. Somehow you are a little bit in here now." He pointed to his chest.

"Truly?" she asked.

"Yes," he replied

With complete honesty she blurted, "Good. Because right now I'm scared, and I do not want to be alone. I think I do need you. Will you stay with me?"

"Yes. Do not ponder on this. I will care for you. You are safe with me. I will not let anything happen to you. Now drink."

"Okay, Handsome." She smiled. She took a drink and almost spit it out but managed to swallow the bitter brew. "That's horrible!"

"I know it does not taste good, but you have to drink it."

Flirting, even in her feverish state, she said, "What will you give me if I do?"

"What do you speak of?"

"If I drink this, will you reward me with another kiss?"

Warmed by her coquettishness, he smiled and said, "Yes, if that is what it will take."

She drank it, grimacing after every swallow.

"Good, all of it," he demanded.

She did and then looked at him expectantly.

After he set the cup down, he turned back to her and while she was still in his arms, kissed her, pulling her close to his naked chest.

She felt his kiss all the way down to her toes. She lifted her fingers and stroked his face. As her strength slipped away, her fingers drifted down to his neck then chest and then … nothing. She was fast asleep.

As her hand made its way down his torso and her mouth went slack, he realized she had succumbed to the pull of sleep. When she touched his chest, every muscle in his body contracted, as if he had been struck by lightning. He could have taken her right then. He had to get control of himself. *She is injured.*

First things first; he needed to find more herbs and get her healed, quickly. He laid her down softly and stood up, intending to start cooking the rabbit, but he just stood there looking at her.

After several minutes his mind decreed, "Mine." Then he turned and proceeded with his chores.

6

A delicious aroma woke Arianna. She opened her eyes and saw Handsome at the fire tending to what was cooking there.

"Hello, Handsome," she said.

He turned to her, smiling. "Hello. How are you feeling?" he said as he walked to her. He crouched down and felt her forehead.

"A little better."

His hand tenderly slipped down her face and lingered there as he asked, "Are you hungry?"

"Yes, actually."

"Good, I have cooked a rabbit."

"A bunny?" she asked.

"Is that what you call them?"

"Yes. They're cute and fuzzy and pets, not food."

"For the Navajo, they are food. Do you have a problem with this? I have dried meat in my pack."

"No, that's okay." *Sorry Thumper,* she thought. "It does smell good and it feels like it's been forever since I've had a warm meal. I'll try it, but I can't guarantee that I'll like it. Can you help me sit up?"

"Yes. And it is good that you try." he said as he got her situated. He then went to the fire and pulled off some meat for her. Because her hand was so injured, he held out a small strip for her at her mouth so she could eat. Reluctantly, she took the meat into her mouth and chewed. After swallowing, she started smiling.

Every time she smiled something ached inside him. "Do you like?"

"I love it! It is so good, who knew?"

"That pleases me."

Arianna smiled again and said, "Can I have some more?"

He went back to the cooking meat and brought it to her. "I like watching you eat. You do it so quietly and carefully. It is not what I am used to."

"What are you used to?"

He thought on that then replied. "Just getting it done."

She smiled and said, "But good food should be enjoyed. Having both of my parents pass away while they were still in their prime forced me to enjoy what I have now. Even the simple, everyday things, you never know if you will have them tomorrow."

He thought of what she said, and he agreed, the state of his people confirmed it. "You are a smart woman."

She laughed and said, "Thank you," then continued eating.

"Do you have any other family still alive?"

"No, my Dad passed first, and not six months later my Mom passed. I'm an only child, so there's no one else."

"I am sorry for their passing. Are you finished?"

She nodded.

She had no family to care for her, but it no longer mattered; he would not let her go now even if she did have relatives living. There were still things that bothered him, though. *He would solve those in time*, he thought.

"I am going to make your fever tea now. You must drink all of it."

"What will you give me?" she asked, smiling.

She is so endearing. How could he have ever thought of letting her go? It has only been two days and already he is unable to fathom not having her at his fire. *I must keep her.* Grinning back, he said, "What do you want?"

Emboldened, she replied, "You next to me all night, kissing and holding me."

His heart started pounding like a war drum, thinking about that very thing. His manhood immediately began to stiffen at her words. He bent down and kissed her thoroughly. He did not want to stop but he needed to fix her tea and then eat himself. He shallowed his kisses and slowly pulled back. "I will fix your tea, then I will sleep next to you." She nodded and he left to do so.

She could not wait for bed! Finally, she knew what all the clamor was about. She had kissed boys before, but it had never been like this; so electric. She no longer cared about her dream job, her car, or anything else. For the first time she felt true happiness and looked forward to what was going to happen next. Sure, she had pain but when he kissed her, she forgot all about it. If she could bottle him, she could make a fortune.

Hashké still could not believe his body's reaction to her. He contemplated that as he ate. She took his very breath away. How could he keep her in his world? There is so much evil that he must deal with, alone, unhampered by feelings of softness toward anyone. His sister and his people are counting on him. He could not let them down. It was his duty. He and his siblings were some of the few Navajo to have escaped the round-up for the Long Walk. He knew that General Carleton was lying when he said the United States government would care for the Navajo in a proper manner if they surrendered peaceably. Hashké had never -- and would never -- trust him or anything he said.

"What's wrong?" Arianna asked as she noticed the stern look on his face.

"Nothing that concerns you. I just have things I have to take care of."

"About me?" She asked. She did not want to be what had caused such a look to cross his face.

"No. It is about my people."

"Do you want to talk about it?

"No, it does not concern you." He turned to check on the tea.

"Can I in anyway, help you? You have done so much for me; you saved my life, for heaven's sake! I have started to care for you and if something is bothering you, then it bothers me. I know we haven't known each other for long but I feel we have a connection." *But, if it is not her place to do so, she would let it go*, she thought.

He brought the tea to her and marveled at her tender nature. "That is not our way. The man is the warrior. The woman takes care of the children and the harvesting of crops. The woman does not concern herself with such things."

"Well that is not MY way," she said. She began drinking; the tea was awful. She could hardly get it down but with Handsome as the prize, she would do anything. "I'm sorry if I have upset you."

"No, you have not," he said with a small smile. "Drink it all."

She did and then she said, "I have to go to the lady's room."

Puzzled, he said, "There are no rooms here."

"No, I have to pee."

"Oh, I will take you." He grabbed the blanket covering her to remove it when she stopped him saying, "But I have hardly any clothes on. Where are they, by the way?"

"I had to cut them off the treat your wounds."

"Oh, of course you did, but I still don't feel comfortable having you see me without my clothes on."

"I have already seen you as you are when I tended your wounds. There is no problem."

"But I still do not feel comfortable."

With consternation, he suggested, "I will take you and the blanket. Will that be suitable?"

"Sure."

He carefully scooped her up, ensuring her modesty was protected by the blanket, and carried her to a fallen tree outside of the camp and set her gently down on her feet.

"Well, go away," she commanded. He scowled. She scolded, "Go."

He turned and walked out of the immediate area.

She did her business and shouted, "Okay, I'm done." He came back, scooped her up and walked back to camp. Once again, he kicked the roll out to the side and placed her on her pallet.

"I have to check your wounds, now." He started to pull the blanket away and she yelled, "No!" He stopped and said, "You are not making sense. I have seen you as you are. There is no worry to be had."

"I was unconscious then. I'm not now. I'm uncomfortable with you seeing me without my shirt on." No man had and the very thought turned her all kinds of shades of red. "You can just look at my arms as they are and you can roll back the blanket from each leg, one at a time."

He blew out a breath and shook his head. "Fine." He did just as she instructed; peeling back a corner of dressing, noted her wounds looked good. They were a little red and there was some swelling, but he believed they were starting to heal. She still had to be very careful, though. Tomorrow or the day after, he would change the dressings. "Do you need the pain medication?"

"Maybe a little, but not as much as yesterday."

He nodded and left to get it.

After she chewed and spit out the plant bits, he settled her in bed. "I have to check on the horses and then I will come back."

"You have horses? I love horses. I used to ride all the time."

"When you are well, I will bring you to them."

"Thanks, I would love that!"

He left and was back before she could miss him. "Can I have some water?"

"Of course." He brought a cup to her and she drank it down. "Thanks."

He nodded, unrolled his pallet and placed it next to hers, then went to put more wood on the fire. He removed his weapons, placing them alongside his pallet as always and then he lay down next to her. His heart was already pounding. He wanted to touch all of her. He wanted to be inside her. He scolded himself, thinking of her pain. "Do you need anything?" he asked.

"You," she said softly. He turned toward her and propped himself on an elbow. He leaned down and began to kiss her, gently to start with, but as the world melted away, he got more insistent.

She didn't remember falling asleep, but she must have, because the next thing she remembered was waking in his arms and smiling.

The new day went similarly to the last, with Arianna napping here and there, throughout the day and then drinking the fever tea.

As they were bedding down for the night, Hashké could only think of one thing, kissing and touching Arianna. He started stroking her hair, then her face. Her skin felt like the petals of flowers. His hand drifted down her neck, then her collarbone. He had an undeniable urge to touch her everywhere. He wanted to know all of her. His hand slipped down further, and his fingers felt the cloth of her underclothes. He slipped his finger under it and skimmed her breast.

Arianna was breathing so heavy that she thought she might hyperventilate. When his fingers slipped under her bra, she held her breath.

He dragged his finger out of the under garment and placed his entire hand on the sweet swell of her breast. She was full and soft and perfect. He heard her gasp. He smiled. But as he squeezed and caressed, something niggled at the back of his mind. His calluses kept snagging on the delicate fabric.

Those unanswered questions about her garments bubbled back to the surface.

"What is this?" he asked, his lips still touching her mouth.

"What?"

"This," he said as he tugged on the fabric.

"Are you kidding? It's a bra."

"What is bra?" he asked while nibbling on her lips.

She pushed at him, so he pulled back and looked at her, questioningly.

"What do you mean, you don't know what a bra is? Even a mountain recluse knows what a bra is. It's time you joined the twenty-first century."

"Nineteenth century, silly woman."

She just stared up at him, dumbfounded. Her mind was blazing: no road, no planes flying overhead, the clothes he wore. It was all adding up, but to what? The sum she was coming up with did not make any sense. She looked straight into his eyes and said, "The day my car had the flat tire was March 12, in the year 2009."

"You do not know of what you speak. It is the year 1864. Maybe you hit your head as well." He said as he put his fingers through her hair to check for bumps.

She elbowed his hand away and said, "No, I didn't hit my head, it honestly was 2009. Are you really saying to me that here, now, it's 1864?"

Nodding his head slowly, he said," Yes."

As she was trying to come to terms with the fact that time travel was a reality, she murmured, "Something must have happened in that cave. I did feel the rocks move but I thought it was an earthquake or something. The air pressure changed; my ears popped. I remembered getting nauseous. Then I blacked out, I guess. I woke and my flashlight was dimmer so I must have been out for a while but in no way was I out for 150 years."

"Flash light?" He asked.

"Shih Tzu!"

"Shih Tzu?" he questioned.

"That's my new non-curse word." She said offhandedly. "Of course, you don't know what a flashlight is, they haven't been invented yet. Grab my backpack and I'll show you."

He did.

She felt around in the pack, carefully trying not to brush her injured palm on anything. There, she found it. She pulled it out. She showed it to him, turned it on. A dim light shone through the lens.

He took it from her and examined it. Light without heat emitted from it. "How is such possible?" he asked.

"It runs on batteries. Batteries store energy, kind of like lightning, in them for use when you want it. I know it's hard to understand, it's hard for me to understand, and I grew up with the darn things."

"So, you come from the future."

"I guess so, 145 years in the future." This time actually doing the math. "I'm having trouble wrapping my head around this. I don't know if it is the concept or the pain meds or the fact that I'm just tired. One thing I do know is that I care about you no matter what year it is." She went on to explain, "You make me feel safe. I haven't felt that in a long time. And right now, I feel like I'm on shaky ground and I just need to feel your arms around me, holding me, please?"

"Yes," he said. Even though it lacked conviction, she would take it anyway.

His mind was going in four different directions at the same time. He lay next to her and put his arm around her. She wriggled closer to him, which felt right.

He did not know what to think. *Maybe she IS a witch. He did not know how else to explain how she could have traveled from one time to another. Maybe she is a spirit, but how could that be, she feels real in my arms.* He inhaled, her natural fragrance hit him and his body reacted. She felt too good to be a witch. If she were evil, would he not sense it? He kept going over things in his head but not coming up with answers, so he just let his mind drift. When he thought about her, it was always with good feelings inside.

He smiled to himself, remembering her saying, "What will you give me?" He did not know what the truth was concerning her situation, but what he did know was that he could not stomach being without her. She touched him deep inside; in a place he did not even know existed. As he fell asleep, he did so smiling, with his head nestled close to hers.

Morning woke him early. He found himself in the same place he was in when he fell asleep. As he removed his arm, she moaned and wrinkled her brow. He smiled, kissed her head, and got up. He's been doing that a lot since she burst into his life -- smiling. He never used to. Life was always one task after another, surviving, without much thought outside of that. But now, all that filled his head was Arianna.

He put more wood on the fire and set out to check on the horses and gather the herbs he would need to change all of her dressings. It was mid-morning when he returned. He found her sobbing. In a heartbeat, he drew out an arrow, notched it to his bow and scanned the area. Seeing no threat, he rushed to her and gathered her in his arms and asked, "What is wrong?"

She sniffed and wiped her eyes with the back of her hand. "That wolf attack has made me irrational, I guess. I don't know. I woke up alone. I called for you, but you didn't answer. I didn't know what to think. I thought that maybe you left or worse, that somehow I got pulled back to my time and wouldn't be with you anymore."

His heart wrenched when he saw her in tears. He did not know what was wrong but knew, as sure as the sun rises each day, that he was going to make it better. Once she told him what thoughts had been plaguing her, he knew he was going to see to it that they would stay together, no matter what.

He kissed the top of her head and said, "It is fine, everything is fine. I am here." He loosened his embrace and when she turned her head up to his, he kissed her thoroughly. When they separated, he explained where he was. "Today is the day to change your dressings, so I left to gather more herbs. I did not want to wake you, you needed to sleep."

"Oh … But can you kiss me some more?" she asked, smiling.

Laughing, he obliged.

After fully satisfying her request, he said, "You need to eat and then I need to tend to your wounds."

"Okay, can you help me sit up?"

He did, then went to get a dried corn biscuit and some water for her breakfast. Afterward, he went to the fire and put water on to boil for the sagebrush mixture. He started preparing the herbs, adding them to the boiling water.

He gave her more pain medicine so that when he began working on her, she would not feel the full force of the pain.

Once the medicine began to work, he proceeded.

While he was tending to her, she wondered out loud, "Do you have any family around here?"

"No. My mother and father were killed during the massacres. I have three brothers and one sister who still live."

"What happened? I mean, I know that Indians were killed for their land, but I would like to know what happened to your family, specifically."

Hashké rebuffed her, saying, "It is not winter, the time of telling stories."

"That's crazy, who knows where I'll be by winter? Where will WE be in the winter."

"It is Navajo tradition to save the telling for times when there is little that needs doing. In the winter months, there is no tending or harvesting of crops, animals are not birthing, and there is plenty of dried meat stored."

"I understand and appreciate the Navajo traditions. They make sense, but I hope you will make an exception this once so I may understand what has happened," she continued, "something brought me here. I'm not sure why, but maybe it is to help you or the Navajo in some way. It's the only thing I can think of to explain my crazy situation."

Hashké thought on what she said about there being a reason for her coming to his time. So even though it goes against the Navajo principle to live life with utmost responsibility, not being wasteful with resources as well as time, he would tell her. This thought gave his mind peace but he would warn her first. "I will make an exception. There is time now while I tend to your wounds to do the telling, but it is an unpleasant story. Maybe you will not want to know."

"I do want to know. I want to know all of it, even the unpleasant, to understand."

"If you are sure."

She nodded with the solemnity required for the atrocities she knew were coming.

Hashké took the sage mixture off the fire to let it cool and began removing her old dressings.

"Before the white man came, my people lived a prosperous life. We had many sheep to trade, abundant crops and orchards that we have cultivated for many generations. There were skirmishes between the Navajo and the white men but the same as with the Apache and Comanche.

"That changed a handful of years ago, when white men started to come to this land to take gold and silver from it, the U.S. Cavalry started harassing my people and killing them more and more. When we would not leave our land, General Carleton gave an order to the army to kill all of our sheep. They killed tens of thousands of them, thinking we would just give up. But few surrendered. Navajo are very strong and resourceful. I think he became very frustrated by the bond the Navajo have with the land. He must not know that it was given to us by the gods and that no man can take it from us."

Explaining further, he added, "The U.S. Government's efforts to eradicate us from the land were not unlike trying to pull an ancient tree from the ground by first hacking all of the branches off, then hitching a team of horses to a chain around the trunk to yank the tree from its bed, exposing the roots. My family was one of those branches.

"Attacks on the Navajo increased. Last year, the cavalry had orders to kill my people where they found them. Their bullets flew farther than the Navajo arrows, ending their lives before the Navajo could fight back. When they found a village, they would shoot the guards, then set fire to our hogans, shooting women and children one by one, as they came out from hiding, trying to escape the flames. In one such attack, my father was killed and my mother was wounded. She died not long after. They had a strong bond."

"Last fall, the cavalry continued to weaken and kill those who survived the slaughter by cutting off all means of sustenance for the Navajo. I have heard that Carleton paid a bounty for Navajo sheep and horses the survivors managed to gather. The troops set fire to our crops and orchards. They even poisoned our wells. Many thousands of my people were murdered."

While carefully pouring the sage mixture over her wounds, he continued: "That winter was very hard for us. My people were starving. We did what we could, but my people's spirits were broken by all of the deaths and hardships. Carleton sent word that the government would take pity on us since we were hungry and feed us, but we had to leave our land to live in the camps the government built. Many gave up and surrendered. They joined the captured and were forced to go on the Long Walk."

Dismayed, Arianna interrupted, "What's the Long Walk?"

"The Navajo were made to travel on foot from Fort Defiance to Fort Sumner in the south. That journey is over 300 miles long. Many died on the way. There are tales that his men shot anyone who stopped to help one who had fallen or was ill. Even pregnant women were shot if they could not keep up. And if they stopped walking because they were in labor to have their babe, they were shot."

Arianna was stunned to silence – then became outraged. She had never heard of such things. This history was definitely not taught in school. "I had no idea that such things happened to your tribe. I am so angry; I can't even come up with the words to adequately begin to tell you how sorry I am. That was so wrong. We are not taught this history in school. We should have been. The treatment of your people by the government is completely unacceptable. I am so sorry this has happened to you. I knew it was bad but this . . . this is hard to even contemplate."

After a second or two, she continued, "I apologize on behalf of the U.S. I know that is not much, but I believe someone should. If I am returned to my time, I will try to do something about it. I don't know what that could be, but something for sure."

Hashké acknowledged what she said but continued to work, now applying new dressings.

She let minutes go by, not wanting to lessen the gravity of the truths he told her.

When he started reapplying the bindings, she tried to alleviate some the heaviness by asking about those who are still alive.

"Where are your siblings? Are they close by?"

"No, they are all scattered. My sister, her name is Shándíín, it means sunlight in your language, was taken captive by Ute raiders who sold her into the slave trade. Your government is fighting over the slavery of the black man but turns a blind eye toward the slavery of my people." He was angry, and Arianna knew it.

"Gosh, again, I am appalled. Slavery is not allowed in my time for anyone in the U.S. I know that doesn't help but at least you know that in the future, no one can be bought or sold.

Things are changing for Native Americans, too. That's the politically correct name we use for the American indigenous people. Some tribes are getting back at the white people in a roundabout way. They now own casinos, places white people go to gamble, they are taking in all the white people's money and becoming very rich. It's a wonderful thing to watch. Many Americans are happy to see this happen."

Hashké half-heartedly smiled at this and continued, "My brothers and I have separated and scattered to avoid being captured. We must stay free to help our sister. We have a plan."

"Please tell me!" Arianna implored.

"We know that our sister was purchased by a man who works for the government. He is the Superintendent of Indian Affairs of the New Mexico Territory. He will not be difficult to find. We do not want more trouble so we will try to buy her back. Once she is safe, then we will try to drive Carleton and his soldiers off our lands."

Arianna took advantage of the silence that followed and said, "As I said earlier, I think that what has happened to you and your people is terrible and wrong. Your enemies should be stopped."

"You speak the truth?" he questioned. "But they are your people."

"The people I considered mine would never do these things. I do not consider Carleton and his men my people. His actions are evil and must end."

Her statements touched him, but he had to focus on finishing her wound treatment. With that in mind, he said, "Your wounds have started healing but you must still take care. Once they are better, we will travel to a safer camp; one that will keep us dry when the rains come."

"You'll take me with you?" she asked, excited.

"Yes. You are a part of me in here." He placed his hand to his chest. She tried to sit up to kiss him, but she was still so weak. Seeing her struggle, he leaned down to her and they kissed. He continued, "I do not want to be without you. I have a dangerous path in front of me, but I will protect you and keep you safe. You are mine. I will not leave you. You are with me now."

Arianna's whole body melted. She loved the feeling of someone so strong and powerful taking care of her, looking out for her. For too long she had been the only one concerned with her care and keeping. It was an amazing feeling to have someone want to. This is the best dream she had ever had, and it was really happening. She had to cross time to have it, but she would do it again and again to be with him. "You are in my heart, as well. I have never felt this deeply for anyone, well, except my parents. I am so glad you have feelings for me, too."

Hashké bent down and kissed her, then smiled. He finished with the bindings and disposed of the soiled wrappings.

Her bladder interrupted her thoughts with urgings she could no longer ignore so she had to ask, "Can you help me go to the lady's room again? I will be so glad when I can do it without your help."

"Do not feel that way. It is not a bother to me." He lifted her and her blanket up and took her to the fallen log.

"Um, I am embarrassed to ask but what do you use to wipe yourself with in the 1800's? We have what we call toilet paper in my time but obviously there isn't any around, so I have to ask."

"I will get you some leaves."

"Oh, okay, thanks. This is so embarrassing."

He returned and set a pile of broad leaves next to her. He asked, "Do you want me to leave?"

"Yes, please. Definitely. I will call you." That had to be the single most horrifying thing ever, discussing bathroom necessities with a crush was awful, but she made it through. After she was finished, she called for him and he came.

He set her back on the pallet and asked if she needed anything. She didn't so he told her that he was going to set some more traps and would be back later. He suggested she sleep and she agreed. She was worn out by the morning's activities. She closed her eyes and napped.

While he was out, he happened upon a doe and her twins. He thanked mother earth, for he could take one and still leave the mother with one. He aimed and shot. The young one dropped immediately; there was no struggle. It was a clean kill. The doe and her remaining offspring leaped away unharmed.

When he brought the kill back to the camp, Arianna was still sleeping. He quietly cleaned the meat and skinned the hide. He also retrieved the needed sinew. There wasn't much but would help if a small repair was needed. He cut some small pieces of meat and hung them to dry. The rest, he skewered and hung over the fire to cook. They were going to eat well tonight.

While the meat was cooking, he went to his pack and pulled out a large tanned deerskin and some thin strapping. He laid the hide by the fire and took some charcoal from the fire pit and marked a pattern on it. He could not make her a proper dress, but he could fashion leggings and a leather shirt. It would not be as fine as her clothing that had been ripped up, but it would be better for riding. He pulled his knife out of its sheath and began cutting.

Arianna once again woke to a savory smell. She looked around and saw Handsome working with some leather. "Good afternoon, Handsome." He looked over at her and smiled. "Can I have some water?" He filled the cup and brought it to her.

Setting it down, he propped her up, gave her the water and asked, "How do you feel?"

"Good. I'm still weak, but I feel like I'm turning a corner."

He stroked her cheek and thought about how refreshing it was being with her. "That is good." he said.

"What were you working on?" She asked.

"Clothing for you. You will need it soon."

"Really?" she asked. "That's so sweet of you. No one has ever gone so far out of their way for me before. You have done so much for me. I don't know how I will ever repay you."

"No payment. I do this for you. It is my place to provide for you."

Her insides immediately turned to goo. Having someone actually do such things for her made her feel so special. "Come here," she demanded. He moved in closer as she leaned up and kissed him. He put his hand around the back of her head and deepened the kiss. He could do this all day long. He moved his fingers through her hair and caught on a snag.

"Ouch," she muttered.

"I am sorry."

"No. Please, you have single-handedly taken care of all my needs, I have not been able to do one thing for myself including the simplest of tasks like brush my hair or bathe my body. I'm sure I look awful. I have just been lying here while you have catered to my every need. It's nothing that a shower and a brush won't fix."

"What is a shower?" he asked

"It's something we have in my time in our homes. It's a small room where the water comes down from a pipe and you clean yourself in it."

"Does your house not get wet?" he inquired.

"No, there's a hole in the floor that takes the water away." He looked questioningly at her. She smiled and said, "If I had a paper and pen, I would draw you a picture to help explain. I'm not doing a very good job describing it.

"Do you have a brush or a comb I could use?" She hadn't seen him use one but maybe he had one in his pack.

"No. I will make one for you."

"Would you? I'd appreciate it. Your hair is so shiny and wonderful. I wish mine were like yours."

"When you are better, I will wash yours with the yucca root. It will be the same."

"That would be awesome! I can't wait! I'm so tired of just lying about."

"You must. It is your time to get well." He stated. "I will carve you a comb to use until then."

"On second thought, that may be a waste of your time. I don't think I could use it anyway. She lifted up her hands in explanation."

"I will do it for you." he declared. "I will be back."

He walked toward the stream. A short time later, he was back with a small hunk of wood. He used a hatchet of some kind and split the wood. He did it again and came up with what she guessed was a suitable piece. Throwing the discarded pieces into the fire, he came over and sat next to her. He took out his knife and started whittling. It wasn't long before he held up a wide-toothed comb to show her.

"That's awesome. You are very handy to have around," she said.

"Thank you," he smiled. "I need to smooth it now." He got up and went over to the leather he was working on earlier. He came back with a strip of the hide and sat down again. He rubbed the hide against the wood repeatedly; he even slipped it through the tines back and forth. He handed the finished product to her and she marveled.

In the same amount of time it would have taken her to get in her car, drive to the store, buy a cheap plastic comb, then drive home, he made a much more beautiful one, a keepsake to be treasured. She looked adoringly at him, saying, "Thank you. I will cherish it."

He took it back and moved behind her. "I will try not to hurt you." Hashké started at the bottom of her hair, working out the tangles as he inched his way higher. She wallowed in the luxury of having a gorgeous man tending to her hair with a comb he made for her. Tension she didn't know she had, flowed out of her with every stroke.

"That feels wonderful," She said, realizing, of course, that a man with long hair knows how to deal with a woman's long hair. It actually hurt very little.

Hashké warmed to his task. He had never combed through another's hair. It was an unexpected pleasure. He doubted it would feel the same with someone else, though. He found himself smiling again. It was a good thing his enemy was not watching. They would not see him as a threat. She turned him inside out; he would never think about doing such things with another woman. He simply would not be bothered with it. But for her, he was constantly thinking about what he could do. If she wanted, he would walk straight up to the chief of her people and ask for her hand. The depth of his feelings amazed him. "It is finished," he said as he tried to distance himself just a little, uncomfortable with the way he felt.

"Thank you, again. Come here; I need to pay you," she said coyly, not noticing his discomfort.

"No payment."

"Just come here," she demanded.

He did and she kissed him.

He smiled, with all thoughts of withdrawing scattered in the wind and said, "You must pay me often." He smiled even bigger, then walked to the fire to check on the meat.

"It smells so good. What is it?"

"Venison."

"I have not had that either. "

"What do you eat in your time?" he asked.

"Mostly chicken and beef." She answered.

"The meat is done. Do you have hunger?"

"Yes, starving." He cut off several pieces and sat down to feed her. "I feel bad always eating first. Will you eat some with me?" she asked.

"If you want."

With every two bites she ate, he took one; still ensuring her needs were met first.

"Venison is good," she decided. "You are such a good cook. You will always have to cook for us because I am a horrible cook."

"You will learn. I will teach you. It is woman's work. I will hunt the meat and you will cook it. That is our way."

Her independent woman hackles shot straight up.

"What if I want to hunt the meat and have you cook it? After I learn how to use a bow and arrow, I mean," she said, raising her eyebrows.

He laughed. "I cannot say no to you, if that is what you want, I will teach you to hunt." She leaned over and kissed him soundly.

"What was that for?" he asked.

"Payment for the correct answer."

"I like payments," he said as they smiled at each other.

Hashké put water in the pot to boil. Then he prepared the herbs for her fever tea and added them to the hot water. Next, he checked on the horses and finished his chores. He was looking forward to this night. For now, he was sure who Arianna is. She is a person from another time, not a witch or a spirit or anything evil. He did not understand how she came to his time, but that did not matter. She is good. That is all that matters, that and the fact she pulls on his heart with a force he cannot deny.

He poured a cup of tea and handed it to her.

Before she started to drink, she said cheekily, "Do I need to ask?"

"No, tonight you will not have to ask. I will give."

She drank, wondering what that meant.

After she finished the tea, he completed his nightly chores and rolled out his pallet beside hers, right where it belonged. After placing his weapons to the side, he turned to her and was sure he felt the sun and moon stop their trek across the sky. The look in her eyes was intense.

Her heart was racing.

He leaned down and began kissing her; softly at first, then it was if they were going to consume each other. Her fingers brushed his face, she was disappointed that her injuries prevented her from doing more.

His hands cupped her jaw and then they traveled. Oh, did they travel! He dragged his finger down her throat and onto her chest. He dragged it straight over her breast and she held her breath. He asked her in a deep, gravelly voice, "Does this come off?"

"Yes, but I can't reach it because of this," she alluded to her injuries.

"Can I remove it?" he asked.

She thought for a moment, as she was in unchartered territory here. She had kissed guys she dated but this was very different. She wanted to but she was a little afraid. But who better to explore this with than Hashké, the man she was falling in love with? She looked up at him and nodded shyly, telling him of the hooks in the back. He put his arm behind her back like he had done so often but this time it was for a whole different reason. He fumbled a bit, then was successful.

Hashké's expression on his face was one of a man who had just single-handedly won the Super Bowl. His grin made her grin, even though she was apprehensive about what was to come. He slipped the straps down and she removed her right hand. He helped her with the left. Then he just stared.

She started to feel self-conscious but then he said, "You are the most beautiful woman I have ever seen." His hand came up and cupped her breast and thoughts of being shy flew away like dandelion seeds scattering in the wind. He started kissing her again and as he did, he leaned her back to the pallet. He started to kiss down her throat and then down her chest too. "Oh God," she whispered. He kissed and suckled her breast and fondled the other one at the same time. She felt like she was floating on a cloud. Then he pinched the nipple he was fondling, and she almost disintegrated right then and there in pleasure.

When he switched breasts, she briefly started to breathe again. This was amazing. She wanted to do this all the time, all day and all night, only interrupting to eat. Why do anything else? As he was still suckling, his hand started caressing down her rib cage, past her flat belly to the top of her shorts. He slipped his hand under her waistband and her breath caught again. But his hand was too big. He pulled back out and pulled at her button until it slipped through the hole. She didn't think they had zippers in the 1800's but it was amazing how adaptable he was. He figured it out in no time. He slowly dragged his hand down and her breath sped up. His fingers touched her panties and he looked at her questioningly. "Panties," she said breathlessly. His fingers inched under them as he resumed kissing her and her heartbeat pounded like a big bass drum. No man had been there before. This was all new to her. His fingers were going to touch … "Oh God!" He rubbed and delved and she came apart. She would have screamed if his mouth hadn't been on hers. As she came down from the clouds, his fingers slowed, and she started breathing again. He gently pulled away from her slightly and smiled. She turned every shade of red possible and said, "Wow!"

"Good?" he asked, still smiling.

"Great!" she exclaimed. "I love the way you 'give.' You can 'give' anytime you want. I have never done, experienced that before. I know you have; you are much too good at it for it to have been your first time."

He just grinned at her.

What was that, a twinge of jealousy, she just felt? Her mind started going six ways to Sunday about how often he had done this and to how many women.

"It is late. You must sleep," he commanded.

"Okay," she capitulated. "But can you get me some water first?" He nodded and got up to get her a cup. As he did, she noticed him tenting his breechcloth. She knew she should do something about it but with her injuries she could not think of what. As he returned, she said, "Should I?" and gestured to his projection, then took the cup and drank.

He shook his head no and said, "When you are healed, we will do many more things. Just sleep tonight. I am here." He took back the empty cup and pulled her blanket up to her shoulders and then grabbed his up, too. But tonight, as he settled up to her backside, he put his hand under her blanket and cupped her breast. The sensation of being cherished washed over her and sweetly nudged her over the edge into sleep.

He lay there holding her bare breast, thinking how long he had been waiting to do this; since the moment he saw her. Now that it is happening, he couldn't be happier. She felt 'right' in his arms. What has she done to him? All he had to do is think about her and he became hard as stone. And when she came, he felt as if he were soaring with her. He had never felt that before. He liked giving women pleasure but it was never like this, soaring with them. He marveled at the depths as he, too, slipped into sleep.

7

The next day was spent in a similar fashion, hunting, cooking, eating. In his spare time, Hashké worked on Arianna's clothing. He placed a piece of hide made from a soft thinner skin over her head that draped nicely atop her shoulders. The whole garment was rectangular in shape with a hole cut out in the center for her head to fit through. The length was past her waist a few inches. It fit fine, but she did not see how to wear it, given the sides were completely open. Not wanting to offend him or belittle his hard work, she said, "It's beautiful. How do I keep the sides from flapping open?"

"If I have enough sinew, I will stitch them. If not, I will use thin strips of hide to lace. This is for you to use until I can trade for a proper Navajo dress."

"Thanks, but I think I will like wearing the leggings and this more than a dress."

He removed the poncho and stared. She was sitting up with only her cut-off pants on and his heart rate shot up to the mountaintops. "You are beautiful," he said. She was still not comfortable being unclothed around him, so she tried to quickly bring the blanket up, but he stopped her. "No," he said, as she tried to wriggle free.

As an intense sense of possessiveness enveloped him, he said, "You are mine. You must listen to what I say." Part of her was offended but another part of her was very excited by a powerful man telling her what to do. Plus, she was thrilled he found her so attractive. She put on her big-girl panties (figuratively) and sat there trying not to fidget with the blanket pooled on her lap. He took a long moment and looked his fill. He leaned over her and kissed her senseless. When he was satisfied, he pulled back and went to do his work.

"Dang," she thought, as she leaned back against the bundle propping her up. Who was she to argue? Her very existence here was completely dependent on him, plus his autocratic attitude had her female bits fluttering. She quickly placed her mind somewhere, anywhere else, not wanting to examine her body's response.

He pounded an awl into the leather that was laid over a piece of wood, which in turn was perched on a rock.

She watched him questioningly.

He explained, "I have a needle for sewing, but it will break if used on this tough hide. I put holes in it, then I will string together the sides of the leggings. I will need to hunt more deer. I will go tomorrow."

When he was finished working with the leather, he checked on the meat cooking. He had snared another two rabbits today. And they were almost done.

"Now that I have a shirt to wear, I can get up and walk around a little," she said.

"Yes, very little, you must be careful with the sutures. Most are good but some I had to use hair to stitch. It is good now but will break if not careful."

"Wow, you used hair? What kind of hair was it?"

"Mine. It is thick and strong."

"I should call you MacGyver."

"Who is MacGyver?"

"He was this guy who could pick locks with a paperclip and blow things up with marshmallows."

"I do not know of him."

"I know, I know. It's really just a saying." Part of her was a little uncomfortable with his hair holding her skin together but a bigger part was grateful for the lengths he went to, to help her.

"Before you go in the morning, can you help me put my bra back on?"

"No." She tingled at that curt answer. Did he want her naked for him to be able to touch whenever he desired or did he just not want to bother with it?

After completing other chores, he once again checked the meat cooking. It was done. He placed a pot of water on the fire, presumably for the fever tea, then brought one of the rabbits over to her and sat down. She tried to quickly pull the blanket up, but he said, "No." She put her hand down and was sitting there bare to the world. He pulled some meat off and she raised her fingers up to take it, but he again said, "No. Open." She assumed he was talking about her mouth, so she opened it. He gently placed the meat in and then got some meat for himself. As she chewed, she noticed his eyes were steely and full of intent but not about the meat. Its impact on her made it almost difficult to swallow. They finished the first rabbit and he went back for the second. She ate some more but was soon full. He finished it off and then leaned down and licked off a small piece that had fallen to her breast. Dear God, she was going to lose what composure she had. There was so much heat between the two of them that she wouldn't be surprised if they both burned to a crisp right there.

He got up, walked to the fire, removed the pot of water, and put the herbs in. He walked back to her and asked if she needed to go to her lady's room. She did, so he took her, this time without the blanket. He brought her back to camp, sat her down, leaned her back against the bundle, and then just stood there staring.

Sitting there in just her shorts, she would have felt self-conscious, but his gaze was so intense she couldn't form a single thought. He went to get her the cup of the tea. No words were spoken. He brought it back to her, she drank it, and he left to bed the horses down for the night.

Arianna wondered what he was thinking. It was like he wanted to take her, but she knew the severity of her injures would make that onerous and she knew he wouldn't hurt her. She was anticipating something decadent, but she couldn't imagine what that might be. He had pleasured her plenty, but she hadn't pleasured him, not once. He was a man, after all. She was surprised by the fact that she was not worried, just anticipating the possibilities.

He got back and finished his chores then stalked over to her. He straddled her, sinking to his haunches! Then he bent down and kissed her. She quickly became putty in his hands. She could feel him rubbing up against her stomach and she ached for him to rub lower. He knelt up, unfastened his belt and removed the cloth. She looked at all of him for the first time. He was huge. Not that she could compare, but big was big, and he was big. His manhood was almost eye level. Her insides were all a-flutter, anticipating.

"Open," he commanded.

Could she do this? She never had before. She was in love with him, she was sure, and she wanted to please him, but he was so ample.

"Open!" He commanded again, and without any further thought she did. He barely fit. He tasted of leather and salt and unbelievably, she wanted more. She tentatively sucked him in, repositioning her lips. Then she instinctively swirled her tongue around the top ridge and moaned. He said something in Navajo, which she of course did not understand. As she sucked and licked, she brought the back of her right hand up over his buttocks. He spoke more Navajo in sharp, short, deep tones as he pistoned in and out of her mouth. For the first time since they met, she could feel him losing control. And she loved it. She rubbed the back of her hand up and down his backside and felt just how powerful he was. He thrust faster and faster, until all of his muscles contracted, and he growled as he came inside her mouth. She swallowed as fast as she could as he jetted his seed. She almost couldn't keep up. It was slippery and tasted well, manly, was the only word she could think of. With her last swallow, he slowly pulled out and sat back on his haunches. His legs were so muscular that he perched a couple of inches over her thighs. He was shaking. She was smiling. "Did I do okay?" She asked, knowing the answer. He answered in Navajo. She did not know what he said but she understood plenty. He leaned down and kissed her almost violently.

He got off her and removed his moccasins and his leggings that had pooled at his knees. He lay down on his side, facing her and began kissing her. This time it was gentle and soft. *I have tamed the beast*, she thought, smiling to herself. He placed his arm along her far side and leaned over and started kissing his way down. Once he got to her breasts, he lingered. She moaned. Then he moved lower and lower, kissing and licking his way down. He got to the waist of her shorts and popped the button like a pro. *Doesn't take him long to learn new skills.* The zipper slinked down immediately after. He pulled her shorts down and carefully brought her legs through the openings without touching a single wound.

He went back up her body and grabbed her panties. The stretch of the fabric amazed him. He took a couple of seconds to test it out, then saw what he uncovered and forgot all about the properties of elastic. He removed her panties with the same care as her shorts. He spread her legs and positioned himself between them. How he wanted to sink himself into her fully and thrust like there was no tomorrow, but he gathered himself back under control and instead delighted in kissing his way from her knees to the junction between her legs. She was the very essence of allure; her womanhood was pink and swollen and begging for his mouth. He looked up at her and puckishly smiled. And then he obliged. He lay between her legs and kissed.

She started to quiver.

He licked.

She jerked.

He forced his tongue inside her and she started bucking. He had to hold her hips down to be able to continue. He chuckled to himself as he thrust his tongue in and out and she lost control. She thrashed her head back and forth. Then she grabbed at his head, dislodging his headband, and sank her fingers in and pulled.

She did not know what she was doing, he was sure. She would never behave like this if she were aware, his little wildcat. It made him want to push her further, to make her lose all of her control completely. He continued his sweet torture and after a few seconds more, her body went rigid and her feminine walls gripped his tongue like it didn't want to let go. He could only fantasize how it would feel once his cock was inside her. Would it do the same, clenching down on him? He would find out.

She quaked and shook beneath him but hovered in the atmosphere. As she slowly drifted back down, he licked more softly, almost like he was petting her with his tongue. When she finally calmed, he looked up at her with his hair in disarray about his shoulders and she was sure she was looking into the face of an angel; an avenging angel to be sure, but an angel just the same. *I love you*, she thought.

He gave her one final, gentle kiss there, then gathered their clothes and placed them at their feet. He stretched out beside her and pulled both blankets up around them. For the first time, they were lying next to each other totally naked, and it was splendid. She snuggled as close as possible to him, not wanting even air to separate them.

He loved how she moved in closer to him. It made him grin. He placed his arm around her and cupped her breast. She sighed. He felt peaceful and balanced inside for the first time in years. And it was due to a bilagaana woman! Maybe that's why his sense of balance was restored, he thought as he drifted into sleep.

8

When Arianna awoke, Hashké was gone. As she looked around, she saw that just above her head and to the side was the rolled-up bundle that she usually leaned against. On it he had placed a cup of water and a corn biscuit. She smiled at his thoughtfulness, her body replete. She would have just lain there for hours soaking in all that had happened if it weren't for the urgent yelling of her bladder. She persuaded her body into a standing position and slowly shuffled her way to an area far enough away from the camp to be sanitary but close enough to not wear her out getting there and back. She didn't think it would hurt so much to walk, but it did. She was grateful she was nude. It made the whole process of relieving herself a lot easier. She finished her business and slowly crept back.

She was sweating by the time she returned to her pallet and with the last ounce of strength she had, set the biscuit and water to the side and scooted the rolled-up bundle into position. Now the hard part, sitting back down. She made it with a few winces and a groan at its completion, exhausted. Grabbing the blanket with her fingers, she managed to drag it across her. Lastly, she reached for her biscuit and placed it on her lap, then the cup of water.

She sat there nibbling and sipping, thinking about her warrior. He was so fierce last night. She thought that maybe he was desperate. It surprised her how much she enjoyed doing what she did to him. And when he went down there, she felt she had shattered into a million pieces that she would not be able to put them all back together. Wow, just wow!

Feeling exhausted, she marveled that the simple act of going to the bathroom could wear her out so much. She thought she'd just lie down for a minute or two, but she soon drifted off to sleep again.

Hashké was out hunting for a deer. He was not having any success. He had been at it a good deal of the morning. He needed it for the sinew along its backbone, so he continued on. After traversing a couple more miles, he did come across a small turkey. It looked to be about five pounds. He silently notched his bow and sent his arrow flying. He thanked mother earth for this gift and removed his arrow. He cleaned it off and placed it back in his quiver. He tied the turkey's feet together with a strip of leather to ease in carrying it and started back. As he walked, he thought about what was left to do before they moved camps. He needed to replenish his bag of medical herbs, finish Arianna's leggings and make a saddle for her.

The thought of her spread warmth inside him. Remembering the way it felt when she was sucking made him hard instantly. He was sure she had not done such a thing before. The way she looked at him, he could tell she was gathering her courage. His little wildcat was not experienced. He liked that; he would teach her all she needs to know to please him. She pleased him well last night.

When I get back to camp, I will prepare the bird and start cooking it, he thought. *Then, find wood for the saddle.* It was good he had been successful the last few weeks hunting, he had many furs and pelts he would sell to the traders for money to use in getting his sister back. *There is always enough when you walk in balance with nature.*

He walked out of the trees and into the small clearing where their camp was. He saw her and smiled. "Yá'át'ééh," he called out in greeting.

"Hi. What does that mean?" she asked, smiling back.

"Hello," he replied.

"It sounds so much better the way you say it. What did you get?

"Tazhii."

"What is tahzji?"

"Tazhii," he corrected. "It means turkey."

"Yum, I love turkey."

"How are you today?" he asked.

"Good. I went to the lady's room by myself. It was difficult but I did it."

He put the turkey down and walked over to her. "No, you must not. You could have done damage." He gently but firmly grabbed her leg to check it over.

"But I had to go. It was fine. I made it. Thanks for the breakfast, by the way," she said, trying to change his focus.

He took off one of her dressings to examine for damage.

"It's fine," she said, trying to pull her leg out of his grasp. "It's a little itchy, though." She could no more pull her leg from him than roll a boulder. It was a good thing he liked her, or she would be in deep trouble. She reached down to rub the side of her wound to try to relieve the itchiness.

"You must not touch," he commanded, blocking her hand.

"But it's driving me crazy."

"I will make a lotion to help. First, I must prepare the turkey. Then I will gather the plant needed. I saw some nearby. Do you need water?"

"Yes, please."

After bringing her some, he set to preparing the bird. As he plucked the feathers, she commented, "It won't be long, and I can help with those things." She pointed to what he was doing.

"Yes, when you are better," he said when he noticed her rubbing near her arm wounds. "You must stop touching."

"But it bugs me."

"Bugs?" he asked, but continued, "if you do not obey me, I will turn you over my knee and . . . " He spanked the plucked bird on his lap in demonstration. She felt a little tingle between her legs that surprised her. *What would that be like?* she wondered., *Scary for sure but a little exciting, too, maybe.*

"Okay. Okay. I will try to not touch but it is hard. Why don't you come over here and distract me?"

He got up, put the turkey down and went to her. He could never deny her. He straddled her, his new favorite position, she guessed. And held her head possessively and kissed her. She immediately got wet between her legs. She didn't need dinner, and this was definitely overriding any itching, so all was good. He could just keep kissing her for the rest of the day, right?

He pulled away and got up, saying, "Be good." He walked back to the turkey.

Dang, she thought, stopping her hand from fanning herself. She wanted him for the rest of her life, thank you very much. He is so fine! When he walked, she could get glimpses of that indentation in the side of his loins, and all she could think about is touching it, feeling how it curves in when flexed.

He finished the turkey and set it over the flames. He turned to her saying, "I will be right back. If you are not good," and he held up his stout hand.

"Yes sir." she replied. Before he could leave, she called out, "Hey, can I have some clothes to put on?"

"No," he stated. And left.

"Okaaay," she muttered to herself. Just wait until I can get up and get it myself.

He was back before she could resolve whether or not she should risk rubbing, darn it.

He had a plant and two rocks. One rock was flatter, a little larger than his hand and the other was a smaller, round one.

He broke apart the plant and put the pieces on the bigger rock. Next, he took the smaller one and began grinding the plant pieces into bits. When it was all mashed up, he pushed the bits into the pot. He did this repeatedly. Once he was satisfied with the amount he had, he poured water into it and set it over the fire. He stirred it with a stick and watched over it. When it was done, he set the pot down to cool.

He walked back to her; kneeling, he began removing her dressings. The wounds looked good but still had a way to go to be completely healed. Some were very deep, he knew it was going to be difficult for her to deal with the limitations they would impose. The wolves had not only taken her flesh but also some of her mobility. But he would help her learn to compensate for any distress it may cause.

After removing both leg dressings, he got up to get the lotion cooling in the pot. For the first time, she was sitting up, her mind clear from fever and got a good look at her legs unobstructed. She drew in a deep and quick breath. She had no idea they were this bad. Her legs were hideous. She started to cry.

He turned back and knew instantly what was wrong. Maybe he should have prepared her better. Her tears ripped him up on the inside. "It will be fine. In a few more days we will start to work on your walk. It will take some time, but you will be able to get around just fine. The newly healed skin will stretch, and all will be good."

What he said was banging around inside her head. But what she couldn't get past was how ugly her legs were. How could he stand to look at her? He was so magnificent and perfect and now, she was not.

"They're hideous!" It slipped out of her mouth before she could stop it.

Empathy filled him as he explained, "I worked many hours trying to make it good but there were so many deep cuts."

"It's not your fault they are ugly, not even a team of plastic surgeons from my time could make this better. The wolves' teeth cut too deep and long. Nothing can make what they did look okay."

"Do not say such things," he said, his heart aching for her. "They will heal, and you will be fine. No one will see."

"You will! How will you be able to stand to look at me? I'm so disfigured.

"You are beautiful to me. Your legs are not you. You are you. That is what I see. I will make you pretty beaded moccasins; they will cover the scars. Others will only see pretty moccasins, not scars."

"But at night when I remove them, you will see. A man like you deserves a beautiful woman to love, that's the way the world works. A good-looking guy would never be with someone hideous, it doesn't happen." She went on, "It would be unfair to you if I stayed with you." She knew she was being superficial, but she couldn't help it. She couldn't stand to look at her legs, how could he?

Hashké rebutted her, saying "I will see them and remember how brave you were when you tried to fight the wolves. My little wildcat did not turn and run and try to hide, she stood her ground and fought. You are very brave like warrior. You are beautiful; you are not ugly. Ugly is coward." He wiped her tears from her cheeks with his thumb as he held her face.

"You are mine. If you leave, I will hunt you down and stake you to my pallet. You will stay with me."

She burst into more tears as he held her to him.

"You will no longer say such things. I will not hear of it. Do you understand?"

"Yes." she said sniffling. But in her heart, she could not believe that a man like him, so capable, so perfect, so handsome, would want to be with a woman so scarred. He could have someone who knew how to do everything that is required of this time; cook and sew, be pretty, all with a perfect body without deformation. She could never be as adept in his time as a woman who grew up in this era. She was out of place, out of time -- and disfigured. To her that was an impossible trifecta to her being of any value in 1864. Sure, she knew she wasn't completely worthless, she would be fine in her time. She could get a desk job or some other work that wouldn't require a lot of walking around but here, she could think of nothing she could do to be of value that would accommodate the physical limitations she now had.

Arianna did not believe him, he could tell. He would show her. It will take time to prove to her that he wanted only her, no one else. Beauty is not just in the face or body, it is all that the person is, their character, their mind, how they treat others, their harmony with all. No one compares to her complete beauty.

"That is enough tears. I will put lotion on now," he said as he pulled away to get the pot. He gently smoothed in the lotion on her legs. It felt better instantly. Next, he went to her arm.

It was ugly, too, but she was beyond caring. She would have to do the right thing and leave him, sparing him a life with such ugliness. Sure, he had feelings for her now; she was helpless without him. But when she was better, she would not let him feel obligated to be with her. She would just walk away. She determined to learn as much as possible from him about hunting and plants and the like, so when she left, she could survive on her own.

That would be her new plan; maybe she could help him get his sister back to repay him for all he has done and along the way, learn all she can. Then once his sister is safe, she and he would part ways. Maybe she would head back to that butte where this all began and try to return to her time, where she belonged. She felt worthless here.

He finished with her hand, then put all of the wound dressings back on and secured them. He could feel her distancing herself from him. He would not allow it. He crawled up her and kissed her ruthlessly. She tried to pull away, but he captured her head and held her until she submitted. He kissed her for a few minutes more for good measure. As he did, tears rolled down her face.

I will miss him, she thought, as she gave in to his kiss.

Later, Hashké was setting the camp to rights when he grabbed the pot to throw out the remaining lotion.

Arianna slowly came out from the turmoil that swirled in her mind as she watched him around the camp. Realizing he was going to wash out the pot, she stopped him by saying, "What are you going to do with the rest? It works great. I will probably need it again tomorrow."

He replied, "I will make more."

"That would be a waste, we can put it in one of my water bottles and just use it tomorrow. Grab one out of my backpack and I'll show you." He did. She poured out the water and gestured for the pot. He gave it to her. She looked in and saw it was still liquid. She said, "Just pour it in. We can screw the top back on, and it will keep."

He did and handed the bottle to her. She put the lid on and turned it upside down, showing that the lotion stayed inside. He said, "This is good." She gave a half-hearted smile and thought, *We do work well together.*

He set the bottle of lotion aside and left to clean out the pot. When he returned, he checked on the turkey. It was cooking nicely. He grabbed his hatchet, turned to her, and told her he was going to look for wood and he would be back shortly.

He walked through the trees and pondered on how things were between them and assured himself that he would just make her see. She would not leave. He would not allow it. She was his and that's all there was to it. He may have to break her a little to his way. He did not want to injure her spirit, but he would do what he had to keep her. Could she have clothes on? Absolutely not. He would keep her naked always if she thought she would leave. He would tie her to him if needs be.

He eventually found the two sturdy pieces of wood he needed. They were comparable to each other and had a bend in them that resembled an elbow. He chopped them to the appropriate length and brought them back to camp. He set them down and once again checked on the turkey. It was done. He pulled a leg off and brought it to her along with a cup of water.

He pulled off the blanket and straddled her again. He held the water to her lips.

She recognized his gruffness and drank, without comment, looking up at him.

Next, he pulled off some of the meat and fed her. She ate. After chewing, she swallowed the meat without tasting it. With his fingers coated in the grease from the meat, he held them to her mouth and said, "Open." She did and he placed them in her mouth. "Suck." She did and there was that familiar twinge between her legs. He pulled his fingers out, pulled off more meat, and put it in her mouth. Again, after she finished chewing, he held his fingers up to her mouth. He did not have to say anything this time; she knew what he wanted. This continued until she was full, and her heart softened. Periodically, he got up to get more meat but always straddled her when he returned. He stayed perched over her eating, staring. She didn't know what to think. He was acting like the savage the white people used to call them. Having such a formidable man exercising his power over her was nerve-racking but it also excited her.

He must have had his fill because he got up and did the nightly chores. He put on a pot of water to boil for the fever tea, she guessed. He walked over to her and put the blanket back on her and told her he was going to check on the horses.

When he got back, he brought her the tea. She took it without comment, in no mood for flirting. He added more wood to the fire and came back to her. He had the comb in his hand. He sat behind her and started to tend to her hair.

It felt wonderful. Her heart softened a little more.

"Are you mad?" she asked.

"I know you want to leave. I will not let you."

"I just don't want to be a burden. You deserve the best and I am not that anymore."

He finished combing, gently but firmly, fisted her hair and pulled her head to face him. "You cannot tell me what I want. You are what I want. Do you understand?"

She nodded and tried to blink back the tears.

He stretched out on his pallet and pulled the blankets up. He turned her to him and kissed her delicately and sweetly. That almost made her start to cry all over again. After several minutes of kissing, he restrained himself, pulling back and then tugging her close to him. Securing her to him with his arm around her. His big shoulders rolled over her as if shielding her. She felt so protected in his arms. Despite her troubles, she easily drifted to sleep, there, in his embrace.

9

Hashké started out early the next morning, it was imperative that he find a deer for more sinew in case they had to leave before her wounds were thoroughly healed. As he gathered her morning meal he smiled. She didn't know what to think when he sat over her eating last night. He knew. He wanted to show her his rightful dominion over her. She belonged to him. He would be the one to provide for her, pleasure her, protect her, and love her, all of her. He would continue to show her his command over her until she surrendered to him. If she still wanted to leave, he would bend her to his way. His path was the correct one.

He walked further upstream looking for tracks. About a mile and a half up, he saw several. He crept forward in the direction they led, arrow in place. It wasn't long before he came upon a small gathering. He aimed and struck a big buck. The others scattered. He once again gave thanks and started butchering the carcass. His attention went to the backbone, along which the sinew would be found. He was concerned about the fact that there was more meat here than he and Arianna could eat. He needed a large mature, individual to get the amount of sinew needed, but it is against the Navajo way to be wasteful. He hoped the gods would not hold this one indiscretion over him in future hunts. He wrapped the sinew and a good portion of the meat in the hide and started back.

The sun had been up for a while when Arianna woke. He was gone. There was the cup of water, corn biscuit, and this time some dried berries on the bundle. She ate, contemplating last night. He was so fierce in mannerism and action. It got her all hot and bothered thinking about it. Then he was the complete opposite once he got in bed. Why? She was so confused. She thought that last night was going to be it; he was going to take her. If she were honest with herself, she was kind of even hoping for it. Her mind told her that she would not have him forever, but she definitely wanted him to be her first.

She hadn't had much experience with men; her dad's illness had a lot to do with that. Then she was trying to get through school as quickly as possible while paying her way. Those circumstances left zero time for dating. That used to be a sore spot but now she was glad for it. Having Handsome be her first was right. She loved him. She loved him? Yes, she did; she realized that yesterday when he told her that her scars were a sign of her bravery. What had he called her, 'his little wildcat'? She was not that little. Five feet, six inches wasn't huge but definitely respectable.

She loved him! That's loony, she had only known him for six days. How can a person fall so completely, madly in love in just six days? Her mind reeled. So much so, everything got all muddled. She pulled out of her introspection and decided to save figuring it all out for another time.

She finished eating and moved her left wrist around to try to see if her arm was any better. Nope. Still hurt a great deal. That was going to take a while to heal.

Studying her surroundings, she finally observed how beautiful it was here. The trees were lush and vibrant. The smaller plants had their own personalities, each standing out from the other in a vibrant way. At night the stars looked so close it seemed as if she could touch them. She could see so many of them, she now understood the term "carpet of stars."

Okay, she put it off as long as possible; she couldn't ignore the need to go any longer. She got up slowly and carefully, shuffling her way to a place that was suitable. On the way back she noticed that it was a little easier to walk today. The pain and stiffness had lessened a bit. She made it back to her pallet and sat there waiting for Hashké to get back.

Now she was bored. Today was the first she felt like she could stay awake and not have to sleep most of the day away. She had no idea how long it would take him to find a deer. She had no doubt that he was an excellent hunter. He was probably great at everything he did, even making love. *Where had that thought come from? That's ridiculous. She would not go there, she would simply think about something else, anything else. But dang, the way he is, all manly, and the way he kisses.* She shivered. Arianna knew that she better not focus on this all day or she would feel like jumping him the moment he gets back. Bad, Arianna, bad! If only she had a book, she could read and not think about him, but alas, no. Oh, well, she might as well wander around, then. *He is so yummy. His face, his body, good lord, his body, she could never date a 21st century man after seeing, being with, adored by, him. She was ruined. She just wanted to touch him constantly. If she weren't hurt, she would have been on top of him so fast.*

"Ta`at`eeh," he said as he walked into camp.

Busted, she thought. "Yah ot eh." She tried to say back to him.

"Good." He said, smiling at her. He was happy she was attempting to speak Navajo.

"Did you get a deer?"

"Yes, a biih."

"You shot a bee?

"Biih means deer in Navajo."

"Oh," she said. "I can say that. 'Bee.'"

"Good," he said but she thought she heard a little placating tone there.

"I wish I could help you," she said.

"I do not need. You need to rest and heal."

"But I am bored," she whined. "I appreciate you doing everything, and I am grateful, but I have been just lounging here for six days and it is driving me crazy. I can't remember the last time I just sat for an entire day and accomplished nothing, much less six of them." She took a second to think and then said, "You could come over here and we could be busy together." She winked.

He smiled and walked to her. He had many things to do but she was naked under that blanket. He knew because he made sure of it. She was so enticing; he just couldn't stay away. He straddled her and started kissing her. He slowly made his way down to her breasts, licking and biting and nipping and kissing.

"Oh!" She breathed. He moved back up to her mouth and lingered there a while longer before he disengaged and stood up to finish preparing the meat.

"Okay, that obliterated my boredom. Can we just do that today?" she asked, all smiles.

"No. I must work. You can talk to me while I prepare. Tell me of your time."

"There is so much to tell. What part do you want to hear about first?"

"You said 'your car had a flat tire'. What is this?"

"Cars are the way most people travel in my time. They are like wagons that don't need horses to pull them. They have motors inside that make the wheels turn." He looked puzzled. She continued, "Inside the machines, there is fuel that is burned and that power that is created is what moves the wheels. It is hard to explain. Again, if I had a pad of paper, I would draw you pictures and I think that would help explain it."

After thinking on what else she could tell him about, she added, "We have phones to communicate with. We can call people we want to talk to and speak to them even if they are thousands of miles away and it sounds like they are standing right next to us. Our voices travel through the air and go to the one you are speaking to."

Discouraged after scrutinizing what she had just said, she added, "I'm not explaining that well either. I know! I will tell you how people live. Most people live in the cities now. Some still live in the country but not as many. The people in the cities live and work in these very tall buildings called skyscrapers; some have over 100 levels to them. And they get to the different floors on elevators. Elevators are these metal boxes that are big enough for several people to fit in and a cable, a really strong rope, pulls them up to the level they want and can lower them back down."

"I do not think I would like to live in your time. Sounds disagreeable."

"Really it's not. It's very nice. Everything is convenient. You can even go to the bathroom inside a house and a pipe takes the waste away." He looked at her horrified. "I am not explaining that well, either. I suck at this."

"You suck very well," he said, smiling.

She blushed and said, "You were the first person I have done that to."

"I know this," he said.

She was mortified and said, "Oh, great, was I bad or something? How embarrassing."

"No. It was very good. I could just see." He put a hunk of the meat over the fire. He cut the rest into thin strips and hung them to dry into jerky.

Next, he gathered four branches and cut them into precise lengths. Using leather strips, he tied the branches together into a large rectangle. He cut small slits in the hide's edge every few inches. Then, he used a thin rope to lace it to the wood. He laid the whole thing against a tree and started scraping the hide.

She was quiet while he worked, lost in her thoughts of the modern world she had left behind.

He stood back.

"Done?" She asked.

"For now, it has to dry."

Being curious, she asked about his plan for his sister's situation.

"I have been thinking on this. First, we had a plan to raid where she was being held, but with Carleton's attacks and the rounding up of my people, these have made that impossible. The Navajo are hunted. We cannot be seen by the white men," he answered as he was working on other things. "Our next plan was to get money to pay for her. I am gathering hides and will capture horses and train them to sell to the traders. My brothers are doing the same. We will gather enough money and buy her back."

"But who will go with the money and do the actual buying? I mean won't you get caught?"

"We will find someone to do this for us."

"But how can you trust them; they could just take your money and not do it."

"We would find them and take it back. We are good trackers."

"All of that will take precious time I'm sure you don't want to waste. Why don't I do it?" Arianna offered.

"No. You are not well. You do not know the way of this time."

"I will be healed soon," she said, adding, "You can trust me. You saved me; I owe you my life. Plus, I can help train the horses; I have ridden and trained most of my life. As a working student at the stables, it was my job to work on the worst horses. The ones no one else would ride. I am good at that."

"No. The wild horses are too dangerous. I will not let you get hurt again."

"Okay, well, you can break them, and I can refine them. With my years of dressage training we can work together, accomplishing in half the time, what it would take one person. It's a good strategy. In this way, I can repay you for all you have done for me. I know my injuries have delayed your plans. I'm costing you time and energy that I want to return."

"No need to return, I told you this," he said rather curtly.

"Please just watch me on a horse, then you will see that I can help. Promise you will just watch me when I am healed? Promise!"

What could it hurt, if he watched her? *She would be no good and then he could deny her plan and this argument would be finished, he* thought. With that in mind, he said, "Yes, I will watch."

"Oh, yes!" She exclaimed. "We have a good plan; we will work well together. I just know it. There was a reason I love to ride. I believe that, you know? That people have desires to do things for a reason. Helping you and being here at this time are my reasons for my love of horses. I just know it. This will be great. I can't wait!" she babbled on.

He had to just stop what he was doing and smile at her. She was so excited and happy. She had a brightness in her eyes she had previously shown only when she was in his arms. He would do anything to keep that look in her eyes. He continued preparing the sinew. He thought about how he would make her saddle very tall in the front and back to secure her there. He was going to protect her even if she did not want it.

"Can we go see your horses, please?" she said interrupting his thoughts. "I'm too excited and I would love to meet them."

He stood up and went to her. Scooping up her blanketed body, he held her close. He bent his head to hers and hovered millimeters away from her lips.

So many sparks were flying between them, she was afraid the trees around them might catch fire. She lifted her head the smallest bit and met him.

That was all he needed. He took over.

Dang, she loved kissing him. Okay, maybe they didn't need to go see the horses after all. They could just continue with this and see where it led. But no, he slowed things down and pulled back. He walked a fair bit and in another clearing were two horses. They were grazing in a grass-filled meadow. He whistled and they both came running. There was a large black appaloosa horse covered in various sizes of white spots followed by a smaller brown and white paint.

"Oh, they're beautiful. What are their names?" She asked as she held her hand out to them.

"The black one with white spots is Bilíí tizhinii. The paint is tįį Náyootbat."

"Let me guess -- the black one is the one you ride."

"Yes."

"He suits you. I'm guessing he's a stallion. He gives off that vibe."

"Yes."

She patted them and leaned to kiss their noses. "I can't wait to get back in the saddle. Riding grounds me. It will all be better when I can ride again."

"Grounds me?" he asked.

"Yes, makes me feel connected to the earth. I don't know how to explain."

He knew exactly what she was talking about. She didn't know it, but she was describing the Navajo way. He was convinced now more than ever that she was meant to be with him here, in his time.

"Thank you, they're wonderful."

"Are you ready to go back?"

She nodded.

He said, "Bilíí tizhinii tehi" and the horses cantered back to their grazing, the black horse tossing his head at the paint.

She giggled, "He's bossy."

"What is 'bossy'?" he asked.

"He tells the other one what to do and how to do it, like you."

"Like me?" he asked and acted like he was going to drop her. She screeched and tightened her arm around his neck. He kissed her.

They got back to the camp and he placed her back on her pallet. She pulled the blanket back in place and basked in the great day she was having.

Hashké went back to his sinew, stealing looks at Arianna. He would tunnel through mountains for her.

Her dressings need to be changed again, but now that she was well into healing, he would switch her to a poultice. That may help with the itching, too. He would need to leave her to gather what he needed but he did not want to. Every day it became harder and harder to do what he needed to do if it meant leaving her behind.

He checked the meat, it was almost done. The sun was drawing closer to the horizon and the nighttime insects were starting their calls to entice mates. All he could think about was Arianna. He would eat straddling her again tonight. He needed to keep showing her his position of authority over her. He would continue to do so until she surrendered to him and adhere to his wishes for their life together. He stood and checked the hide. It is drying nicely. He still needed to split a couple of logs for the side panels of Arianna's saddle. He could do that while the meat finished cooking.

After crafting the panels, Hashké checked on the meat. Finding it was fully cooked, he could get to the best part of his day. He walked to her and removed her blanket. She took in a quick breath. This time he straddled her and immediately went to her breasts and bit at them, lightly.

Her nipples responded like little soldiers saluting their superior officer, traitors! She wanted to touch him, kiss him, anything, everything. But he abruptly stopped, got up and walked to the fire. After slicing off pieces of meat, he took his place over her again.

"You know it is not fair that you have all of your clothes on, but I have none," she brazened.

"It is this way because I want it so."

Her response to that was a sarcastic, "Well, okay then."

"Eat."

She did.

"Suck."

She did.

As he got up, she snuck a look at his crotch, and yep, at least it was affecting him as much as her. She secretly smiled.

Things had been progressing this evening much as the last two had. But she hoped for more tonight. She couldn't help it; she lusted after him with a depth that surprised her. She would give anything, everything to be his.

As he placed the last piece of meat in his mouth, she sucked and licked and swirled his finger mercilessly. He closed his eyes and groaned.

That's right. I can do that, she thought.

He attacked her. Even before he removed his finger from her mouth, his tongue was there, too. Both at the same time, it made her quicken between her legs. She surrendered completely, his mastery over her body overwhelming her.

"Please!" she heard herself saying as he took in a breath.

"You are mine. Say it," he demanded.

"I'm yours," she capitulated.

"Say you are mine for the rest of our days."

Tears started falling as she softly forced out, "I am yours for the rest of our days."

He got up, pulled up her blanket and left to do his chores. He did them in record time, getting back to her as soon as humanly possible. He sat and pulled his moccasins off; his leggings soon followed.

"I want you," she said.

He looked at her with a pained expression, "We cannot. Your wounds are not healed. But I will take care of your need and you will take care of mine," he said, always in command.

There he was, naked in all his yum. He got in his preferred position and kissed her senseless, pinching and caressing her breasts. Oh, she wanted him. He slipped his knees back a few inches and his cock found her entrance like a heat-seeking missile. It nudged her and she spread her legs. She even tilted her pelvis, trying to angle herself just right to aid him in entering her.

He could not help himself; he flexed his muscles and slipped in just a tiny bit. It was exquisite torture. He wanted more of her, more than he wanted anything else ever. And she was willing. But, but if he opened her wounds, he would be furious at himself. He knew if he took her right now, he would not be gentle and soft, he would pound into her relentlessly for what he was sure, would be hours.

He growled, sat up, moved his knees forward and shoved his cock at her mouth and demanded. She obeyed. She performed the motions she had earlier on his fingers, and he seemed to enjoy it. He held her head in his hands, not pushing his cock into her mouth further, just holding. While she was trying to drive him over the edge, she brought her fingers up between his legs and dragged her nails along his sack slowly, lightly. That did it. He lost it all in one big rush. It was hard to keep up with him, but she did. *I'm gettin' good at this*, she thought smugly.

He pulled out and wanted to tell her right then that he loved her, but he stopped himself. He decided to wait until he was seated deep inside her for that telling.

He removed the bundle from behind her back and laid her flat. He straddled her and bent forward to kiss her. He placed his hands on the sides of her shoulders, capturing her beneath his powerful body, and began kissing.

She wanted action, now.

He could feel her impatience and chuckled. He said, "You will wait, my little wildcat." He moved on to her straining nipples. As he licked and squeezed, he took his free hand and, pointing two fingers out, he started dragging them down her cheek, down her throat to her breast. He circled there, then ever so slowly continued down her sternum to her belly. It tickled, her muscles jerked. She tried not to laugh. Then his fingers went lower still and circled the area between her legs. Her hips jumped, trying to push his hand onto where she craved. Just as she was about to scream with frustration, he plunged those two delicious fingers deep into her sex. As he did, he sucked her breast almost fully into his mouth. She tried to stop herself from coming, to draw it out, but she failed. Her entire body contracted with every thrust of his fingers. She came for so long she thought something might be wrong with her.

She finally started floating back down. He released her breast and kissed it. His fingers slowed. He smiled knowingly at her and she knew he was hers and she was his. He covered her with the blanket and he again pulled her against him as close as possible. She fit into his side perfectly; she was meant to be there.

10

Arianna awoke to Hashké touching her. He was fully aroused; she could feel every inch of him along her backside. He reached down and positioned himself in the crack of her bottom cheeks. He was kissing her neck behind her ear and down to her shoulders. Then he caressed her breast. How delightful. *This is the best way to wake up ever!* she thought.

He started to rub himself back and forth in the cleft of her bottom. His hand was now at her sex, petting and circling.

She moaned.

"Yá'át'ééh abíní." He said softly, kissing her ear.

Mmmmm," she mumbled. "Oh!" she continued as he put a finger inside her. "More, please."

He obliged and said, "Yes, my wildcat, take." He quickened the pace of his rubbing both in front and behind. She was there in seconds, her body shuddering, shaking, gripping his fingers rhythmically. As her orgasm ended, his began. He removed his fingers from inside her, gripped her hips and soon lost himself entirely. As his movements slowed, he slipped his hands from her hips to her breasts.

He tightened his powerful arm muscles and squeezed her close. He just held her there.

She could have stayed there for hours. Several minutes passed; she thought he might have fallen asleep. Then he said,

"I will clean you. We have to change your dressings today and I will wash all of you then." As he was speaking, he traced his fingers up and down the side of her body.

She wasn't sure how she felt about this. That was a whole other level of intimacy she did not think she would be comfortable with. No one had washed her since she was in diapers. To change the subject, she asked, "What was that word you said to me, earlier?"

"Yá'át'ééh abíní."

"Yes. That one."

"It means good morning."

"It is so beautiful when you say it in Navajo. I could listen to you speak all day in your language. I would not understand a thing, but I would love hearing it."

"You will learn."

"I don't know. It sounds so complex."

"I will teach you."

"Good luck with that. I think it would be easier to train a buffalo to sit."

He stopped his fingers movement and tickled her side.

"Stop, stop!" she cried in between giggles.

"Say you will do as I tell you,"

"Okay, I'll do it, I'll do it!"

"That is better." He turned her onto her back and kissed her.

If only every morning could be like this, she thought as he kept kissing her. Her conscience reminded her it could be if she stayed. She tried to suppress that thought. Oh, how she wanted to stay with him. He slowed and then he got up with a satisfied growl. He went to his pack and brought back a small cloth. He wiped his seed from her backside as she blushed. "I will get water," he said as he started getting dressed. He rolled up his pallet and blanket and placed it behind her. "Then we will have breakfast."

"Okay." She said with a bit of longing in her voice. She was completely happy with what they were doing and really could have stayed that way for at least another hour or three. So much so that if she was in charge their bodies would probably die from starvation and neglect.

He soon returned with the water that he put over the fire. "I have a surprise." He held up what looked like bulbs that flowers grow from. He brought them to her. "What are those?'

"They are Sego lily bulbs. He peeled the outer layer and handed it to her. "Eat." He peeled another one for himself and took a bite.

She tentatively took a small nibble and was surprised. It was very sweet. It reminded her of vanilla cookies. Not that they tasted like that, there was just something about them that made her think of yummy cookies. "These are great!"

He nodded and continued eating.

"I could eat these every day," she said.

"I will bring them to you every time I find them," he assured her.

After finishing his bulb, he unwrapped the last one and gave it to her. She gladly took it. As she was nibbling on that one, he started removing her wound dressings. Once they were off, she couldn't stop herself, she looked at them like looking at a wreck you pass on the highway even after swearing you won't. Her appetite instantly disappeared. "Here, you have the rest." she said dispassionately as she tried to hand the rest of the bulb remnant back.

"Thank you," he said and popped it in his mouth. Then it occurred to him why she didn't finish eating. He looked at her sternly. "Did you go to the dark place after you saw?"

"Please don't yell at me. I just can't see how you can stand them -- or me."

"I will turn you over my knee if you say any more on this. I have stated how I see them. It is good. You must listen. If you do not, I will punish."

"Okay, okay, I will not say more." But in her heart, she knew her feelings about her disfigured body stayed the same. She would just hide her feelings better.

"I will wash you now."

"First, can you take me to the lady's room?"

"Yes, of course." He picked her up and hugged her close, once again kissing her.

She thought with a smile, *He could make me forget about a hurricane if he just kissed me.*

When they got back, he laid her out on the pallet, then walked to the fire to check on the water. Afterward, he pulled something out from his packs. He grabbed it and the water and brought them to her pallet. He dipped the clean chamois in the warm water and then proceeded to gently wash her body off, even where she was not quite comfortable with him washing. He made her roll over exposing her backside to him. He continued his ministrations.

When he got to her bottom, he commented, "You have a nice backside."

"Thank you. I think I have riding horses to thank for that asset."

He leaned down and bit then kissed each cheek. She squirmed, not used to her butt getting so much attention. "Then you must keep riding," he said as he continued washing her. The warm water felt nice. She soon got used to his attentions and started relaxing. Actually, she turned into a big pile of mush. When he told her to turn back over, she didn't want to.

"If you don't, I will have my way with you, your beautiful ass, to be more specific."

She tingled in anticipation.

He spanked her lightly and she yelped.

But that did do unexpected things to her.

In her foggy state of mind, she rambled, "You know that I will probably have to stay here in this time now; you've ruined me for men in my time."

His heart fell to his stomach. Did she think that she would go back to her time? No, no she will stay with him. He would not accept anything else. He wanted to spank her again for even thinking that was a possibility.

Focusing back on the task at hand, he said, "I have to dress your wounds before they get dirty," he said as he rubbed around the wounds with the lotion.

Gratitude filled her; she said, "That feels so much better."

"They are healing well. Some have closed completely but not the deepest ones; we still have to continue to take great care with them. That is the only reason I do not have my way with you right now. I will put a moist poultice on this time, so the scabs do not crack and start bleeding."

"Okay. But can I start walking a little each day. I think I will need to start to stretch the new skin as it forms, or it will be too tight."

"Yes. I believe that would be best."

"Can I get dressed then?"

"You can wear your small top, that which you call a bra and the small pants. I have saved your boots, but you may not have them."

"Why?" she asked.

"If you have your boots, maybe you would try to leave. I will not allow."

"What if I promise?" she said feeling like she was a child seeking permission to go out to play.

"I will think on it, but not today. The poultice needs to soak in first."

"Okay," she said not wanting to lose the little ground she had just made. She would push for more in a few days. Let him get comfortable with her moving about for a while first.

Hashké sat on the rock where he did all his work. He pulled out the pieces of hide that Arianna knew were going to be her clothing. He started sewing her leggings.

Is there anything this man can't do? she thought. *He doctors her wounds, hunts for food, makes her clothes, trains horses, and loves her like a professional.* Mulling him around in her mind, she asked, "Do you have a girlfriend?"

"Girl friend? I have many women I am friends with."

95

"No. I mean, a woman who you love." She never asked if he were married. Oh God, what if he were married?! She remembered hearing that Native American men were not always monogamous. She remembered reading about some chief having three wives or something.

"No. When I was old enough for such things, it was not a good time, the attacks started, and I was too busy defending my people. I could not devote my time to one person when the whole tribe needed all of my attention to protect them."

"Oh." She was gleeful inside; not for the reason but for the fact that he was unattached.

"What about you?" he asked, garbled because he had put sinew in his mouth, moving it around to soften it, except for one end, which stayed dry and stiff, held out in his lips. Once the rest was fully softened, he used the still hard end as a needle pushing it through the holes he had already punched in the hide. She was amazed at how well it worked.

"I was too busy for those things, too. In my time, people wait to get married until much later than they do in your time; 25 to 30 is the usual age for marriage now." He was glad she was not married but he would not have let her go back to her husband even if she was. She was his now.

"Isn't that late for women to have children?"

"No. Women can have children as late as their '40s in my time. They are too busy with school and their careers to start earlier. With life expectancy in the upper '70s, there's no reason to start so early. Plus, men and women are not considered mature until they are in their '20s.

He was struck by that news; he could have her for 50 years! But he thought that even that length of time would not be enough.

He finished the first legging with the sewing of a tab of leather at the top that he looped over and stitched in place. A belt would go through them to hold them in place. He started on the second.

"Don't you want children?" she asked.

"My people have great desire for children. Many children in a house is considered a great blessing. But now, our children are in danger of being captured by the cavalry, enemy tribes, and Mexican raiders. Before, there was many warriors to guard them but now, they take them if the man goes to hunt. It is wrong and we will stop it. Now it is not a good time to have children."

"That is awful. They would go to jail for a long time if they did this in my time. Stealing children is severely dealt with." She felt horrible for those Navajo families who have lost children. She could not imagine.

It wasn't long before he had finished both leggings, saying, "It is finished. I will go look for things for dinner. Then I will finish your shirt."

"Kiss me before you go?" She had sensed his mood becoming dark after they talked about the children and she wanted to lighten it. He walked to her and knelt down. He kissed her tentatively first but then it deepened. By the time he left, he was smiling.

After about an hour, he returned with what looked like some wild potatoes. He put them into the pot with some of the meat they hadn't finished last night. He went to his packs and got out some dried corn and put it in there as well. He added water and put the whole thing over the fire.

He sat back down on his rock and started working on her shirt. She couldn't wait for it to be done. She was tired of always being nude.

He started to use the sinew to lace up her shirt but then stopped. As he thought about it, he decided to use something more flexible but still strong. He had some wool yarn that he could braid into a thin but strong cord. But to sew using a yarn cord, he needed a needle. It didn't have to be strong, just something to guide the cord into the holes. He thought he could whittle a sliver of wood or use a piece of bone from the deer. He decided to start with the wood. It would be easiest to work with. He looked around for a small twig on the ground. He found one he liked and using a smaller knife, started shaping it. He ended up with something he thought might work. He went back to his packs and retrieved the yarn. He cut several strands into the same length and tied them at one end. He brought them over to Arianna and asked her to hold onto it. He then started braiding them into a cord. She did not know how he did it; she can braid with three sections, anyone with long hair can, but he used several. When he finished, he had an honest to goodness cord that was about three feet long and knotted the end.

"Thank you," he said.

She just smiled marveling at his handiness. Who needs a Target when you have Hashké around? He laced the cord through the left side of the shirt and back down. He left a large enough opening for her to get her splint through. On the other side, he used the sinew to sew it up permanently.

When he finished, he brought it over to her and loosened the cord side. "Put this on."

She placed her left arm through first then her right arm and head. He helped by gently pulling the entire thing down. The leather was so soft and buttery. It fit well. He tightened the cord and it fit even better.

She smiled and said, "I love it. Thank you so much. It's perfect." She kissed him. He smiled.

He carefully helped her out of it and brought it and her leggings to his pack. Returning, he stirred the stew, then tasted it.

"It smells good, how much longer until it's done?" she asked.

"An hour or so. Hungry?"

"I wasn't until I started smelling it simmering away. You are a great cook."

"Well, you have to wait a little more. The potatoes have to soften." He added more water and stirred it again. "Now I will remove the hair from the buck hide that has dried." He walked to his packs and got out a flat, hand-sized maroon and grey marbled rock that had chipped-off sides.

"What is that?" Arianna asked.

"It is one of my prized possessions. It is a scraper flint that was passed down to me. It comes from a tribe long ago called Antelope Creek Tribe. They lived about a month's ride to the east. It was made a long time ago. Sometimes the ancient's way is still the best. This is very strong and perfectly sharp still, after many years of use." He used it to expertly scrape the hide clean.

He was teaching her so much, but she still had an enormous amount to learn. She might have to stay with him longer than she originally thought to learn everything she needed to survive. *Darn, even more time with Handsome, the crosses I must bear.* She giggled at herself. She was the luckiest woman in the world right now.

After he was finished with the hide, he came back to the stew, tasted it again, and nodded. He grabbed a scrap piece of leather and picked up the pot's handle with it. He brought it over to her pallet and set it down. He left again and brought back some water. He sat next to her and spooned out some of the stew and blew on it. He brought it to her lips. She made noises of appreciation as she ate. He ate the next bite. They continued until they were both full.

After drinking some water, she was curious and asked, "Why didn't you pull down my blanket this time like you usually do?"

"If some of the stew were to have dripped off the spoon, it would have burnt you. I would not let that happen. It is my place to keep you from harm. I will do my looking of you later."

Of course he thought of that. She knew down to her toes that he would never knowingly let any ill threat come to her.

He spooned out the last of the stew and got up to wash the pot out in the stream. He went to check on the horses and came back to spend time with Arianna. He picked up around the camp and then asked her if she needed anything. "Lady's room, please." He smiled and leaned down to scoop her up.

When they got back, he sat down with her and checked on her bandages.

Arianna said, "They are fine. You need to sit here and relax. You are always busy going here to do this, going there to do that. Just sit and relax for once."

"A lazy man is no good; he is ugly. Being responsible is the Navajo way."

"You are the opposite of lazy. You are what we call a Type A Personality in my time."

"What is this?"

"It is a person who works too much and doesn't take time to just sit and enjoy what he has done."

"I enjoy, very much, taking care of you. Helping you get better is a pleasure for me. We have spent a lot of time together. I have not done so with another."

She was touched by what he said. To have this big powerful warrior telling her such sweet things was overwhelming. The sun had set and all she could think about was having this man touch her. *This can't be normal,* she thought. But she really didn't care; while she was with him, she would hold nothing back.

Hashké stiffened. He grabbed his bow and quiver and turned to the east, crouching. It was dark; she didn't see or hear anything. Noiselessly notching an arrow in his bow, he pointed it out in front of him.

There! A huge cougar sprang out of the darkness at him. He shot the arrow, ducked and rolled, all in one smooth motion. He lunged on top of the cat that had fallen to the ground, with his arrow lodged deep, and pulled out the knife he always had in a sheath on his belt and slit the cougar's throat. It died immediately.

"Shit!" She exclaimed, but it was over before she knew exactly what was happening. Once it was over, she noticed how much she was shaking.

Hashké cleaned his knife, sheathed it, then walked to Arianna and knelt down to gather her in his arms, knowing this could trigger bad memories for her. But all Arianna was thinking was that her own personal warrior just saved her life again and now his foremost concern was to comfort her. If he didn't before, he owned her heart completely now. Due to the adrenalin coursing through her veins, her mind was jumping around from subject to subject like a dragonfly at the water's edge, Arianna's next thought was of his abilities; her warrior was a killing machine.

She pulled away and said, "You are amazing."

"It was nothing, but I have to go and take care of this now. Will you be all right?"

"Yes. I think so," she said, trying to make herself stop shaking.

"I will be as fast as I can, but I have to take the carcass far from the camp. We do not want any other predators to scent the kill and come."

"Yes, of course."

"Here," he said, handing her his knife. "I will leave this with you. You will be fine, but you will have it to help you feel better."

"But don't you need it?"

"No. I have others."

"Okay, be safe."

"Rest," he said, removing the bundle from her back so she could lie down. "I will be back soon."

I love you, she thought again. But she did not say it.

Hashké left her to get a rope from his pack and tied the cougar's back legs together with one end. He whistled loudly and she heard the thunder of hooves. Both horses came running up and stopped right in front of him. He said something to the paint and patted his neck. He turned to her and said, "He will stay here with you so you will not be alone."

"Okay, thanks. I think that will make me feel better." She was relieved.

He then tied the other rope loosely around the stallion's neck. He grabbed the mane and tossed himself up on its back. Using only his legs, he guided his horse out of camp, dragging the cougar behind.

After she was sure he was far enough out, she rose to her feet and made her way to the paint. "Hi," she said as she held out her still shaking hand to his nose. "Sorry, I had a fright." But he sniffed and nudged her anyway. "Easy, I'm not a hundred percent."

She awkwardly ran the back of her right hand down his neck. "You are beautiful. I can't wait to ride you. I just know you will be a good partner. It must be hard for you, always living in the stallion's shadow." She gently rubbed his silky chest. "But you are very strong, that is why you carry the pack," she assured. He snorted. Somehow, she knew he understood her. She stepped to his withers and eyed his height. "What are you, about fourteen-and-a-half hands? A good height." She stepped back to his face and kissed his nose. "Thanks for keeping me company. He was right once again; it does make me feel better to have you here. I would have you lie down and sleep right next to me if I could figure out how to get you to do it. But just having you near is the next best thing. I better go lie back down, I'm getting tired now." She kissed his nose and he nudged her lightly. "Good night," she said and turned to make her way back to bed leaving him to graze quietly.

She lay down, pulled the blanket up and fell asleep. In the middle of the night, she felt Hashké snuggle up next to her; contented, she fell back into unconsciousness.

11

Hashké woke up later than usual the next day. His first and only thoughts centered on his beautiful Arianna. Bowing to his body's urgings, he immediately started running his hand lightly up and down her side. She moaned. He gently pulled her to her back and started tonguing her nipples. She moaned more urgently as her head rolled back and forth slowly. Possessing her was his only thought. He straddled her thighs and began rubbing himself from tip to base. He dripped some spittle onto his erect shaft, lubricating his movements. She woke to the sight of the gorgeous man astride her, stroking himself while looking at her! The sight brought moisture between her legs. Did she turn him on that much that he would get off by just looking at her?

She raised her right arm to brush his butt cheek with the back of her hand. His butt was hard as a rock; one that had been honed smooth by its journey down a mountain stream. She just knew he would be powerful in bed. His hand movements quickened. He strained and then shot his seed all over her stomach and breasts. She was taken aback. She did not know people did such a thing. It was unsettling on one level, but compelling on another.

"Do not move. I will clean you up. He walked over and grabbed the chamois and wetted it. He came back and wiped up his seed and set the cloth aside. He lay down next to her and started kissing her all the while his fingers lightly ran over her body. She wanted his hand between her legs, forget everything else. He touched her everywhere except where she craved it the most. His mouth moved to her breast. She went crazy. Finally, his two gifted, strong fingers found her sex and plunged inside. She could hold her orgasm off no longer and came with fervor. She was so loud, she probably startled the horses. His mouth went from her breast to her mouth and she got lost there for a bit. Starting the day with a mind-blowing orgasm was her new favorite pastime.

As he kissed her, his thoughts were about making her come two or three times when he was finally able to have actual intercourse with her.

He begrudgingly pulled his mouth from hers and said, "Today, we work on your saddle." His abrupt change was meant to get his mind off her body and on to the day at hand. They had slept well into the morning and he needed to get things done.

"Okay. But these types of mornings make me hungry. Before you start constructing and laying the Transatlantic cable, can we have breakfast?"

"Yes," he said, grinning. He did not know exactly what she meant but he knew that tone of hers when she was joking with him. It made his heart smile. She poked fun and played with him, totally side-tracking him. He continued, "I have something new for you to try."

"I can't wait."

He got up and walked up the stream. When he returned, he cut up one of the bulbs she thought tasted delicious and dropped the pieces into the pot. Next, he poured some kind of grain into it. He followed with some water. He stirred and placed it over the heat.

"This will take a few minutes to cook. Do you need to go?"

"Oh, yes, please."

She was always so prim and proper. He loved that, too. The things he loved about her were accumulating into a quite an edifice.

When they returned, he sat her down and checked breakfast. After tasting it, he brought it to her, sat and pulled her blanket up high to her neck. Bringing a spoonful out, he blew on it and fed it to her.

"Mmmm." She murmured. "It's delicious. What is it?"

"Rice grass seeds and lily bulb. I saw the plants last night when I was disposing of the cougar."

"You are so resourceful. It blows me away. I don't think I will ever get as good as you at foraging, even with you teaching me."

"You do not have to worry about such things. I will always be with you. You have me, I will do it for you."

She blinked back tears. *What a man; I could love him forever, she thought.*

Soon she was full; the porridge seemed to expand in her stomach. He finished the rest of it as usual. Then washed up. Walking toward her, he said, "I must finish with the buck hide, then I will work on your saddle."

"Okay. I can't wait. I'm so excited to ride again. I will probably be sore at first; it's been a few years since I was in the saddle."

"We will take it slowly. Do not worry; I will not push you hard. Today, I will also put more poultices on you to keep the wounds soft."

"It already feels better. It doesn't pull as much when I move."

"Do not move very much! Be good."

She smiled mischievously and said, "I will be good."

He looked doubtfully at her.

"Really, I promise." The term "honest Injun" popped in her head. She couldn't believe people used such a derogative statement. It was unacceptable stereotyping. We were so wrong and in return wronged these people. She determined to do what she could to make that better in any way. Changing the past and therefore, altering the future, be damned. She did not set out to come through time; it just happened. She was determined to make the most of it, to right some of the wrongs that were done.

He shook his head as he walked to his packs. After collecting his scraper, he started again on the buck hide. It took him another half hour to completely remove all the hair. He took it off the rack he made and folded it up and placed it in pack.

"Is it finished?" She asked.

"For now."

Next, he started to string up another hide on the stretcher.

"What hide is that?" She asked.

"The cougar."

"Oh." Of course he skinned the predator, as well. He would use whatever he could from every kill so as to not be wasteful.

"I removed the claws and some teeth, too. Good for decoration."

"Oh."

"Tonight, we will have to eat corn cakes and jerky. I do not have time to hunt."

"That will be fine with me. I would rather have you here with me than out hunting. If eating jerky makes that happen, then I am a happy girl."

He turned to her and smiled. *She is the best woman ever to have been created.* He knew of no other woman who was pleased to eat tough, dried meat just to spend more time with her man. "Can I get you anything before we start on your saddle?" he asked.

"A kiss."

He walked to her, knelt down, leaned over her, placing his hand down on the other side and kissed her with such tenderness that she almost swooned. Yep, swooned.

"Shall I bring you my saddle so you can see how the Navajo make them? I am sure it is different than what you are used to if you jump in the one you had. It would be very uncomfortable to jump in mine."

"Sure."

He got up and went to retrieve it.

After sitting down with it in his lap, she scrutinized the primitive saddle's construction of wooden slatted sides, very high pommel and cantle, leather bindings and a woven wool girth. She took a moment to marvel at the carved wooden triangular stirrups.

"Can you make mine just a little different?"

"How?" He asked.

Pointing to the pommel and cantle, she said, "These lower. The front only this high," using three fingers, "And the back four fingers high."

"I want you secure in the saddle. We will be traveling on dangerous trails. Anything can happen. You must be safe. I am just getting you healed. I will keep you this way."

"But I like to jump, and you cannot do that with this so high," she said, pointing to the cantle piece. Actually, all I need is a saddle pad secured with a girth and some stirrups attached to it."

"I do not like riding in a saddle either, but on long journeys, it is safer. If a deer springs across our path startling the horses, it will hold you more securely. I will make this saddle to protect you. Maybe, we can make you another one when we get settled. One that you can jump in."

She reached up and hugged him. "Really? Thank you! Then I will gladly ride on the one you want to make for traveling. And I won't complain or anything." She kissed him.

She warmed his soul. He would make her the jumping saddle as soon as they got to his secret camp.

"You know, they still use a version of that girth in modern times. It is a good design and has held up over time."

"Yes, it keeps the horse from getting rub sores that happen when just a leather strap is used. I must get to work."

"Okay." She said and started absent-mindedly scratching at her arm wounds.

"We will change the poultices, too." Thinking on it, he said, "Maybe I will do that first. It seems to be bothering you."

"Now that you mention it, it is. Thanks."

He left to put his saddle away and get more of the wet poultice. When he got back, he removed the old dressing and put on the new. "I think that tomorrow we can remove the bandage from your hand and keep it off. It is almost all the way closed. I will make a salve and put it on and that should be enough."

"Great!" she said.

"The same is true for some of the other ones but not all. The wounds that were the deepest, we will still bandage. I will take out some of the stitches in the ones that are healed in a couple more days. I want to make sure they hold without bandaging. It is important you be good until we are sure they will stay closed. Understand?"

"Okay, I promise. I like the damp dressings. They are soothing; my wounds don't itch as much."

"Good. I will work on your saddle now."

He got up, put the medicines away and got out his carving knife. He gathered the two wood planks for the sides and started carving. Satisfied with the end product, he rubbed them with leather to remove any splintering rough spots. Next, he carved out two holes in the front part, one over the other, about an inch apart. Now he worked on the pommel and cantle. He removed the bark, then tapered the ends, holding the planks up to them, to ensure a good fit. Then he carved two corresponding holes in the tapered ends, making sure they lined up.

He got up and went to the edge of the clearing, looking at the ground as he walked. He picked up a few sticks and brought them to his work rock. He worked on them until he came up with eight dowels, all about the same size. Standing up, he placed a side panel on the rock and lined up the pommel and pushed a dowel into the holes that aligned and pounded it with the blunt side of his ax. He repeated his actions for the other side and then affixed the cantle. He held up the saddle and inspected it. Satisfied, he brought it to her.

"That looks great!" she said.

"Metal pins are best to secure it together, but I do not have any, so I had to use wood ones," he explained.

"It is fantastic. I can't wait to use it. I don't think it will be possible for me to fall off that. Thank you."

"Now I have to carve the stirrups and then wrap it all in a thick rawhide. Are you getting hungry yet?"

"Sure, I could eat but I'm not starving. If you have other things to do, you should do them first."

"No. It is a good time to sit and eat."

He brought back jerky, a few corn biscuits along with some water. They sat and ate until full, discussing their day.

12

The next two days were filled with hunting, finishing her saddle, and sensual pleasures. He was preparing for their journey to his secluded camp where there was a permanent shelter.

Arianna's wounds were healing; just a few bandages remained. She was walking a little every day. He allowed her to wear her shirt, shorts, and boots. She refused to walk otherwise. Her stamina increased daily. On their walks, he took the time to point out plants that were of note.

They had just returned to camp when Hashké heard something. He stepped in front of Arianna and whisked his bow from his shoulder. He was grabbing an arrow when a very distinct bird whistle came to them. He lowered his bow and whistled back.

Out of the trees came another Native American man on horseback. The man resembled Hashké but was taller and broader. Intimidation surrounded him like a cloak. They had similar facial features, except the new man had a larger brow and his chin was harsher. But they both had the same long deep black hair that shone when the sun hit it. He was handsome, of course, but not as handsome as Hashké to her.

They spoke in Navajo. The man slid off his horse and hugged Hashké roughly. Malicious sounding words came from the stranger as he looked Arianna's way. They argued and Hashké held him back when he tried to walk toward her. More angry words were exchanged. Arianna did not know what to do, so she just stood there, not backing down or cowering even though he frightened her. She found courage in knowing she was Hashké's and Hashké was hers. When the men seemed to calm down, she questioned, "Hashké?"

He turned to her, softening the furrow in his brow as he did. "Arianna, this is my oldest brother, Bidzii, He Who is Strong."

"Hello." She said cautiously. "Nice to meet you."

Hashké translated.

"Does he not speak English like you?" She asked her Handsome.

"No. He refuses to. He has hatred toward white people."

"Oh.

Handsome walked over to her and motioned for her to sit on her pallet. She did and he covered her with the blanket. "I am going to explain to him why you are here. So, I will be speaking Navajo for a while. Then I will translate for you."

"Okay."

"Do you need anything?" he asked.

"No, I'm fine. Please do not think about me now, talk to your brother. He looks upset." She looked at his brother who was still scowling at her.

"We will unsaddle his horses and bring them to the meadow. We will be back soon."

"Okay, please, take your time."

He nodded and walked back to his brother. They unsaddled his mount and removed the pack from the second one. They walked the horses to the meadow while Hashké tried to explain everything. He didn't know how he was going to accomplish it; the story was truly unbelievable. Arianna being white, made everything worse. His relationship with Bidzii was already strained. Hashké did not agree with his brother on a number of issues, not the least of which was his brother's raiding. And he had told him so a number of times. Hashké believed that raiding caused much of the bad relations his people have with the settlers. He knew his brother and his friends were doing it to try to drive the silver and gold seekers (Mineralies) back out of the Navajo land but it wasn't working. Instead of the white people leaving, more soldiers came, and then even more settlers. His brother's way, while noble and brave, was not slowing the inflow of the white men. Hashké did not have all the answers but something had to change. Too many Navajo had lost their lives already.

He took a deep breath and started. He told of how he came upon Arianna, her bravery and what she had done trying to fight the wolves. He spoke of how sweet she was, of her good nature. How she tried to leave him when he accused her of being a witch. His brother asked why he thought her one.

They had reached the meadow and released Bidzii's horses. The newcomers immediately trotted over to the two already there, sniffing each other with an occasional squeal and stomping of hooves. He took another deep breath and blurted that she was actually from another time, from the future. The look on his brother's face told Hashké all he needed to know about the insurmountable task he had in front of him. He told him her stories of cars, phones, and tall buildings. He told him that he would show him her pack, her boots, and the flashlight.

He then told him what he knew would be the most difficult part for his brother to take. He told him of his deep love for her and that he planned to marry her and never live without her.

Bidzii's face was a deep red, flushed with anger, when he started in with how he thought their parents would never allow such a union. Especially since their father had been the chief and therefor his sons had a responsibility to hold the clan's well-being foremost. Certainly not to invite an enemy into their midst.

Hashké rebuffed him by saying that it did not matter anymore since most of the clan members had been either killed or rounded up by the soldiers.

"So, you are deserting us and our plans to save Shánddíín," Bidzii accused him.

"No. Arianna wants to help. She has knowledge of training horses, which she did back in her time. And she hates what her people are doing to the Navajo and wants to try to make it right however she can."

His brother scoffed.

Hashké continued, "You can believe us or not. It matters not. I will protect Arianna with my life and if that means we fight, so be it. I will not leave her, ever. You will see, she is good and true and deep in my heart."

His brother looked unbelievingly at him.

They reached the camp and Hashké pulled her backpack out and showed him the fabric, the zipper, and the flashlight that had dimmed but still gave off light. It startled Bidzii. Hashké put the flashlight up and handed the pack to his brother, eager to prove his words. His brother examined it and was fascinated by the zipper. He kept zipping and unzipping it.

Hashké walked over to Arianna and knelt down grabbing her hands in his. "He does not think you and I should be together, but I told him that I would never leave you and that what he thought did not matter."

She smiled at him and asked, "I take it that you told him that I'm from the future, given his attention to my backpack. What did he say about that?"

"He was not believing me, so I showed him your things. We will see what he thinks now."

"I'm so sorry you have to go through this. I do not want to cause you any more trouble than I have already. If it becomes too much, you can just drop me off near a town and I will figure out something from there."

Steam seemed to rise from Hashké as he said, "Do not say such things. We will not separate. You are mine. I will not talk of any other way. Do you understand me?"

"Yes, I just don't want to come between you and your family."

"You are my family too, now. We will still work with my brothers to get Shándíín back. We will not leave them alone in that fight, but I will not have any talk of you going away from me. If you do try to leave, I will find you and then punish you for leaving me," he said sternly.

Given his state of agitation, she thought it would be best to let that statement go, but she would bring it up again when they were alone. *He is not master over me.*

"I will check on the meat now and we will all eat together."

"Okay."

He walked to the fire to check on the meal. It was ready. He asked his brother to sit and eat. Bidzii put down the pack and did so. Hashké went to get Arianna, explaining it is taboo for his people to eat while in bed so they must eat near the fire.

"Oh. Why didn't you tell me this before? I would have respected your ways and done so earlier."

"It was not necessary before. I do not care of such things. Plus, I like you best without clothing, in bed," he said with a mischievous grin.

He carried her to a fallen log on the side of the fire. Hashké cut hunks of meat off for Arianna and himself. He sat back down and tried to feed her. She turned away and said. "I want to do it myself."

Hashké replied with a curt, "No. You will get your wounds dirty. They are almost healed. I do not want them to become red and angry with infection because you are impatient."

She didn't want to appear helpless in front of his brother but now wasn't the time for an argument, so she gave him a look that said she was not pleased.

He chuckled. His wildcat is not happy with him. He fed her anyway. She ate. His brother asked why this was happening and Hashké pulled her right arm toward his brother, showing him her stitches and wounds. He nodded, agreeing.

Hashké's brother had such a formidable presence she could not relax with him around. She felt like he might assault her if she turned her back on him. She did not want Hashké to ever leave her alone with his brother. She ate until she had her fill, then she sat there listening to the two brothers talk to each other in Navajo.

Once the meal was over. Hashké stood and picked her up and carried her to her pallet. He arranged the blanket over her and knelt down at her feet to take her boots off. He set them aside.

"Thank you," she said.

He nodded and smiled, then got up to set the camp up for the night. His brother bedded down on the other side of the fire. Arianna was just fine with that, the farther, the better!

Bidzii watched his brother help the white woman. He could see his brother's fond feelings for her in the care and attention he paid to her every need. He could not imagine feeling that way toward any woman, and never a white one. He would have to think on all of this. *There is much to contemplate.* He lay down and closed his eyes.

When Hashké finished his chores, he lay next to Arianna, pulling her close to him as always. He tried to ignore her shirt, but he couldn't do it. He loosened the laces and signaled her to pull her arm through. She shook her head. He said, "Yes" very firmly and she reluctantly gave in, knowing this was a battle she wouldn't win. He tossed it to the side and pulled their blanket back up and said, "Better." He turned her face to him and kissed her. She tried to turn away; their cozy love nest was now contaminated by another. But he would not allow it. He insisted on them keeping their connection. She understood why and was grateful that he cared so much to ensure they did not drift apart. But his judgmental brother was just over there. She thought she might have heard a chuckle from across the fire, but the more he kissed her the more she forgot all about Bidzii. Hashké persisted until he was contented. He tucked her close, covering her breast with his hand. They drifted off to sleep.

Bidzii woke before dawn. He stood, rolled his pallet up and set it aside. He looked toward his brother and the white woman. Hashké was holding her close and smiling in his sleep. He hadn't seen his brother smile since their parents' death. He had come looking for Hashké to tell him that they had received word that Shánddíín had been sold again, this time to a woman who owned a boarding house in Santa Fe, so she had changed specific locations but was still in the same town. Coming upon his brother with a white woman had diverted his intention. He could not believe his brother's actions as he had watched undetected from the cover of the foliage yesterday. Hashké was pointing out plants to her, holding her elbow to lead her about, kissing her so frequently, it was a wonder they got anything done. He would not have believed it if he hadn't seen it for himself. He acted like he loved this woman. He was so consumed with her that he didn't even sense he was being watched. That was unacceptable. Hashké's inattention to his surroundings could lead to him being killed or captured. He had to be more aware, especially now, during the time of killings and round-up. His disappointment fought with his anger for supremacy toward Hashké, both full of vigor. He would have to shake some sense into him. But there he lay, happier than he had ever seen him before. Was it wrong for his brother to find love during the horrific times they live in?

Then there was the traveling across time issue. She did not seem to be from this time. Her mannerisms, the way she speaks, how she treats his brother; no white woman from this day and age would behave in such a way. The way she looked at Hashké seemed to indicate true feelings of fondness, but it was hard to believe that was so. When white people treat you so poorly, like you are an unwanted, stray animal, it is difficult to think that one might be different. He would have to think on these things some more.

~~~

When Hashké and Arianna woke, His brother was already up and gone. They saw his rolled-up pallet still on the other side of the fire, but he was nowhere in sight. Arianna asked where he was, but Hashké just shrugged. He helped her put on her shirt and wrapped the blanket around her legs, then took her to her lady's room. He carried her. He did not want his brother coming back and seeing her with so little clothing on. She understood without having to bring it up. They returned to a delicious aroma, as his brother was back and cooking breakfast. He was making scrambled eggs.

How he found them, she had no idea. Hashké sat her near the fire and gave her a cup of water. She thanked him and told him to tell his brother how happy she was to be able to have eggs for breakfast. Hashké did and it was the first time she saw his brother look at her without contempt in his eyes. While he didn't quite smile, the scowl disappeared briefly when he nodded.

Hashké threw out the remaining water in her cup and scooped up some of the eggs into it and handed her the spoon. He and his brother ate out of the pan. Was it her imagination or had the tensions eased a bit? She even saw Bidzii smile while talking to his brother. He was more attractive when he smiled. She realized how Bidzii must think of her, but she was determined to prove that she was very different from her ancestors.

At some point they must have switched topics to her wounds because after they finished eating, the men stood up and approached her. Hashké took the empty cup and spoon from her hand and set it aside. He showed his brother the cuts on her arm and hand. They spoke and nodded their agreement, Hashké picked her up and brought her to her pallet, telling her that he was going to show his brother the other injuries.

Bidzii walked over; both men knelt at her legs. He folded back the blanket from her left leg first. The wounds on this leg were almost all healed; they were not as bad as the right. He explained to her that he and his brother agreed that these stitches should be removed today. He then folded back the blanket from the right one. Bidzii did not hide his grimace as he saw the damage there. She was once again reminded of her disfigurement. She blinked rapidly, trying to prevent tears from escaping.

Sensing the atmosphere around them had changed, Bidzii looked at her face and saw shame there. The depths of it moved him. He felt sympathy for her. For the first time since knowing of her existence, his heart opened to her. He was finally seeing her soul and the trauma she had been through. He softly squeezed her right arm, the only place she was not damaged.

When he touched her so tenderly, she lost the battle and her tears silently dripped down her face. She staunchly held back all sound from leaving her lips; she would not sob in front of him or anyone else. This was her problem, hers alone. She was determined that she would bear it alone.

Hashké looked at his brother and knew he finally understood how he could love her; he was seeing her for who she was not what she was.

Bidzii gently lifted her leg up to examine it more closely. He said something to his brother in Navajo, to which he agreed. Hashké turned to her and said, "He is giving you great respect. For you to have endured such pain and still have a pleasant nature moved him." They went back to discussing the wound itself. He carefully probed around the wound and said something to Hashké and then smiled. Hashké laughed.

"What did he say?" she asked.

"He said that maybe I should become medicine man because I have cared for you so well. He did not realize that I did so because I had love in my heart, even when I was stitching your wounds." He smiled warmly at her.

Bidzii continued his commentary. She looked questioningly at Hashké. He told her that they both agreed to remove some of these stitches, but to leave others in place for a few more days.

Next, they moved to her left arm. Hashké removed the splint and bandages and gently raised it for his brother's inspection. They discussed it. Hashké must have told him what he saw the wolf doing when he got to her. He was simulating a bite toward her arm, then shook his head back and forth twice. Bidzii nodded, then asked a question about her right arm while pointing to it. Hashké answered, his brother smiled at her nodding, then continued talking. She looked to Hashké for interpretation again. He told her his brother asked why her right arm was not injured. "I told him that you had wrapped cloth around it to protect it, and he said you are a very smart woman. I agreed." He softly smiled at her again.

Hashké and his brother discussed it further, and he set her arm down carefully. He turned, telling her they decided to remove all of the stitches in this arm since it was being held immobile by the splint and that his brother suggested they keep their eyes open for clay during their journey so they could use it for making a better splint.

"Oh," she said. She did not realize that Native Americans had the knowledge of casting. It shouldn't surprise her, given the level of care she had already received.

Bidzii went to his pack and returned, sharpening a small knife. He said something to Hashké and handed it to him. Hashké turned back to her and said, "We are going to remove the stitches that we think should come out now. It shouldn't hurt but if you become uncomfortable, tell me and I will get you the pain medicine. Yes?"

"Okay," she replied. He bent down and kissed her, and she smiled.

He then nodded to his brother and they turned their attention to her arm. Bidzii positioned it to give his brother the best view of the sutures. Hashké was very careful. She felt a twinge of pain only a couple of times as he placed the knife's edge under each suture, tipping it up, slicing easily through the sinew and then placing his finger over the knotted end, pushing it against the knife as he moved it away, freeing the stitch from her skin. When he finished with her arm, they moved to her left leg, then her right hand, followed by the right leg. Here, they spent the most time. His brother pointed out which one to take out next, as they worked seamlessly together.

She experienced the most pain here. This wound bled the most and so there was more scabbing, which made it difficult to free the sutures. She drew in deep breaths when the pain intensified. Bidzii softly patted her arm when she seemed the most uncomfortable. There were a couple of stitches that needed to come out but were imbedded in the flesh that had grown there. They discussed it thoroughly.

Since there were only a few in this condition, they decided Hashké would distract her and Bidzii would remove them instead of waiting for the pain medication to start working. Hashké straddled her and she looked at him puzzled. He explained the situation. He asked her if she was willing to try and she agreed. He then bent down and started kissing her. His brother chuckled and waited a minute for her to get fully involved in Hashké's seduction before starting. When he heard her moan softly, he knew now was the time. She flinched a few times but when she tensed, Hashké was there, deepening his kisses. Before she knew it, it was over and Bidzii was tapping his brother on the shoulder, telling him he could stop. Hashké nudged off his brother's hand and ignored him.

Laughing, his brother got up and went to get the salve he had in his packs. When he got back, Hashké finally relented, pulling back from her and telling her it was finished. The brothers laughed, as she turned beet-red. Hashké swung his leg off her and helped his brother dress the wounds she had left, no doubt receiving a ribbing from him the entire time, given the way they were speaking to each other and the looks they were trading. When his brother pointed out Hashké's state of arousal, Hashké punched him.

Bidzii spoke seriously in Navajo. Hashké agreed. Arianna asked what he said. Hashké told her that his brother thought that the waters near his cabin would be good for her recovery. She didn't fully understand but let it go, the entire ordeal had left her very tired.

There was a wonderful sense of camaraderie now in the air. She smiled at the brothers. They put her splint back on and seemed pleased with their efforts. They discussed something and Hashké nodded turning to Arianna and told her that they were going hunting for dinner and that she should rest. She ardently agreed. He removed the bundle from behind her back and she lay down. He pulled the blanket up to her chest and they left.

As Hashké and his brother walked along the stream, he told him how much she liked the turkey he hunted earlier in the week, so he was looking for those tracks.

Bidzii was half-heartedly looking for them, but mostly studying his brother. It was sinking in how good he and his woman were together. She surprised him with her poise and discipline. He was glad his brother was happy. He opened up a line of communication by stating that he was impressed with her self-control.

"Yes, she is very strong. But she is very tender, too."

"Why the tears when we looked at her leg?" his brother asked.

"She thinks they are very ugly. She believes that she is too ugly for me to be with her. I have told her this is not true, that when I see them, I see her bravery. But she would not give in on this. I will bend her to my way. She wants to help us get Shándíín back to repay me for saving her. Then leave me, so I can be with someone who does not have scars. This makes me very angry. I will not let her leave. She is mine. If she tries, I will hunt her down and bring her back."

His brother nodded and said, "I have seen your strong feelings for her, but are you sure she wouldn't be better off with her own people? This is a very dangerous time for us."

Hashké looked at his brother sternly and said, "I believe she was given to me by the gods; that is why she has traveled to this time. I do not think she would be happy with the white people. She is happy with me. She does not agree with how her people have treated the Navajo. I know it is not an easy time; maybe after we free Shádíín, we will leave Navajo Land and go elsewhere."

"You cannot leave, you have responsibilities to our clan. Father would not stand for it."

"Father is dead. Our clan is scattered. There is no need for me here, past what we have already decided to do."

"What you say is not true. You will always be needed to help with our people."

"No. You are the oldest; it is your responsibility. I am not."

"And what if I am killed, then what?"

"I do not know. Adika'í can stand in your place. I will not give her up."

"I understand how you feel, but you do not have to leave, we will figure this out. If I can see how you feel about her and understand, then maybe the others will, too."

"I would not hold my breath for such," Hashké said, ending the conversation. He pointed to the tracks he was looking for and signaled his brother. They soundlessly followed their trail for some time before coming upon the large birds. Hashké notched an arrow, pulled back, affirmed his aim and released it. The turkey dropped. He removed the arrow and they gave thanks for the kill and started back to camp.

"We will need to catch another horse for the journey." Bidzii said.

"I agree. I was tracking a herd when I came across Arianna. I could not leave her in order to capture them. Her injuries were too severe. I planned to scout for some when she was able to get around better. But that hasn't happened yet. She is almost there."

"I will leave tomorrow and bring one back to be a new pack horse. She can ride the paint you have. He is a nice mount. We will work on the new horse together, to get it ready faster. We can search for more horses to sell after we get to the cabin. It will be easier to journey without them."

"I thank you for the help. I did not feel good about leaving Arianna alone for the few days it would have taken to track them down."

They walked the rest of the way in silence, not needing to fill it with unnecessary words. They had said all that needed saying.

After getting back to camp, Arianna woke as they were working on the bird. Hashké walked over to her with a cup of water.

"Thanks," she said. "Did everything go okay?"

"Yes, we were successful. How do you feel?"

"Good. I didn't know I was that tired."

"Your body knows it must rest to heal. Do you need to go?"

She shyly said, "Yes, please."

He would never get tired of hearing her say that in the endearing way she does. He smiled and picked her up. She wrapped her right arm around his neck and as they passed his brother who was plucking the feathers, she noted, "You got another turkey!"

"Yes, for you."

"Thank you and thank you!" she said smiling at him, then his brother, who smiled and nodded back.

As he carried her, Hashké told her of his conversation with his brother. "I told him how I feel about you and about my plans for us. He knows and understands. You have impressed him with your ways. It is good."

"I'm glad things are better. I did not want to come between you and your family."

"If my people do not understand then we will go to other lands. I believe the Holy People want us to be together. We do not have to stay on Navajo Land."

"I would hate for you to have to leave your home," she said.

"Where I live is no longer important. You are."

She kissed him. She shouldn't want to hear that statement from him, but she couldn't help but admit to herself that she secretly loved it.

They got back and the turkey was already over the fire and starting to cook. Hashké and his brother busied themselves with chores and preparing for his brother's trip.

The sun was heading down, and the turkey was cooked. They sat down for dinner. Hashké explained to Arianna that his brother had offered to go track for a new horse to carry their packs, since the paint would now be her horse to ride on. She thanked him and told him how much she appreciated his offer of help.

He nodded to her.

After a few more bites, Bidzii said, "It is time I tell you the reason I was searching for you. Word made its way to me that Shándíín has been sold to a woman in Santa Fe who owns a boarding house. She has changed places but still in the same town. She will not be surrounded by guards at the boarding house. We could save the money and raid the house at night, under the cover of darkness, then sneak her out of town."

Hashké interpreted for her.

Arianna spoke up and asked, "Wouldn't that be very risky? I mean the soldiers are already looking for you, it's not like you can blend in if you are seen. I'm sure they will shoot first and ask questions later, if ever. Plus, even if you get her out and you all make it back alive, once word hits the army that an Indian has stolen a valuable slave, I'm sure the entire garrison will pour out of the fort and be on your tail. How far do you think you will get? All they need is the slightest of excuse and they will be out scouring the countryside again. It just sounds like what we, in the future, call a suicide mission. There has to be a better way."

While he was telling his brother what she said, she was mulling it around in her head. She was once told that everything you need to accomplish what you want to do is already available to you. She didn't know if that were true, but it did start her thinking of what they had at hand. They had two warriors, and a white woman. Being a white woman was a negative in some instances, but she could walk right through the middle of Santa Fe and no one would even bat an eye. SHE could go in and get Shándíín.

She raised her hand like she was back in school again. It interrupted the men. "*I* could walk down the street and go completely unnoticed."

Hashké immediately started shaking his head. His brother asked him was she said. He reluctantly told him. Bidzii raised an eyebrow. They argued, heatedly.

Hashké would not hear of Arianna being out from under his protection and control, much less endangering herself for them. What if she decided to stay with the white people once she was back around them? He felt her heart's distance at times. He could not risk that. He told his brother as much. Bidzii explained that her interaction with the white people was not dangerous in and of itself. They would not know that she was actually an ally of the Navajo.

Hashké was pissed. His worry that he could lose her was bigger than his desire to save Shándíín. He knew it wasn't right but there it was. "I will not allow you to be in danger," he said.

"I wouldn't be in any danger if I go to Santa Fe to buy her back. I would just be conducting a business transaction."

Hashké reluctantly told his brother what she said.

This sparked a new round of heated discussion between the brothers.

"Even if it is a good plan, I would not let her go and risk her not coming back," Hashké insisted.

Bidzii reasoned, "If she did not want to stay, then she was not yours in the first place. If you hold her against her will she is not your wife, she would be your slave, like our sister is now."

"That is fine with me; I know she is meant to be mine."

"If it were meant to be then she will come back to you."

Hashké stormed off.

She looked at Bidzii questioningly. She could tell that Hashké was upset so she called after him using her nickname for him. "Handsome, come back and talk to me, please! Please?"

He couldn't resist her delicate pleading. He slowly walked back with his face disheartened. She hated to see him like this. He sat and looked at her with a dispirited expression. She took his hands as best as she could and said, "It's a good plan. We can all work together to free your sister. Isn't that what you want?"

"Yes, but I have fear that you will not come back to me."

"If I promise I will come back, will that make it better?" She still reserved the right to leave after she brought his sister to him. But to sooth him she said, "You know how I feel about you. There is only you." Which was true.

"Yes, but you have also said that you want me to have someone who does not have scars." He looked at her pointedly.

"Yes, I said that but more important, I told you that I wanted to help you with your sister. We can talk about the other later, after I get your sister back, safe. I promise I will bring her to you in person, then we will discuss the rest." She couldn't even say it out loud; the thought hurt so much.

He reluctantly agreed to talk about it. He released one of her hands and told his brother that he consented to discuss the plan, but he was still not happy about it.

His brother nodded sympathetically and said, "While I am searching for another horse, I will send word for Adika'í. We will need the money he has gathered. When I return, we will leave for your hidden camp." His camp was located in a heavily wooded and very secluded area in the foothills. Being closer to Santa Fe, it would be the ideal place to bring the plan together. Hashké agreed.

With the meal ended, Hashké brought Arianna back to her pallet and then tended to his nightly chores, while his brother readied for his trip. Hashké crawled into bed, took her shirt off and tossed it to this side, as he always did. He held her with a fevered intensity. She melted into him.

13

The next morning, Hashké woke and raised his head, looking to make sure his brother had gone. He guessed he would have but Hashké's plans demanded he make sure; he was going to have Arianna fully, completely. He had to make her his to keep her from going back to her people.

He started with light kisses on her forehead, she responded by snuggling in closer. He slowly moved down, kissing and nipping his way. He was at her chest when she regained wakefulness. The smile she felt assured her that this was indeed her favorite way to start the day. Bidzii must have left already; Hashké would never be this amorous if his brother was still there.

He removed her shorts and panties, then turned his attention to her breasts. He attacked them like they needed conquering.

She could hear her mind's chatter in the background, cautioning her to keep some distance between them; to be able to leave him to a better life without her. But her body was begging her to give in. She knew deep in her soul she didn't want to curtail his physical attentions at all. It wasn't but a second more before her physical desires had taken over and eclipsed all thoughts.

The only thing that vexed her now was the fact that she couldn't touch him back the way she wanted to. Her wounds still wouldn't allow it, if she didn't, she would undoubtedly reopen them. So she placed her hands over her head to squelch the temptation to use them.

With his ferocity to have her finally unleashed, he was single minded in his goal. Hashké was determined to possess all of her this very moment. When he could no longer ignore the pull to attend to her womanly core, he licked and nibbled all the way there.

She was squirming, tightening and releasing her abs. She wanted his fingers, his mouth, anything in between her legs right now! Discerning her urgency, he slowed. He kissed all around her most intimate area, teasing and heightening her pleasure. He could see that her vagina was weeping, actually crying for attention from his efforts. When he sensed she was about to scream in frustration, he allowed his mouth to plunder. His tongue dove into her woman's flower and she came instantly. He licked and stroked her until her tremors ebbed.

That was the first, he thought. Like a cougar, he crawled up her body, his expression conveying his intentions. As she became aware of his movement, she started to shiver slightly, her body contemplating what was coming next. He settled over her, his cock just kissing her opening. Wanting to rule over her, not hurt her, he propped on his elbows, gripped her upper arms far from her injuries, holding them down.

With her body somewhat appeased, Arianna could finally hear her mind's niggling. She still wanted him, true, but there was also some reluctance; wouldn't this catapult their relationship onto an entirely new, deeper level? "Hashké?" She started to ask but he claimed her lips with a forceful kiss. As she succumbed, he drove into her.

She tensed; his intrusion was very uncomfortable. She tried to bring her arms up to his chest to push him off, but he wouldn't relent although he did cease all motion.

Hashké stilled his body to let her get accustomed to him; her taut channel was very narrow. He waited for her body and passion to unfurl and fully bloom, while occupying her mouth and mind by ardently kissing her. He refused to hear her arguments for keeping their physical joining from happening; their souls were already irrevocably entwined. Even the gods wanted them to be together that is why they sent her; to be with him, to be his.

With the realization that she did love him as she would never love another, Arianna felt the tension slowly ease from her like a piece of chocolate left outside on a hot summer day.

As she relaxed, he started moving slowly, shallowly. Her body responded to him at the cellular level, moistening her passage, resulting in a sensual glide. She moaned in pleasure, so he eased back his kiss. She immediately whispered breathlessly, "We should have talked about this." His answer was a deepening of his thrusts. Her sigh hitched with unexpected ecstasy and he knew he had her right where he wanted her. With his mastery of muscle control, he drove her into such a state that she forgot what day it was, her name, and just about everything else, including her intention to retain some distance.

She went to wrap her legs around him but remembered her bandages and relaxed and let him dictate. He was relentless in his motion. She reached higher and higher, matching her pelvic motion with his until she was about to fly.

He felt her reaching her pinnacle. In response, Hashké stuttered his action with shallowed thrusts to hold her just before the precipice and demanded, "You are mine. Say it; say you are mine." She would have said anything at that moment to get him to just move a little deeper, faster, something! His lack of impulsion had insanity knocking on her door. She shouted, "I'm yours! I'm YOURS!" He responded at once, plunging fully into her, pulling back, then plunging in. She flew higher than she had ever been and detonated. Her orgasm had her inner walls gripping and releasing him rhythmically, milking him in the most delicious way. He jettisoned so deep inside her; he was sure his seed would take a couple of days to make its way back out.

He collapsed on her in utter contentment, then immediately raised himself off her onto his elbows, not wanting to hurt her. She came back to her body completely satiated for the first time in her life. He released her arms and she carefully rubbed his back with her fingers.

Still inside her, he looked into her eyes and said, "I love you."

Tears started trickling down her cheeks.

He continued, "You are mine, I am yours."

She smiled through her tears and nodded.

Hashké was hard again at her capitulation. He bent his head down to hers and kissed her softly, tenderly, and resumed moving inside her.

Her eyes widened.

"I will have you when I want you and you will have me when you want me from now until the end of our days." He said as he continued with his love making.

They lay in each other's arms, spent. She wondered if they would stay in bed all day. If she had her way, they would. He eventually stirred and rose saying, "I will clean you." He added wood to the fire and put the water on to heat then retrieved the chamois.

Once he left their bed, she could finally think about what had just happened. He had declared his love for her, and she gave in and acquiesced to it. She knew she loved him even before this, but she wasn't going to tell him, to keep that small bit of space left between them. But he obviously bulldozed right through that.

Her breath caught as it occurred to her, she had no protection. What if she just got pregnant! Her mind was in full gear now and anger started to rise. He should have asked, or they should have discussed all of this at the very least. Why had he taken her like that? Sure, it was amazing. It definitely wasn't a random night out on the town, their judgement impaired from making sound decisions or anything remotely like that. But she thought her first time should have been all soft, sweet, and tender.

Hashké brought her some corn cakes and a cup of water. He put on his breechcloth and sat down next to her to wait for the water to warm.

"Hashké, why did you do it like that?"

"Do what?"

"Have sex with me without asking."

"You are mine. I have taken you. No one else can have you now."

"But don't you think that we should have decided that together?"

Still terrified she might leave him once she was back around her people, he declared, "I have saved your life, it is mine. I will let you help my brother and I with Shádíín's recovery, but all other decisions about you are mine to make."

"You mean to say that the cost for saving me was my virginity and servitude!"

"No, I could not, would not let you go back to the white people without marking you as mine."

Her brain reeled trying to understand what he just said. She lay there silently, wanting to form her thoughts into words that made sense.

Thinking her silence was acceptance; he got up and checked the water. Bringing it to their bed, he motioned her to spread her legs. She complied, preoccupied with trying to come up with an appropriate response. He began gently washing her.

How could the same man be so hard-lined one minute and so tender and thoughtful the next? Not being able to come up with the words to adequately express her feelings, she let it go for now but would definitely give more time to contemplate it when she was alone, without him around to cloud her mind. But the pregnancy issue is a no-brainer and would definitely be discussed immediately.

"I have no protection. I'm not on the pill or anything, now. They are in the 21st century in my bathroom cabinet."

"Yes you do, I will protect you with my life if needed."

"No, that's not what I mean; I could get pregnant."

Hashké wasn't going to let her know that the Navajo have herbs that can prevent conception because the thought of her pregnant with his child pleased him greatly. He responded by saying, "If you do, then it is meant to be."

"But I do not want to be pregnant right now; I'm too young."

"No, you are late to start such things."

"Not in my time. And that is what matters. My wishes are what matter to me, not what chance dictates. In my time, women decide when to get pregnant, not fate; well, for the most part. Sometimes there are accidental pregnancies but that doesn't matter. What matters is that you do not decide when or if I get pregnant. It is my choice."

"Children are never accidents. I saved your life; you are mine to decide what I will."

She growled in frustration. "You do NOT own me, I own me. Even if you did save my life, I do not owe you it in return. Yes, I want to help get your sister back; that is how I will repay you, not with me but with my help. Besides, you told me there was no need to repay you for your efforts."

"I changed my thinking."

"You can't just change it like that."

"I can and I have. Your life is mine now." He normally would never have said something like that to anyone, especially someone who needed his help, as she did, but he could not let her go back to her people to buy Shándíín back unclaimed. Nor was it the Navajo way to be dominating over one's mate. In his culture, man and woman are on the same level; it was a matriarchal system after all, with the women retaining all the wealth. But making love to her was the single most amazing feeling in his life. He wanted it again and again for the rest of his days. He would do anything, say anything, to keep her. If that means playing dirty, he would, gladly.

He would take her again, right now, if she wouldn't be too sore, but he knew she would be tender at the very least. So, he must do something to put his mind's attention elsewhere.

He could go hunting; that would be a good distraction. He got up and said, "I am going to hunt. Do you need to go to your lady's room?"

"I will go by myself. I do not want your help."

He bent down, picked her up and started walking. She kicked her legs trying to get him to put her down, but he was so strong it didn't faze him. He said, "Stop, you will hurt yourself."

"Put me down this instant."

"No. You will do as I say."

She didn't of course. He looked for an appropriate rock and finding one, sat down and put her over his knees.

"Don't you dare!"

"I told you to stop so you would not hurt yourself. You disobeyed. There will be punishment." The blanket had parted over her lush bottom as he sat. He was either going to plow through her fields of desire or spank her; he wasn't sure which would win. He laid his hand on her bare flesh, all the while trying to restrain his carnal urges and said, "Will you obey me?"

"No!" She shouted.

His little hellcat was taking a stand. As much as that pleased him, he had to make a statement about her disobeying him. He felt he had to gain her compliance to keep her from leaving. His hand landed with a smack. "Will you obey me?"

"No, you jerk."

Smack. Smack. "Now?"

Her defenses had her gritting her teeth. It hurt but she would not cry even though tears welled. When he began to softly, sensuously rub her stinging flesh, she started getting aroused but didn't understand how she could be anything but mad. If she really wanted to know her truths, she would have to examine herself, deeply, without the usual safeguards and obstructions; lay it all out in the open, bare.

As she picked apart her feelings and looked at what was causing them, she came to the realization that maybe trudging through all of the trials she had been through had taken a toll on her brain's resolve to be strong and independent. She knew that she had every right to stand up for herself and not go along with Hashké's dominance. But there was another part of her, a feeling actually. A feeling she had never felt before she entered his world that she acknowledged now. That part of her heart didn't mind being bossed around by him; his commanding attitude comforted her. Hashké loved her and had her best interests at heart.

With that realization, a sense of peace flowed through her and she exhaled deeply. She could now see the difference between her old life alone and this life with Hashké. In her world before Handsome, she had to steer her ship through life's storms with her hands tightly clenched around the helm all alone, day in and day out. Her brain in firm control but it was exhausting. With Hashké, she had experienced the wonderous sensation of trust when you love another and the feeling is returned. In that kind of reliant relationship, you know your partner may not be perfect but will look out for you and hold you above all others. There's a relief that comes from letting go of that white knuckled hold. But giving into this "passenger" way of going, even briefly, also felt like she was a traitor to herself, her sex, and all of the women that came before her to fight the just and hard-fought war for independence and equality. Didn't she have a duty to womankind to stand on her own? *All of this back and forth with introspection is in itself, exhausting.* Didn't she think his life would be better without her dragging him down with her ineptitude of this time? And after all, a Navajo man could be shot for just being seen in the company of a white woman. That thought jolted things into perspective; if she loved him, she needed to keep some distance between them so she could leave him for his own safety at the very least. With that settled, she ignored her heart and body's desire for more to shout, "No."

Smack, rub, smack, caress. "Now?" his voice was husky and low. Her sex tingled.

"Hashké." She said his name; beseeching him.

He turned her over and cradled her in his arms. He kissed her brutally, with stern passion. She responded in kind, without thought. He wanted her anew. His hand roamed down her body to her sex. It was open and inviting. He took in a sharp breath; she wanted him, too. He played with her there. She said his name again. He had to be inside her. He lifted her up, pulled the blanket out from under her and tossed it to the ground. He placed her on it and had her roll over onto her stomach. With all his attention in the last few minutes focused on her bottom, he wanted to see it as he entered her. "Spread your legs."

She did.

He pulled his breechcloth to the side, freeing himself. Kneeling between her legs, he touched her sex with one hand and stroked her ass with the other. He wanted to make sure her body was prepared for him to try to lessen her tenderness. She whispered his name again and that was the signal he was waiting for; he entered her slowly, carefully.

"Oh," she said softly, drawing it out. He again waited for her to get accustomed. Once she did, he moved slowly, but firmly, in and out. With each round, he ratcheted up his intensity, building her desire. Her breaths quickened. She emitted a little sound with each deep thrust. He cherished that sound. One of his new goals in life was to hear it as often as possible. He could feel her starting to grip him. He surged in deeper, harder; she came apart but he held his release back. He wanted her to grasp every last second of pleasure. Once she became relaxed beneath him, he allowed himself to attain his. Her woman's nectar from her release enabled him to drive in a little farther without causing her discomfort. He took advantage of that and stroked deep. It felt spectacular. Hashké wanted to figure out a way to stay here inside her, permanently. He ground his hips to feel all of her. Her sex tightened and grabbed him, he could hold back no longer. He thrust in and out determinately, and she came for a second time with him seated fully within.

Once he had spent every last drop, he rolled to his side taking her with him, again her back to his front. He had one arm underneath her neck and bent to hold a breast in his hand. The other spread possessively across her lower stomach. They lay there, replete, the argument forgotten.

She should not have been so turned on; she was mad at him for being all caveman-like and punishing her. But when he started rubbing his hand on her bottom and then spanking her again, with his voice all low and gravelly, she couldn't help it. She would still have to clear things up between them but right now she really couldn't be bothered.

Several minutes passed before they started getting up. He secured his breechcloth back in place again and helped her stand up so he could shake out the blanket. Once clean he wrapped it around her, and they continued on their way, neither saying a word, not wanting to spoil the atmosphere of tranquility.

When they got back, he set up her "lounger" and placed her on it. After he kissed her, he left to go hunting.

She had so much going through her brain. She was overwhelmed; her mind jumping from one topic to the next, all without resolution. It was wearing her out. And not having a good reason not to, she declared peace between her warring thoughts and took a nap. Maybe she would dream a solution. She loved him, craved him, but he drove her crazy with his overbearing ways. Then there was all this, "He'd be better off without her", stuff. She still had no answers when she gave into sleep.

As Hashké walked, looking for tracks and listening for sounds, he thought about how satisfied he was with things between him and Arianna. Sure, he was a little rough with her to start with but if he waited for her consent, it could have been months until she gave in. He did not have that time. He was confident she would enjoy his body once he started -- and she had. His little wildcat responded to him well. He knew she would. He would never allow only one release for her; she would have at least two to every one of his. He would make sure of it.

He knew she would be starting her cycle soon; she had to. Arianna had been with him for two weeks now and she hadn't had it yet, so the chances of her conceiving were small. True, it would not be good for her to be training horses while carrying his child. But he did want her pregnant after they retrieved Shádíín. He told himself to look for the snakeroot plant to prevent pregnancies from taking hold. He would make her drink the snakeroot tea every week until their mission was over, then never again.

As he walked, a distant bleating reached his ears. He silently crept toward the sound. He noted the wind direction and altered his path, to have the wind carry his scent away from the sheep he was stalking. He was within range when he spotted the perfect one. It was not yet full-grown. He did not want to waste meat again. He aimed and shot. The herd scattered. He walked toward his prey, slit its throat and gave thanks. They would eat the meat and he would use the pelt for the seat of Arianna's saddle, giving her cushioning for the long journey ahead. He was pleased with the day.

Arianna woke to the sun directly overhead and the sounds of the water babbling. She had a lot to consider. She did not want to face Hashké barrier-less, physically AND emotionally, so she searched around the camp for her clothes. Putting on her new leggings was still out of the question, but she would put on everything else she could. In his packs she found her clothing folded neatly. She pulled them out. She could feel her arm was mending; it was not as painful. She would use it sparingly and not at all around Hashké. She did not need to add more fuel for his protective fire. She would not be in this state of dependency much longer, but she must be patient to prevent prolonging the healing. She pulled her panties and shorts on. Next, her shirt, forgoing her bra, since she still couldn't fasten the hooks. She left her boots off, as well; they were too much trouble. The statement would be made well enough without them.

Hashké made it back not long after she sat back down. Her heart started pounding the second she saw him. She knew he would not be happy with her sign of defiance.

He entered camp smiling, happy with his success until he saw her. His smile changed from a real one to a front. She had put clothing on. He would have to deal with this. She thought she could keep him away from her? He would show her just how wrong she was.

He finished butchering the meat, arranged it over the fire and hung the skin up. He would tend to it later. He advanced toward her without words. His presence felt like a giant boulder rolling menacingly closer. Tension encompassed him and it was palpable. Without words he loosened the laces on the side of her top. He circumspectly pulled it off her. He unbuttoned, unzipped in a single motion, lifted her butt off the pallet and removed her shorts. On seeing her panties, his faced tightened even more. He expertly removed those as well.

Her heart was still pounding, waiting for the retribution that didn't come. He picked up the clothing and brought them to his packs, folded them and put them back. While there, he grabbed his hide scraper.

She pulled the blanket up. She didn't know what was worse, the immediate explosion or the delayed one. She wished he'd just get on with it. He turned his attention to the sheepskin. He worked on it until he was satisfied. He modified the rack and strung the hide up to dry. He turned the meat and got a drink of water.

Once he finished all that needed tending to, he turned to Arianna and thought, *Must be that I need to back up a step and remind her that my wishes had be adhered to; I am in command.* He did not like breaking his rule concerning the orgasm tally, but this wasn't going to be about pleasure but rather their power struggle.

He again pulled the blanket from her and was hard instantly. She was so beautiful. He straddled her and pulled his cloth aside and commanded, "Suck."

She did. She knew there would be a price to pay for defying him, but she never expected something so delectable. She loved taking him in her mouth. She felt an immense sense of power performing this act. She knew he didn't realize that. She would keep that thought close to the vest. Hiding her smile, she sucked, then licked. His entire body trembled; she knew she had him in the palm of her hand. And when she tongued around the ridge of his head, he shuddered. She moaned and the sound vibrations toppled him; he shot his load into her mouth while lovingly cupping her face.

He withdrew from her, shoved the tender feelings she elicited from him down deep, and got up, moving his cloth back in place and left camp. Putting out the traps he needed to set for tomorrow's meal would give him time to compose himself. She undid him. He could feel her sense of triumph. She was unlike any other woman he knew. She was strong and willful. He must tread cautiously with her.

As he left her, she bit the inside of her cheek, trying to stop the smile threatening to show. She took delight in knowing that she, in fact, held all the power she needed.

He returned and checked the meat again. It was almost done. He messed with this and that, not letting his eyes find hers even once. She would not be rewarded for today's defiant actions. They would eat, then sleep; there will be no pleasure tonight.

When enough time had passed for the meat to fully cook, he brought some to Arianna and straddled her. He pulled down the blanket, exposing her breasts. He was very pleased with them. He schooled himself and proceeded to feed her. She ate without talking. She understood he was trying to prove a point. She did not accept it, but now was not the time for more confrontation. She would just say the same things she already had, and he would say what he already said in response.

Her enchantment over him was almost impossible to resist, though. They finished in silence. She thanked him. He got up and brought her another cup of water.

She had to go to the bathroom again but this time when he picked her up, she went quietly, without protest.

He finished cleaning up and checking on the horses. He came to her and removed the bundle she reclined against and tenderly helped her to lie on her back, then rolled out his pallet.

She longed to touch the ridges in his stomach, but she could tell he was in no mood for it. A part of her wanted to anyway, just to push on the wall between them to test its steadfastness.

While it was true that her body twinged with tenderness, that fact couldn't dampen the blatant awareness that the most drop-dead gorgeous man on the planet was getting ready to climb into bed with her. She was torn; on one hand, she couldn't get enough of him but on the other, she had to start disciplining herself and not reach out for him. Then again, she didn't want him going to sleep still mad at her.

He pulled her in close and she could feel his arousal in her bottom's cleft. She wriggled her hips slightly. He groaned and grabbed them to keep her still. She smiled then moved her hips more overtly.

"Arianna," he admonished.

"Handsome." She drew out and teased while rubbing against him.

He roughly turned her toward him and laid her flat. He kissed her and she kissed back more fervently. He groaned again and his hands could not stay still; he started caressing her breast. Her sounds of enjoyment snapped him back to his rational mind, reminding him that he was not going to pleasure her tonight. He broke their kiss and jerked back quickly. He told her, "No." But he noticed his hand was still caressing her and abruptly stopped it.

"Please, Hashké. I desire you."

His face softened. "Not tonight. Your body might be sore and needs time."

"But I want you," she pleaded. She had become totally wanton; if not for the physical pleasure, then for the mental reassurance of their connection.

"Not tonight. It will not be good for you."

"So, you're not mad at me?"

He thought for a moment and said. "I do not like having to show you why doing what I have told you is better than the consequences of not doing it. I will be strong and firm to help you if I must."

She rubbed her hip against his erection and smiled up at him as she said, "You are very strong and firm."

He grinned at her before he even realized it. He was putty in her hands and he feared she knew it. He kissed her with all the love in his heart, rolled her to her side and held her close as they slipped into sleep.

14

Arianna was the first to wake. She found herself, actually half on top of Hashké. Her left arm was draped over his chest and onto his arm, her left leg between his, her head pillowed on his chest. It was hard to think he could sleep with her scratchy splint undoubtedly poking him, but he did. She smiled to herself impishly and proceeded to take advantage of her situation by softly dragging her fingers down and back up his stomach and chest while admiring his form. He should be on billboards; he was so defined. And he was hers ... for now.

As she stroked him, he moaned. She went lower; his muscles clenched. Now her fingers had furrows to bump down which led her to trace that lascivious V shape of muscles that insistently directed her to his sex, which was thickening as she watched. She wanted to touch, explore, to feel every inch of it. Her injuries had prevented her from doing so, until now! She propped herself up on her elbow next to him and started at the base of his sex. Without a thought, she very lightly stroked up to the tip. It was weeping.

He growled. She smiled, realizing she had awakened the beast. But she wanted to play with him on her terms. His skin was so soft; how could someone so tough be so soft?

She swirled her finger over the dew seeping out of the slit in the head. It was like naughty finger painting. Her mouth was jealous of her finger, so she bent her head over him, her hair dragging along his torso in her wake. She stuck her tongue out and tentatively licked her painting. She wanted to lick all of him.

Back in the 21st century, she would have never thought of herself as one of those sex-kitten types who lounged around all day in bed just waiting for her man's beck and call; one who had no purpose in life other than sex. She could see the possibility now.

After toying with him with her tongue, she wanted more so she put her lips around him and sucked him in as far as she could, then back up to the tip. With her fingers, she explored his sack. She was amazed by its response to her touch.

He fisted her hair.

As she sucked, she could take no more, she had to have him right now, the way she wanted. Her mouth withdrew with a pop as she extricated herself and carefully straddled him directly over his cock and began caressing herself along its length.

He grasped her hips and spoke words she was unable to translate.

Apparently, when she drove her Navajo crazy, he forgot how to speak English. She chuckled inwardly. She moved back until he was at her entrance and slid him in with a gasp. He was large, she knew, but in this position, he felt like he took up more than she had to offer. She was unsure if it would even work like this now that she had started.

He regained his English and said, "Sit up slowly and let your body get used to me."

She did, then, swiveled her hips slightly, trying to get more comfortable.

He moved her up, just a little, then back down. Their efforts were eased, as she became slicker. He moved her even further up and then back down slowly.

Oh, when she came back down, and he was so unbelievably deep in her and touching her right in that perfect spot! It triggered a domino effect she had absolutely no control over. With a couple more strokes, she exploded.

He held himself back until her orgasm started. Once it did, he let his passion and action have free rein. He stroked into her a few more times, then flung his seed deep, hurling her even higher.

Utterly spent, she collapsed on his chest.

He held her constricted to him. The entire encounter took less than three minutes. *She would be the death of me*, he thought, knowing he was totally acquiescent to the control she had over him. She might as well put a rope around his neck and lead him about. That realization left him feeling more than a little unsettled. He had to do something to push his discomfiture away, so he pulsed inside her and hardened on demand. In response, she moaned. He sat up with her in his arms. Then lifted her by her folded thighs off him and placed her to the side on her knees. He rose over her. He carefully positioned her on her elbows and knees to not put pressure on her broken arm and mounted her from behind, ensuring his control was reestablished.

In her groggy state, she was unaware of his intention until it was a done deal. She quickly drew in her breath. He was definitely more domineering in this position. She knew he wouldn't harm her, but it verged on intimidating.

He grasped her hips and started plunging in and out. She was so excited and he was so, well, savage that she was close to coming in seconds. He reached around her and circled her clitoris. She immediately took flight in ecstasy. He pounded into her. He moved his hands to her hips again and quickened his pace. He was still careful to hold her in a way to keep the weight off her arm. Her ass was so perfect. He loved taking her this way. With that thought, he came with an unexpected fierceness that he felt to the soles of his feet.

She was mindless as she floated back down.

Finally satisfied, he pulled out of her and tugged her onto his chest. They lay there for minutes while he tried to slow his breathing.

With his arms around her, she marveled at this new facet to her life. Sex was fun! She could become addicted. She wondered if it would be the same with someone else and seriously doubted it. She knew she was ruined for the rest of her life. There was no way sex in the 21st century was even close to sex with Hashké. She found men of her time to be the opposite of the pendulum swing, either too refined or couch potatoes. And if they had muscles, they were usually self-obsessed. She had not met nor knew of any men who were even a tenth of the man Hashké was. Yep, she was ruined. Her stomach growled. Sex made her hungry.

Hashké chuckled. "Do you want to eat?"

"Yes," she said sheepishly.

He rolled them to their sides and got up. He brought her a corn cake and some jerky for an immediate fix.

"Would you like some cereal and lily bulb?"

"No, this is fine. Can we have it tomorrow?"

"Yes. I will go looking for more later."

"Great!"

"I will clean you now," he said as he walked to put the water on to warm. He added, "Today I will wash your hair for you. Would you like that?"

"Yes! I'm sure it is a mess."

"It is fine, but I thought you might enjoy it. I have some things I have to do first but then I will do this for you."

"Great." She was happy.

He got dressed and brought the chamois and water to her. He washed her body with the kindness that never stops surprising her.

"Lady's room?" he asked.

She nodded.

When they got back and settled her in, he said, "I will go check the traps now."

He wasn't gone long and came back with two rabbits. He cleaned them and put them high over the fire to cook them slowly.

He brought her saddle to his work rock. He sat down and placed a sheepskin over the seat.

"Is that for my saddle?" She asked.

"Yes, to soften the ride for your beautiful bottom. I do not want it rubbed raw and sore from the long days in the saddle on our journey."

"My bottom thanks you," she said with a cheeky grin.

"I will still spank that bottom, if it and you, do not behave," he said, trying not to smile.

"Promise?" she asked. His grin was all-encompassing.

But not paying the attention to the task at hand, he smashed his thumb with the back of the axe head he was using to tack down the skin to the saddle. "Yauow!" he said, then sucked hard on it trying to bring the blood back into where it had been squished out. She laughed. He rose and stalked to her and started tickling her, saying, "Did you find that funny?"

"No, no, not at all; I promise." she said as she tried to squirm away from his probing fingers.

"I don't think you are truthful," he said as he got up and went back to work. He looked at her. She held her lips closed with her fingers, showing him she wouldn't say anything.

When he finished, he told her he was going to get what he needed for her hair and that she should rest. She was tired of resting but she wasn't going to say anything to risk not getting her hair shampooed by her lover.

~ ~ ~

Hashké rode his horse past the end of the tree line where he knew he could find the yucca plants. Coming to the first one he saw, he loosened the dirt around the base of it and pulled it partially up from its dirt bed. He chopped off only a fist-sized part of the root and nestled the plant back into place and tapped the soil around it, securing it back into its home. He slipped the root fragment into the pouch at his side.

He rode back and released the stallion in the meadow, walked to the stream and rinsed the root of dirt. He placed the root on his work rock, then checked on the meat. After turning it and lowering it closer to the flames, Hashké went to the rock where he pounded his palm down on the root to break the bark covering it. He peeled it away and placed the naked piece in a bowl that had some water warmed by the fire in it. He rubbed on the root like it was a bar of soap while it was in the water, which started to suds-up. The suds turned into lather as he continued rubbing. Once satisfied with the results, he left the bowl to pick Arianna up to lay her on a rock by the stream that was warmed by the sun. He went back for the bowl of lather. He put the bowl under her hair as it hung over the side if the rock and gathered her hair into it. He splashed the lather up onto her head and rubbed it in repeatedly. She moaned with utter enjoyment. He continued rubbing and swishing her hair until he was pleased with the result. He threw out the soapy water and rinsed the bowl out in the stream. He filled it with clean water and rinsed her hair with it. It was a little cold, but not bad. He continued until the water flowing off her hair was clear. He told her to wait a minute and left to get a clean chamois.

After rubbing the excess water out with the chamois, he wrapped her hair in it and carried her back to the pallet. He retrieved the comb and sat behind her, alternating combing through her hair with rubbing it dry with the chamois. Before long, it was only slightly damp. She reached up and ran her fingers through the strands and was amazed by the softness. Her hair flowed through her fingers like water; it was so silky.

"Wow! It feels so amazing."

"I'm glad you're pleased."

He kissed the top of her head and left to check on the meat. Returning, he said, "It's almost done. Now I will look at your wounds."

"Okay."

He inspected her right hand. There were only small scabs left. "Good."

"Ya, I thought I could start using it more now," she said.

"Yes, a little more." He looked at her sternly.

She smiled.

"Let's look at your leg." He removed the dressing. "It is better, but these still need to be treated with care. I will leave those few stitches that remain in for a couple more days." Hashké was relieved that even where his brother and he had to extricate the embedded stitches, the overall appearance of the wound was good.

He looked at her and caught more than a glimpse of sorrow in her eyes that she could not hide. He bent down and kissed the scars to show her that they did not disgust him, far from it.

She teared up demanding "No, don't."

"I love them. They are a part of you now. I love you, all of you. I saved the wolves pelts so when we get to my cabin, we will put them on the floor for you to walk on."

"Really?!" She laughed through her falling tears.

"Yes, for you to have your revenge every day."

"You are the best!" And to herself, she thought, *I love you.*

He moved to the other leg. "This one is almost well."

Moving on, he removed the splint and thin coverings on her arm. "I think that now we can just put some salve on and then cover with cloth to protect it from getting rubbed by the splint."

"Okay."

He put salve where it was needed and redressed the few places that still required it, but they were shrinking in size. He wrapped the piece of cloth around her left arm and replaced the splint.

"Now let's eat," he suggested.

"Yes, it smells great."

As they snuggled up in bed, she fought hard not to tell him that she loved him. She didn't know how much longer she could hold out.

The next day, they enjoyed cereal and the sweet lily bulbs. He carried her to the lady's room so she would not need to put her boots on and could stay completely naked. He loved the thought of her naked all day.

After she finished going, she noticed blood between her thighs. She was mortified. She hadn't given her period any thought with all that had happened. How could she have forgotten about it? What was she going to do? She had no other choice; she would have to tell him. God, she would rather lie on a bed of cactus than discuss something as repugnant as her period with him.

"Arianna?" he asked as he came towards her. He saw the blood and said, "Ah, it's your time."

She teared up again, damn PMS. "I don't have any tampons or anything. I feel so ashamed. I didn't even think about it with all that had gone on." She was blithering as she does when she felt insecure.

He held her face in his hands and smoothed away her tears with his thumbs and said, "It is fine. I do have a sister, remember? I know of these things and I knew your time of flow would soon be so I have what you will need." He didn't know what tampons were, but he figured they had something to do with catching her flow.

"How did you know?" She asked

"You have been with me for over two weeks, it was just a matter of time."

He kissed her and carried her to the stream. He splashed water to rinse the blood off then set her on her pallet. He went to his packs and got out a cloth made from cotton and folded it and handed it to her.

"Thank you," she said, embarrassed. "Can you get me my panties, too? They will hold this in place."

He reluctantly handed them to her but understood her need.

"Thanks, that's much better. I have never discussed my period with any man before. I was not very comfortable doing it, but you are so understanding. Thank you for that and for thinking about it ahead of time. I would be lost without you."

She kissed him.

He hoped that what she said was from her heart and she truly realized that she would be lost without him. He knew it to the bottom of his soul. He would be lost without her, as well.

That night he gave her another cloth folded up and asked her to give him the soiled one. She didn't want to.

"No, I will wash it out, myself. I don't want you to touch my bloody things."

"Yes, give it to me. You cannot wash it out; you would have to move your arm too much. We cannot risk it. I have washed your blood off before."

"Yes, but that was different; I was hurt. It was different blood."

"Blood is blood. Stop arguing with me," he said sternly. "I love you and all that makes up you, which includes your cycles. It is the way of life. It is what makes you a woman and should be revered." He forcefully grabbed it out of her hand and walked to the stream before she could do anything about it.

She was astonished by his willingness to perform such an act. She marveled at this man who was most assuredly secure in his manhood as well as his love for her. What wouldn't he do for her? *Let her go*, she thought. Her heart melted a little more. There was hardly any hardness left to it at all. She had to search long and deep to find any to hang on to.

When he finished, he hung the now clean cloth over a branch to dry and joined her in bed. They held each other. When she thought he was asleep, she whispered, "I do love you." And joined him in slumber.

He heard what she said, and it took every ounce of control he had not to react. Every fiber of his being wanted to kiss and hold her tight all night long after hearing those words. But he knew she only uttered them it because she thought he was asleep. He treasured those words even though they were not said to his face. Some day she would. He held onto that thought as he fell asleep.

15

Late afternoon, on the third day, Bidzii arrived back at camp with a stunning golden palomino mare in tow. After greeting his brother, Hashké brought Arianna her shirt and shorts and helped her put them on. His brother laughed, knowing Hashké wanted to keep her naked all the time. After she was dressed, he showed Arianna the mare. She was a nice-looking horse. Her coat was similar in color to Arianna's hair. He pointed that out and his brother just smiled. He knew that Arianna had wiggled her way into his heart, too.

"She's beautiful!" she said. He smiled, knowing she was pleased. "Can I pet her?" she asked.

Hashké wrapped her with the blanket and brought her to the mare. The new horse was skittish but soon let Arianna lightly stroke her nose. "She is wonderful," She told Bidzii. He smiled at her.

After Hashké returned her to her pallet, the brothers walked the horses to the meadow. Bidzii put hobbles on the mare to restrict her movement while she got used to domestication. Hashké caught him up on all that had happened, letting him know they would need to take out the rest of the sutures soon. He asked his brother how his search for the herd went. He told him that there was no incident to report.

"Good," Hashké said, clapping him on the back.

The next morning, after they ate, the brothers wanted to start working with the new horse. Arianna would not be left out. She insisted on going to watch. Hashké gave in. She still couldn't wear appropriate clothing on her legs so Hashké gladly carried her wrapped in a blanket then set her on a nearby rock at the edge of the meadow.

As Arianna looked on, the brothers tried to put a bridle on the reluctant mare. When she gave in and took the bit, they rewarded her with pats and soothing tones. Arianna recognized that training a horse had not changed much over the years. After getting her used to the feel of the saddle blanket, next they put a saddle on her. She tried to skitter away from it, but the men had it cinched up before she could. Hashké stepped away while his brother led her around. The mare hunched her back and took a couple of bucking steps before she settled down.

Hashké whistled for his horse and jumped on him. His brother tossed the mare's reins to him and he urged his horse into a canter, pulling the mare along. The change of pace elicited more bucking. She soon settled and they returned to the walk. After a few minutes, he cantered them around again, but she only bucked once.

He slowed them to a walk and nodded to his brother, handing him the reins. Bidzii put the reins around the mare's neck. He grabbed her mane and jumped on. She was not happy and tried to do all she could to remove him, but she was not successful. He had an excellent seat and anticipated her moves brilliantly. After about 10 minutes of trying, the mare realized her efforts were futile, gave in, and settled. He squeezed her with his legs urging her forward, but she pinned her ears. He squeezed harder and smacked her rump with his hand. She kicked out, then acquiesced. The brothers looked at each other and laughed. She trotted, then cantered. He patted her and rubbed her neck. He pulled back on the reins and she tossed her head. He pulled harder and she gave in and slowed. He rewarded her with more soothing words and petting.

The brothers continued a few more times, then switched riders and repeated the process. By noon they had cooled her out and brought her to the stream to drink. After drinking her fill, she was led back to the meadow where they hobbled her again and left her to graze. As Hashké carried Arianna, the brothers talked about the mare's antics and discussed her ways. They agreed she would make a good horse, but she was no push-over.

Hashké interpreted for Arianna.

Arianna said, "I can't wait to ride her. I like her stride and way of going."

"It will be a while before I will let you. She will need a lot more work before I will allow you up on her." Hashké said.

Her hackles rose. He had no idea she had ridden horses with behaviors much worse. She remembered one horse in particular who would go around a course of jumps nice as you please, then, just as the rider started to relax, would stop dirty at the base of one of the jumps and spin; most of the time leaving the rider in the dirt.

If the horse weren't so beautiful over fences, they would have sold him a long time ago into another line of work that didn't involve jumping. But Arianna did not want to give up on him. She wanted to solve his issue so he could have a good life being pampered and appreciated. It was too bad she had to quit riding before she could fix his problem. She often wondered what happened to him. Maybe it was best she didn't know.

She would just show Hashké as soon as she was healed. Actions spoke louder than words.

After they had finished lunch, the brothers went off to hunt. She rested until they returned.

~ ~ ~

The brothers walked back into camp with a kill and put the meat over the fire. Next, they turned their attention to Arianna. Hashké removed the remaining dressings and his brother remarked on how good the wounds looked and decided to take out the last of the sutures. Luckily, they came out without much drama. Afterward, they applied the salve but kept the dressings off.

Now she was down to just a soft leather piece to protect from rubbing and the splint. She was thrilled. She could glimpse freedom from restrictions. She pumped her fist in the air and exclaimed, "Yes!" The brothers looked at her with uncertainty and mirth. "It's what we do in my time to cheer – show great joy. Guess you had to be there," she mumbled. They just smiled at her.

Arianna was now able to put her leggings on and walk around dressed. The leggings came up over her shorts and were longer than Hashké's; they went from below her ankle to the very top of her thigh and looped around a braided belt that he made for her. They fit like a glove. She loved wearing them.

~ ~ ~

Two more days passed with hunting and gathering what they would need for their journey, and on her twenty-first day in the nineteenth century, they left the temporary camp by the stream for Hashké's secret cabin. Arianna was told the journey would normally take three days but Hashké and his brother decided to take twice that, for her comfort.

They had fashioned a sling for her splint to rest in and she found the ride only mildly uncomfortable. The sheepskin saddle seat helped!

Daily, they traveled until evening, when they would eat and let the horses forage. Not wanting to draw any attention to their presence, they put on more blankets to counter the chill of the night without a fire.

The mare did well, getting the hang of things easily enough. Arianna thought she was a little put out by being used as a pack horse, but she would work with her when her splint came off and turn her into an exceptional riding horse.

Arianna was a little saddle-sore the first couple of days, but her muscles soon stopped griping, accepting that they were not going to get out of the work. The paint was a gentle ride. She told the guys they didn't have to take it so slow, that she was tougher than that, but they wouldn't hear of it.

16

The scenery gradually changed from flat plains to gentle rolling hills and into increasing inclines with ponderosa pines dominating the topography. A deciduous tree snuck in here and there, as well as the sight of blue-green needled branches from a few Colorado blue spruces.

And so, on the sixth day, around noon, just as the brothers had planned, they came upon a serene clearing, forty or so acres of grass carpet nestled in the midst of the vast forest of evergreens. There was a small shack off to the side that did not look like any Native American dwelling she knew of. She looked at Hashké questioningly.

He rode up next to her and said, "One time when I was being chased by soldiers, I rode up into these mountains trying to tire them and came across this cabin. It was in ruin; whoever had built it had long since gone. The roof had caved in and the door was off its hinges. I doubled back and rode widely around it, making sure the soldiers did not see it. They did eventually give up looking for me. That's when I came back here and thought it would be a good place to hole up while things calmed down. There were no Navajo around so I knew the soldiers would have no reason to come back up here. I repaired what was falling down and sent word to my brothers that this is where we could meet without danger of being discovered. It became our safe place to gather. It is very remote. No one happens upon it, but it is not far from Santa Fe, an ideal location for our plans.

"It's perfect, but I bet it is cold here in the winter."

"Yes, heavy snow. Best for times other than winter."

He dismounted and she allowed him to help her down, not wanting to jar her arm.

After patting the paint, she walked inside the cabin. It had a dirt floor and was about 20-30 square feet in size. It had a rock fireplace along the far wall that would be helpful for cooking and heating. She was surprised by how accustomed she had become with living out of doors. She especially loved seeing the stars every night, something she never did in her time. The light pollution made it very difficult to see any but the brightest stars. When it rained, she would be very grateful for this little shack.

The horses were unsaddled and let loose to graze. They went to the small stream about 50 yards from the shack and drank before snacking on the lush grass. The packs and saddles were brought inside and the brothers left to hunt. A warm meal sounded great. She did what she could to straighten their things up, but her efforts amounted to very little; one-handed moving in was frustrating. Plus, there really wasn't much to do, but roll out a pallet or two.

Worn out by the journey, her legs ached and she was filthy. She would go to the stream and wash up in just a moment. She was sure it was going to be cold, but she had to get the layer of trail dirt off her. While she was glad it hadn't rained much during the time they were traveling, it made for dusty, dirt-filled days. She felt like she had an inch-thick layer of smut on her skin. What she wouldn't give for a hot shower. But the stress of a long journey caught up to her at that moment so she, in her filthy state, sat down in the middle of the floor with her head on her knees and just rested.

The men were successful early on and came back just after an hour and found her still there on the floor. Hashké rushed to her and asked her what was wrong.

"I'm not very useful. I tried to set up the house and got nowhere. I'm dirty and I need to wash up but I'm dreading that cold stream. I know I have to man-up and just walk into the water and get it done. I was trying to muster up the energy for it. I'll do it. It will be fine." Not wanting to sound ungrateful for this wonderful shelter and all he had done for her she said, "Really, everything is great, I'm just a little tired and dirty."

He looked at her and smiled. "I have something to show you." He gave his brother a knowing look and helped her up. He led her about 200 yards to the west where she saw what looked like fog through the brush. She held her breath. He continued, leading her to a small pool that had steam rising from it! "I think you will like this," he said confidently. "It is not like your shower you spoke of, but it is very pleasant and will help your body heal fully."

"Oh, this is what you and your brother spoke of at the other camp. Please tell me I can get in it right now."

He smiled at her and nodded. He helped her get out of her clothes and removed her splint. She was buck naked in seconds, then slowly stepped into the water. It was very warm, and she sighed loudly as she sank her tired body into the steaming pool.

She proceeded to immerse herself, rinsing her hair out. She looked up at him standing there and smiled the biggest grin she could. "It is the best ever. Can I just live in here?"

He laughed and said that he was glad she liked it.

"Get in here!" she commanded.

He smiled and started taking off his clothing. He stood there, naked, watching her like a predator, fully erect.

It had been close to two weeks since they had sex and she was so ready and by the looks of it, so was he. Having a slow start to sexual activity, she was willing to make up for lost time. She gazed back at him in appreciation of his exquisite body. The man was sin on two legs. She batted her eyelashes at him and smiled coyly. He rushed toward her, splashing through the water violently. She heard of those kinds of things working but she never believed it; boy, was she wrong.

He moved them toward a rock in a shallow part of the pool and sat, pulling her onto his lap, kissing her. She wrapped her legs around him. The new position put his tip directly at her entrance. He growled. She sank down on him. She moaned. He put his hands under her bottom and lifted her up, then pushed her back down. Her vaginal walls throbbed with an awaking sensation of a too-long dormant period of activity. She almost came the moment he entered her. Her nipples were peaked, straining to be touched. As if he heard their cries for attention, he ended their kiss and sucked one in hard, pinching the other. She came apart. God, she was so easy. Her orgasm, in turn, pushed him over the edge. He gripped her hard and shot for what seemed like forever. The man was virile.

They just sat there breathing heavily. Then they started laughing. Apparently, they felt the same about their abstinence. She said, "Let's never go that long again."

He agreed. "It was very difficult for me to have you so close and not be able to be inside you. I cannot tolerate such things."

She smiled and said, "It's agreed then, we will never let that many days go by without making love, my big handsome man."

He swatted her butt, not an easy thing to do under water. Her vaginal walls gripped him after his hand made contact with her skin. It made him hard again. They loved each other until they were replete.

They walked back to find Bidzii working diligently. He prepared the birds they had hunted and set them over a fire he made about 15 feet in front of the house. They smiled at him as they walked up; he smiled knowingly back and gestured for them to keep walking. He was happy for his younger brother.

Arianna asked as they entered the house, "Why doesn't he use the fireplace inside?"

"He does not like to stay in a white man's house. He prefers to be out under the stars and in touch with the land. Traditional Navajo houses are very different than this cabin. They are rounded in shape, having many sides, with the door always facing the east to catch the blessings of the sun's first rays. It is not forbidden to stay in a white man's house, so Bidzii will come in if it rains. But you should know, no Navajo will stay in a dwelling where someone has died."

"Oh, okay." As she thought about the housing situation, it occurred to her that she and Hashké would be alone inside the house and therefore would be able to resume their love-making nightly, yippee!

They arranged the saddles and packs and as promised, Hashké rolled out the wolf pelts on the floor. They almost made a wall-to-wall carpet. He gestured for her to walk on them. She did so, dramatically, grinding the toes of her boots into the fur with every step. They laughed and went back outside to see about helping his brother.

Bidzii had things well under way so they sat around the fire, going over their plans, waiting for the birds to cook. They told her that after she was settled and felt comfortable, the men would go to a known grazing area and scout for a herd of horses. Bidzii intended the mare to be Arianna's personal mount now since he found one that matched her hair, so another horse or two would need to be trained and then sold.

She asked how long it would take and Hashké told her that it should take a couple of days. At least she had four walls around her and a roof over her head when she would be alone. She felt much safer being able to shut the door on anything that unsettled her. She used to not be so fearful, but being attacked by wolves had changed her perspective.

After dinner, they parted ways with his brother and went inside the cabin. Hashké made love to her softly, sweetly, christening their home with warmth and love.

The next two days were spent once again gathering supplies, this time for her to eat while they were gone. Hashké took her for walks around the surrounding area to teach her which plants were edible and which plants not to touch. He taught her how to set traps and how to clean the animals they caught; her least favorite thing to learn. She told him she was very happy to eat the jerky until they returned. He laughed at her and shook his head.

He told her that he would also make her a bow so she could learn how to hunt and defend herself. But because her arm still needed another week to mend the bone completely, he would leave her a big knife to use for now. She was to have it on her at all times. He strung it onto her belt and taught her the best way to hold it for defense and for killing.

She felt pretty confident that when they left, she would be fine.

The final task on his agenda was to make her special tea to prevent a pregnancy while they trained the horses. He took the snakeroot he had gathered while on their journey from his medicine bag and brewed the tea. After explaining what it was for, she gladly drank it.

The next day, Hashké and his brother were mounted and started to leave when Hashké turned back to Arianna and said, "Be good."

"I will," she shouted back as she watched them leave the clearing. They took only the two horses they were riding, leaving the remainder behind. Arianna was very happy with the situation because she had plans to work her mare while they were gone. Her secret plans helped ease the discomfort of watching Hashké leave. She intended to make the most of her time-out from under his over-protectiveness.

She waved good-bye and as soon as he was out of sight, she went into the cabin to look through the packs to find what tack was left. All she really needed was a bridle. But today, the first day, she would use her saddle too, just to be on the safe side. She would never hear the end of it if she got hurt being thrown from a bucking horse.

She pulled out her saddle and found a bridle, but it had a very severe bit attached to it. She thought that for today it would be fine, but as the mare got the hang of things a plain snaffle would be best. She did not want to create a horse with a hard mouth.

She was so excited, that she had to take a minute and settle herself down. She needed to establish a calm environment to accomplish her goals.

After schooling herself into a more relaxed state, she hid the bridle behind her back and walked out to the mare. She got close but the mare stepped sideways away from her and snorted as she got within arm's reach. Arianna just crooned, telling her of the fun they were going to have working together. And of how she was going to learn way more than that pushy stallion ever knew. She inched closer to her and slowly put the reins around her neck. Once she had her secured, she patted her neck and rubbed her forehead, telling her what a good girl she was.

Arianna led her a few steps to get her used to Arianna asking something from her. She complied, so Arianna faced her and slowly inched her splinted arm up toward the top of the horse's head, getting her accustomed to such a bulky presence. The mare had to get used to the splint setting in between her ears so she could hold the bridle in place, enabling a smooth ascent of the bit into her mouth. If the mare did not readily accept the harsh bit on her own, she would have to force her teeth open with her fingers, so it had to be done this way.

It took more than 30 minutes, but the mare finally lowered her head with Arianna's arm still between her ears.

Next, she lifted the headstall of the bridle to her left hand and let the bit rest just under the horse's mouth. She positioned her fingers of her right hand at her jaw just behind the front incisors. As she pulled the bit higher, it pressed against her teeth, signaling her to open her mouth. The mare did not comply, so Arianna pressed into her jaw in the tender place in between the incisors and premolars, and the mare finally opened. She quickly but smoothly pulled the bridle into her open mouth and slipped the crown of the bridle over her ears.

After this success, Arianna rubbed on her and praised her. She again led her around.

She knew it would be best to do the whole thing over again so the mare would get the process down, but she was impatient and wanted to get on with things. She ended up giving into the voice of reason and slipped the bridle back off, then did the entire process over again. The mare became more accepting as time went on.

The saddle was next. She slowly slipped the saddle pad onto the mare's back. The horse accepted the pad easily, so she reached for the saddle; holding the pad steady, she slung the saddle onto the mare's back. The placement wasn't perfect on her first one-handed attempt, so she jostled it into the correct position. Next, she tightened the cinch, loosely at first, letting the mare get used to the pressure around her belly. Then she pulled it to the proper tightness. The mare accepted everything like she was an old ranch horse. Arianna was very pleased.

She untied the mare and walked her around a bit. The mare hunched her back for the first few steps, then relaxed. Arianna lined her back up to the big rock and stepped on top of it. She twirled her earrings and contemplated the possible outcomes. If the mare bucked her off and she broke something, Hashké would be so angry. That thought bothered her, but it wasn't going to stop her.

This was it; it was time to see if the horse remembered her earlier riding lessons. Holding the reins and the front of the saddle, she put her foot into the stirrup and smoothly lifted her other leg over the saddle and slipped that foot into the stirrup. At least she was firmly seated now. She felt confident in being able to stay on at this point, even if the mare had a bout of bucking unacceptance.

She reminded herself to relax and not transmit her tension to her mare. Once she was convinced she was in a good, centered place, she squeezed the mare with her legs. The mare walked off like a pro, not knowing what all the drama was about.

Arianna chuckled and rubbed the mare's neck, telling her what a good horse she was. Tomorrow, she would leave the saddle off for sure, and just ride bareback, enabling better communication from her body to the horse. For now, she just enjoyed a nice walk around the clearing.

As they walked, she started using one leg at a time to put pressure on the mare's side, cuing her to move away from it. Once she did, Arianna removed the pressure and rubbed her neck and praised her. She repeated this until she was sure the mare understood. She did the same on the other side. The mare was smart and caught on quickly. Arianna was very pleased.

She walked the mare around for a few minutes without any cues, letting her relax. Next, she squeezed her into a trot. She had a lovely flowing trot. Once she had settled in at this pace, Arianna again applied pressure to the mare's sides. First one leg and then the other, asking her to move away from the pressure at the trot. The mare performed brilliantly. Arianna was so happy that she brought her back down to a walk and rubbed both hands up and down her neck, telling her how wonderful she was. They walked around a few more minutes, relaxing, enjoying their success. When it was time to end their workday, Arianna dismounted and took the saddle and bridle off. She rubbed the mare's face telling her how dazzling she was. The mare looked haughtily at her like, "Of course I am." And Arianna laughed. She was disappointed she didn't have some peppermint candies to give her as a treat for such a good day.

She smiled as she walked away, truly pleased with how her morning had gone. It was still early; maybe she would work the paint after lunch. That settled, she left the saddle and pad by the rock and walked back to the cabin to get some jerky and water, she was parched. Stress made her thirsty.

After eating her fill, she rummaged back through the packs, looking for a softer bit. Eureka! She found an O-ring snaffle; just what she was hoping for. The snaffle was what she preferred to use. It was the most basic of bits, but it was the best. Rarely, she used a specialized bit if a horse had a certain issue but, in most cases, a plain snaffle would do. She brought it out to the bridle she had used earlier and switched out the bits.

Walking it out to the paint, she had no need to hide it behind her back; he was used to the process. This was nothing new to him. She slipped the bridle on with ease and walked him over to the rock. Not needing a saddle, she swung her leg over from atop the rock and sat up. The paint stood still like the gentleman he was and waited for her to get situated.

She patted him on the neck to thank him for his patience and squeezed him forward. He responded with deftness. She knew he had been taught riding fundamentals, but she wanted to play with him to see if she could get him to do some dressage. It felt great to ride bareback. She could feel all of the horse's movements without the barrier of a saddle to get in the way.

She squeezed a little more and he picked up the trot. His short stride made his trot easy to sit. She loosened her lower back and let it follow the paint's movements. She pressed him into the bit, and he rounded nicely. She then asked him to turn a small circle while on the bit, which he did after only evading a couple of steps. The circle to the other direction was even better. She brought him back down to the walk and slackened the reins and let him relax.

After a couple of minutes of relaxation, she gathered him up and got him back on the bit. She asked him to move away from her leg pressure as he walked, this movement making him cross one leg over the other as he traversed the field. She then equalized the pressure, asking him to just go straight. After a few strides she pressed with her other leg, and he crossed back, then straight again. After this success, she relaxed the reins again and let him stretch out.

"Now for the same thing but at the trot; sometimes it's easier at the trot," she told him. He performed nicely, only once getting confused. She just kept her cues at a constant and he figured it out. She brought him back down to the walk and rewarded him.

Next, she practiced lengthening and shortening his strides at the walk and trot. He did as she asked but she could tell he was just humoring her. He had figured out long ago that doing what he was asked meant a shorter time being trained.

"Well sir, you have catapulted yourself well into first-level dressage. Congratulations," she said to the paint. He was unimpressed. "Wait until you show off your new moves to that pompous stallion, then you will care," she said, patting him. She dismounted and unbridled him. "You are so fun!" she said, kissing his nose. "We will play more, tomorrow." She rubbed his forehead and sent him back to get a drink and graze.

Thrilled with how her day was going, she smiled while carrying the tack into the cabin. After putting away the bridle, she straightened and stretched. Feeling the workout on her body, she thought of the hot spring and grinned. With that in mind, she looked through the packs for the chamois. She took it and her tired muscles to the pool.

Gosh, did the warm water feel good. It was even better than a bath because it never got cold. She would stay in there all night if she weren't afraid of falling asleep and drowning. After an hour or longer, (she lost track of time), she got out and dried herself off with the chamois. Life was good!! She slipped on her shorts, shirt, and shoes and walked back. It was getting dark and she was hungry.

Back at the cabin, she grabbed some more jerky and dried berries and walked out, looking at her surroundings. If she had a glass of wine, it would be perfect. After she finished eating, she walked to the horses, petting each of them, telling them good-night. On her way back, she thought about how happy and fulfilled she felt. The only thing that would make this day even better would be having Hashké make love to her tonight -- that and a glass of wine. Oh yah, and some dark chocolate; Hashké, horses, a glass of wine, and dark chocolate, these were all she needed for a perfect life.

She rolled out her pallet, grabbed both her blanket and his, pulled them up, and snuggled in for the night. "*It was a good day*," was her last thought as she drifted off into sleep.

17

The next three days were filled with riding, eating, soaking, and sleeping. She was so content. She could stay here for the rest of her days. She did miss some modern conveniences like a toilet and a refrigerator, but really, she was pretty satisfied.

On the fifth day, she was working the mare, bareback, when she saw them. She had the biggest smile on her face and she waved, squeezing the mare into a canter to get to them quickly. When she got close enough, she saw the scowl on Hashké's face. She rode up, pulling the mare to a smooth stop and asked, "What's wrong?"

"What are you doing?" Hashké shouted.

"I'm training my horse. She is so smart." She said smiling at him and his brother. Bidzii looked pleased; Hashké, not so much. "Watch what she has learned," she said as she rode off to demonstrate, not waiting for a reply. She cantered the mare in a small circle, changed leads through the trot and circled in the opposite direction. She brought the mare back down to a trot then she asked for the leg yields the mare did so well. On cue, the mare extended her diagonal limbs appropriately across the field, then turned and repeated in the opposite direction. After bringing her down to the walk, she dropped the reins and walked toward the men throwing her arms out to the sides and yelling, "Ta-dah!" and bowed at her waist. When she got to them, she said, "Whoa," to the mare and she stopped without any cues from the reins. She gathered the reins and said, "You have to be impressed with that. She's the best."

Turning her head toward Bidzii, she said solemnly, "Thank you." He nodded and said something in Navajo. She looked to Hashké for interpretation and he said disparagingly, "My brother said that you have done very well."

She beamed, and then asked, "What's wrong?"

"You do not have a saddle on the horse, and you should not have been riding her at any rate, she was not worked with long enough for it to be safe for you."

"We got along fine, as you can see. Wait 'til you see the paint. He has his own talents." She slid off the mare, pulled the bridle off her and jogged to the paint. She slipped the bridle on and made the adjustments for a proper fit and jogged him over to her mounting rock.

She jumped up on him and cantered toward the guys, stopping about 20 feet from them. She grabbed his mane and said, "Watch this!" She cued him and they spun in a tiny circle very fast. She said "Whoa." He stopped immediately on demand and she almost lost her seat. She started laughing as she scrambled back in place and looked up.

Bidzii was laughing too, but not Hashké. He had jumped off his horse quickly, trying to get to her before she fell. He reached her side right before she was firmly seated back in place on the paint. He pulled her off the paint's back. Because she still held the reins in her hands, the process caused her to pull back on the reins accidentally. The paint hurled backward trying to do what the reins were asking. Seeing this, she quickly released them, and he stood still. Hashké glared down at her.

"What if you had fallen while I was away? What would you have done? What if you had broken a leg or worse?" he asked, all hundred ways pissed.

She patted the horse, telling him she was sorry for rudely grabbing his mouth and turned to Hashké and said, "It was fine. I am fine. I'm not some china doll you have to cover in bubble wrap. I'm hardier than that. Sure, you had to care for me while I was healing but I'm fine now, and I'm going to behave accordingly." She turned back to the paint and removed the bridle and patted his head, telling him to go and play. She shooed him away and he trotted off. She turned to Bidzii and gestured to the paint asking his opinion of him and he clapped in response. She bowed, smiling, and then turned to Mr. Scowly Face and stuck her tongue out at him.

Chuckling, Bidzii, seeing what was happening, reached down and grabbed the rope that was around the horse Hashké had been leading and rode off to water the horses, giving the couple privacy he knew his brother would want. Hashké reached for his horse's reins and Arianna's right arm and pulled both of them to the cabin.

He unsaddled and unbridled his horse and sent him off. He dragged Arianna inside and shut the door. "I told you to be careful while I was gone. Can I no longer leave and expect you to stay in line? I cannot trust you. When we rode up and I saw you on the new mare without a saddle, all I could think about was paddling your behind."

"But I was fine; it couldn't have gone better. I rode all day, then soaked in the hot spring in the evening. It was wonderful; I enjoyed every day. But I did miss you." She said to try to appease him. As she spoke, she ran her hands up his chest, savoring every ripple of muscle. He closed his eyes shutting out everything but her touch.

Knowing she had him where she wanted him, she upped the ante and let her hand drift toward his breechcloth. She dragged her hand roughly over the bulge there. Before she knew what was happening, he picked her up by grabbing her butt with both hands and urged her to wrap her legs around him. She did, of course. He kissed her hard and rubbed himself between her legs. She moaned; she needed him.

He had to have her right that instant. He set her back on her feet and whipped her belt off, then unbuttoned and removed all that was in his way. She stood there exposed, her leggings pooling on the floor. Inspired, he pulled the leggings back up and threaded the belt back through then and cinched it back in place. He made her turn around. She hesitated; he grabbed her hips and turned her. Her ass bare, framed by her leggings, made his blood boil. He treasured the view in front of him. But he was conflicted; should he take her from the front with her legs wrapped around him so he could kiss her while cumming deep inside her, or from behind, giving her the reprimand she deserved?

His manhood jumped at the thought of him spanking her while he drove deep in her sex. The decision was made. "Bend over and put your hands on the wall." He commanded.

She looked over her shoulder at him questioningly, but complied.

He wet two of his fingers and plunged them into her. She closed her eyes and her knees started to buckle. He took hold of her hips to steady her and guided his cock into her entrance. Once seated deep, he took one hand and brought it down on her ass cheek. She let out a yelp and looked back at him, shocked. "That and the others to follow are for putting yourself in danger and disobeying me." He pulled back out almost fully and then slammed back into her and followed it with another smack on her ass.

She was so turned on she could have come with the first stroke/strike. She held out as much as she could but after the fifth piston, she could feel him about to lose it, too. He reached his hand around her, and lightly petted her clitoris. They came together as he pumped in and out of her. Her legs started to give way, but he was there to catch her and hold her up. After they had spent their passion, he pulled out of her and turned her. He held her close as he bent to pick her up and while she was in his arms, her head nestled against his chest, he kicked out her pallet and placed her on it, following her down.

She pulled him toward her and kissed him. He took over, kissing her until she could think of nothing else.

After the tension eased, he pulled back and looked down at her. "Do you understand now what will happen when you do not follow my orders?" She looked at him puzzled and then it occurred to her: the spanking. She thought she would disobey him at every turn if what had just happened was her punishment. But she would never tell him that. She tried to look sufficiently chastened and nodded.

His mind kept returning to the vision of her ass framed by her leggings and said, "Seeing you in your leggings and nothing else was so beautiful." She smiled, then it occurred to her: of course he thought she was beautiful; her scars were covered up. He only saw the unblemished parts of her. She withdrew emotionally, going for the bunker deep inside her, far from him and everyone.

He could feel the moment she left. Sure, physically, she was still right next to him, but her soul was no longer anywhere to be found. He sat up abruptly, and Mr. Scowly Face was back.

"What?" she asked.

"You left. Why? Where did you go?"

"Nowhere. I'm right here," she said sarcastically.

He looked at her unbelieving, seeing right through her. Frustrated that she did not speak truth, he decided to take a walk and give both of them some space. He would go wash up in the warm pool of water to clean off the last five days. He got up and walked out the door without saying a word.

Once outside, he saw his brother preparing the meat they hunted earlier that day, knowing Arianna probably hadn't had a warm meal since they left. They both knew she didn't have the heart for hunting yet and wouldn't have eaten anything but jerky. He thanked his brother for taking care of everything while he dealt with Arianna and asked if he wanted to go with him to the warm waters. He agreed and they both left to wash while the meat cooked.

Entering the pool, their long journey slipped off them as they immersed themselves in the water's warmth.

Bidzii asked, "What is wrong little brother? You should be proud of your woman; she is a good rider and has trained the horses well. Any man would be happy with such a woman."

Hashké sheepishly smiled at his brother and answered. "She is a very good rider and trainer, but I told her to not be reckless and she disobeyed. She always disobeys. She will continue doing so especially after bringing Shándíín back to us. I cannot accept this. It saddens me to know that she will continue to defy me and maybe even try to leave. I feel this inside her."

"If she tries to leave, I will go with you, and together, we will track her down no matter where she is and bring her back." His brother told him this in an unemotional, matter-of-fact manner.

Hashké smiled a genuine smile at Bidzii. "Thanks, big brother," he said sincerely, comforted by their close bond and his brother's pledge.

Having completely soaked their travel-worn bodies, they left the pool for dinner.

Hashké walked inside the cabin and Arianna was lying on her side, elbow bent, head propped on her hand, waiting for him to return. His hair was wet, so she figured he had gone to the hot spring. "Time to eat. Get dressed and come outside."

"Okay." She did so and joined the brothers around the fire for dinner. "You cooked?" she asked.

"Bidzii did. We thought you would like a hot meal after eating only jerky for five days."

"Yes, I'm so hungry. It smells wonderful. Thank you," she said gratefully.

They ate and she asked about their trip. They told her they were able to catch the two horses they thought would be good riding mounts. One was a chestnut and the other a dark bay. Both were just over 15 hands. While the Indians like a smaller, more agile horse, the cavalry prefer a taller horse, solid in color. They chose the horses they did, due to their wider appeal. And if the horses eventually ended up in the cavalry, so be it. Their primary goal is to make the money needed, not worrying where the horses ended up.

After dinner, Hashké made love to Arianna slowly with every kind of tenderness. She couldn't help but soften. Satisfied with some of her walls coming back down, Hashké pulled her close and drifted asleep.

The next day, while the men were off hunting, Arianna saw a mouse skittering across the cabin's dirt floor. She screeched and jumped away as if it had the power to cut her down where she stood. It was unbelievable that it had been months of living outside and the first encounter with a rodent was in the cabin. She shivered as she thought about how much she hated the things. She knew her feelings toward the tiny mouse were irrational, but she didn't care. She would tear the cabin apart to evict the thing if she had to. Carefully, she searched but couldn't find it. There was no way she would be able to sleep if she knew the intruder was still in there with her. She was determined to find it. She was well into the process of getting everything out, when she heard a shout. Walking outside, she saw Bidzii holding his brother back from going to the cabin.

Hashké was shocked into immobility. After hunting a turkey down for Arianna, he returned home to see all of his possessions outside the cabin they shared. His mood went from utter contentedness to one of complete bewilderment. Why did Arianna no longer want him? His brother tried to console him, but he would not accept her divorce.

Bidzii held tight to Hashké, knowing Navajo ways were clear, if a woman no longer wanted to be married, she placed her husband's possessions outside their home and the marriage was ended.

Hashké struggled to get free of his brother's hold and demand Arianna keep their union intact. He did not care if it was Navajo tradition; he would not abide by it. Sure, he felt her pull away yesterday, but later she felt like she had come back to him. Was he wrong?

Arianna stepped outside to see Hashké very upset. He looked devastated and she had no idea why. She rushed to him and he clutched her to him, painfully so. "What's happened? Are you okay?"

"I will not let you go, Arianna. I do not care if that is what you want. I will not comply."

"What are you talking about? I don't understand."

"You have put my things out, you want to separate, a divorce."

"I still don't understand, I don't want you to leave. Why would you think such a thing?"

"It is Navajo custom that if a woman no longer wants her marriage, she puts his things outside the house. Once done, he is not allowed back in. Their union is over."

Finally realizing how things looked from his perspective, Arianna explained, "There was a mouse inside the cabin. It creeped me out! I hate those things! I was trying to find it so I could get it to go outside. That's why I put everything outside. It was a mouse, that's all."

Hashké was so relieved he nearly dropped to the ground. He looked back at his brother and explained and Bidzii started laughing. Hashké scolded, "It's not funny!" His brother ignored him and just kept laughing.

Arianna said, "Seriously, you guys have to go get that thing out!"

~ ~ ~

The next few days were spent with the brothers working on the new horses while Arianna continued working with the paint and her mare, the latter continuing to surprise her with her intelligence and willingness to show off in front of the boys. She was a bit of a diva and Arianna loved it. She would just giggle after completing a demanding movement with flair. This palomino mustang was putting to shame a lot of the more nobly bred warmbloods of her time. It just made her giddy inside. She was thrilled to be a part of her blossoming into a remarkable mount. The brothers were impressed, asking her to teach them how to elicit some of the moves the mare so easily performed.

Over lunch, she explained that the movements she and the mare performed originated in Europe hundreds of years earlier to aid in battles. Being able to evade a sabre attack with quick, balanced movements of their mount on demand was very helpful. The brothers understood the principle of schooling a horse to perform certain movements in battle because often Native Americans have done such things. They teach a horse to move without use of reins, off of knee pressure, so their hands are free to shoot with bow and arrows. That made sense to Arianna. She said that dressage evolved from the same idea, it just developed into a very intricate way of training, a lot of the moves now for show and not useful in combat. It does however develop a supple, balanced horse.

Their training continued and at the end of two weeks, they had four lovely mounts, with the mare and paint excelling in a more demanding regimen. Their plan could now move forward. The money they would get for two good riding horses plus the sale of all of the hides, would give them enough for the purchase of a typical female Indian house servant.

It didn't sit well with Arianna that a woman's worth was put in such monetary terms. She itched to take down the entire system that would allow a human to become a material possession. Maybe that would be her focus after she left Hashké. She had to do something to try to fill what would undoubtedly be an empty life without him.

Toward the end of the second week they had an unexpected visitor; their youngest brother, Adika'í, rode into camp. Introductions were made, the brothers took Adika'í's horse to the pasture and explained all that had happened and why they needed him.

Later that night, in the cabin that was now free of any unwanted rodent guests, Arianna asked Hashké about his younger brother.

He told her, "Adika'í's name means, 'One who plays with cards or gambles.' Navajos look down on gambling. They think it is a bad thing to do, so Adika'í has lived away from our clan ever since he started playing with cards. He does not hold the Navajo way close. They say he is good at cards, that he wins often."

"So that is why he doesn't hate me. He's an outsider, too."

"Yes, probably, but also because as he told me earlier, he thinks you are beautiful and understands why I have helped you."

"Really?" she asked.

"Yes, but do not get too close to him, he always stays apart. He is not for you. I am."

"I am a one-man woman, and that man is you, only you."

He gathered her into his arms and their night progressed in a most delicious way.

~ ~ ~

Over meals the next few days, their plan for Shándíín evolved. Hashké knew a trader he did occasional business with about a day's ride away. The trader was not a threat to the Indians; he was more concerned with making money than skin color.

Given all their resources, including Adika'í's gambling winnings, they were confident they could adequately fund their endeavor. First, they would need to purchase an inexpensive prairie dress and fittings for Arianna so she would blend in easily when she arrives in Las Vegas, New Mexico, the closest big town on the stagecoach route; it was big enough that she could enter and not be noticed. Once there, she was to purchase two dresses as well as a proper pair of shoes, befitting a lady of wealth. Then she was to purchase a stagecoach ticket to Santa Fe at that Las Vegas stop. Thus, when she arrived in

Santa Fe on the stagecoach, it would appear that she was a well-to-do woman traveling from back east.

Arianna told them of a Las Vegas in Nevada in the future, that they would be amazed at all the lights. They looked at her like she was crazy.

Once in Santa Fe, she would stay at a boarding house. It was a two-story building with white wood paneling and blue trim that was at the end of the north side of the town. Her story would be that both of her parents passed away and having no other family and wanting an adventure, she came out west where it was all happening. She was an artist and fell in love with the landscape of New Mexico and was looking for a house or property to buy. After a couple of days of pretend real-estate shopping, she should attempt to purchase Shándíín.

They knew from Bidzii's earlier reconnaissance that a signal could be easily seen from one of the second-floor windows. They decided Arianna would hang a colored cloth from one to signal when the women were ready to be picked up. In the middle of the night under cover of darkness, Hashké would bring two horses and wait for them to come out of the back of the house, then they would all ride away and head back to the cabin. They agreed it was a good plan.

Now that all of the details were agreed on, it was up to Hashké to sell the horses and furs to the trader he knew. He left the following day. He was expected to be back late that night.

It was the longest day of Arianna's life. After dinner she went into the cabin, fixed their pallets and sat there waiting. She couldn't sleep even if she wanted to. After what seemed more like three days, the cabin door opened and Hashké stepped in. She jumped up and ran into his arms. He stumbled back a step and laughed as he wrapped his arms around her and hugged her close.

"Good to see you, too," he said.

"How'd it go?" she asked.

"Very well. After purchasing everything needed, adding that to Adika'í's money he has won gambling, we have $343.00."

"Is that enough?"

"It should be, we have heard that an Indian woman house slave goes for $175 to $200, so there should be plenty for the purchase and your expenses."

"Great, I'm ready to get her back."

"Yes, I am too, but I will worry for you while you are gone."

"I'll be fine. It's just a business deal. Now come and play with me."

He obliged, shutting the door behind him.

They made love with a ferocity they hadn't visited in a while, attacking each other in a frenzy like animals. They only had one more night to be together before this phase of their journey was over; they were to leave the day after tomorrow.

The next day was a quiet one. It was spent loading the paint's pack-saddle with the supplies they would need, along with the small traveling case that would hold the dress and fittings for her cover. She also put her backpack in there for the ride back. She would stuff her leather shirt, leggings, and shorts there so they would be handy in case a quick get-away was needed. The meal that night was also a quiet affair, the gravity of the next week weighing on all of them.

Bidzii, consumed with trying to account for all outcomes that could occur, was aware of the possibility of Hashké losing the one person who gave him the most happiness his brother had ever experienced. If she did not come back, there would be hell to pay. It would take all he had to keep Hashké from doing something foolish and dangerous just to get her back. He would try to be prepared in case that happened.

Hashké, sensing the atmosphere, piped up, reminding Arianna, "I will make you that jumping-saddle when we are all back at the cabin. Then you can demonstrate your skills over obstacles."

"That's right, you do owe me another saddle. I forgot about it, concentrating on our project," she said.

He rebuffed her, not able to suppress his ever-present protectiveness. "But do not think I won't stand in your way if I think it is too dangerous."

His brothers smiled at his attempt to give her more freedom only to snatch it right back.

"You will always be the same, I fear," she said.

"I will try to be accepting of this if it makes you happy. I want you to be happy." He said earnestly.

After finishing the meal, they said good-night to his brothers and entered the cabin. As soon as the door shut, his mouth was on hers, consuming her. Her body melted as she gave in to him, completely.

He laid her out on their pallets and removed her clothes and shoes. His eyes never left her as he undressed himself. He crawled up her, positioning himself at her entrance with his body weight on his forearms at her shoulders, caging her in. He bowed his head down and resumed kissing her. His intent to possess her entirely was evident. She had decided to give herself to him unreservedly, thoroughly, completely tonight.

This very well could be her last night with the man she had fallen completely in love with. It was going to rip her heart apart when she left him, but she had to be strong; she owed it to him to allow him the best life possible with a woman who would be unmarred and good for him, not one who was so needy, with a disfigured body on top of that.

He pushed into her slowly but deliberately, and all thoughts she had been having were dissipated. His actions intensified but didn't seem to quicken. Whatever it was, it was driving her to the edge. She felt like her entire body was being consumed by his fire. Just then he drove unbelievably deep into her and she took off. He followed her and they soared together in what was for her the most soul-wrenching orgasm of her life. She lost track of time and space.

At some point, she didn't know when, he rolled with her and put her on top of him, while still staying inside her. He held her to him, not wanting to let go. He bent to the side, grabbed up a blanket and pulled it over them. He enveloped her again and she gave into the pull of sleep.

He stayed awake, not wanting any of their time left to be wasted in sleep. He felt himself softening and starting to slip out of her, so he contracted his muscles to push back into her, stiffening him in the process. He wanted to stay inside her as long as possible, keeping them connected as one. All night, he made sure they stayed like that, joined.

Just before dawn she awoke on top of him. He was hard, moving in her. She loved waking up like this. She sat up, thrusting him deep. She wanted him to remember her like this; strong, sexy, giving him pleasure, so she cupped her breasts, displaying them for him. He lost it, clutched her hips and drove powerfully into her. She fell apart as he jetted his seamen deep. If he could figure out a way to plug her, keeping part of him in her for the entire time she was away from him, he would. The way she looked holding her breasts flung him over the edge. If any other man saw her like that, he would disembowel him. She is astounding. She is his.

They were interrupted by a knock on the door, his brother saying something. She had a feeling that if his brother hadn't interrupted them, they would just make love all day, delaying the mission indefinitely.

She rose off him and his seed started running down her leg. Noticing it, he said, "I will clean you, wait."

He pulled out the chamois and wetted it and tenderly cleaned the evidence of their night off of her body. She smiled sadly at him as he returned it; they both were feeling the encroachment of their impending separation.

They slowly got dressed and walked out of the cabin to find the horses tacked up, ready to go. Hashké lifted Arianna onto the mare, then pulled up onto the stallion. They rode off to the east in silence.

18

Hours before dawn of the fourth day they arrived near Las Vegas without being seen from the town. Hashké dismounted and helped Arianna down. His brothers respectfully turned their horses around, so their backs were toward Arianna, giving her privacy.

She changed clothes from her comfortable riding attire to the prairie dress Hashké bought for her. Arianna decided to go without the corset. She refused to wear such a torture device. She had her bra on, that was good enough. The dress felt so odd on her body; she hadn't had a dress on in more than two months. He held her while she put her shoes back on. Once she was done, she pulled her hair back and pinned it up into a bun. Putting her riding clothes into her backpack, she placed it in the small case and shut it.

She looked up at Hashké, they both knew it was time. The thought of good-bye made it difficult to breathe. Her mind told her to make their last kiss as quick as possible, but her heart was screaming, grasping for him as their lips met. She slowly, painfully, wrenched herself away, her head the victor in the battle against her heart. His sister's life was at stake. She had to be the strong one.

Hashké lifted her up onto the mare, his hand lingering on her leg. She gathered the reins in one hand, the other clenched around the satchel handles, and she urged her horse away.

When she reached the outskirts of the town and dismounted, she tied the mare's reins around the horse's neck and waved back at the brothers as if all was good.

Hashké whistled, signaling the mare to return to him. The mare wouldn't go.

Arianna told her, "I have to do this. Hashké will care for you. When I'm done, he will bring you back to me, I promise. Now go." She pushed on the horse's neck and with Hashké's second whistle, the diva in the mare re-emerged, so she turned and cantered back to him. She watched as they retreated. She pulled in a deep breath and wiped her face of the telltale tears.

The town was still asleep as she walked up its streets looking for a hotel while marshaling her emotions back under control. The first one she encountered had lights on, so she stepped inside.

Walking up to the front desk, she asked for a room. She filled out the registry and was shown to her door.

After the bath she requested, she walked down to the lobby and had breakfast. This was the first time she would eat more than a few bites since they left the cabin. Her appetite had been diminished but after three days of just nibbling, the aroma of breakfast caused it to return. She ate scrambled eggs, potatoes, and toast. She also had her first cup of coffee in two months. It wasn't Starbucks, but it hit the spot just the same. While she ate, her mind kept wandering to the meals she had with Hashké. She would give up coffee and eggs for the rest of her life just to have breakfast with him every morning. She loved their simple life at the cabin.

She suppressed the tears that threatened. She had work to do and she couldn't do it with a red nose and puffy eyes. She paid her bill and asked if there was a local dressmaker. She was directed down the street two blocks. She walked into the little shop and was greeted by Clara, a middle-aged woman with a pleasant smile.

"How may I help you?"

"I need to purchase two dresses, yesterday."

"Well now, what has you in such a hurry my dear?"

"I have some people waiting for me in Santa Fe and my luggage was stolen. As soon as I can get proper clothing, I have to catch the stagecoach to finish my journey." Arianna was proud of herself for her quick thinking.

"Let's see what we can do for you. My name is Clara by the way." She smiled with a knowing look, and eyed Arianna, for what she assumed was her size, then left for the back of the shop. She returned with two bundles. "You and I must be living right. A lady came in and ordered four gowns two months ago. She paid half down and then I never heard from her again. She was slightly larger than you but with a nip here and a tuck there, I think they will do nicely," Clara explained.

"Are you sure? I don't want to take someone else's order."

"You would be doing me a favor, sweetie. I fear I will never see her again and would be stuck with only the fabric paid for. I will even make you a bargain if you want them. I will sell them to you for half price. They were very expensive; the lady had ordered the best of everything I had. With her paying half and you hopefully paying the other, all of my expenses will finally be covered. It would put me to rights again."

"In that case, I would love to purchase two of them."

They examined each of the four dresses. They were actually full, floor-length skirts with jacket-like tops.

"They are so beautiful. You are amazing. Did you really make these?"

"Yes, thank you," Clara beamed.

"I love the purple, and it buttons up the front, which makes it easy for me. I will take it for sure. I will also take the peach with the black trim. It is so smart-looking. Your beautiful creations will make me look so pretty. Thank you so much."

"No, dear, thank you. Now let's get you into the fitting room and get these alterations marked. The lady who ordered these was shorter than you, but if we fix the hoops so they have less flare that should work to drop the length down."

"I would prefer no hoops at all, actually," Arianna confessed.

"As you know, that is not done in today's fashion. I agree with you, I would rather not wear them either but what can be done?"

After trying on the garments, it was evident that the alterations that needed to be done would be slight and should easily be finished by the end of the day. They picked out stockings and undergarments and soon Arianna was on her way to the shoe shop.

There, the clerk almost showed a look of horror when she told him her shoe size, but he caught himself and cleared his throat to try to cover up his faux pas. She would be damned if she were going to apologize to him for the size of her feet. She had to hold herself back from saying that a size eight-and-a-half is perfectly normal in her century.

But then, a look of "Ah ha!" came over his countenance, interrupting her thoughts. He said, "I might have something, just a moment, please." He rummaged around a while in his shelves and held up a pair. "Yes, yes, I have them," he said triumphantly as he used his short apron to wipe off the thick layer of dust that had accumulated. "They are only one size smaller than what you have requested, maybe if I stretch it some, they will work until you can get a proper pair made for you. They are discounted due to their overly large size. I take it by your request that you do not have the time for me to make you a pair?"

"That's right, I'm trying to leave tomorrow on the stagecoach to Santa Fe. My luggage was stolen, and I have to make do. Please stretch them and I will come back and pick them up. When will they be ready?"

"I should have them done by the end of the day."

"What time would that be?"

"4:30 will do," he said.

She paid him and asked direction to where she could buy her stagecoach ticket. He pointed the way, she thanked him and exited his shop to check the last item off her list.

She bought her ticket and was informed that it would leave at 8 o'clock the next morning out front. She thanked him and left to eat lunch. She made her way to a cafe and ordered the special, roast beef and potatoes, with tea to drink.

As she sat there her mind wandered to Hashké, of course. She needed to keep busy, to keep from thinking about him. Her food came and she forced it down even though her appetite had waned; she had ordered it and didn't feel right wasting the money, knowing how hard his brothers worked to get it. She finished and paid her bill.

Next door was a shop that looked like it had a little of everything, a tiny version of Target. She walked in and a man yelled a greeting to her; she greeted him in return.

She was amazed by the variety of things offered. The labels on some of the goods were great. Truth in advertising had definitely not been implemented yet. There was everything from hair-growth tonic to ox collars for plowing. Down one of the aisles she saw books. Maybe it would be all right to buy a small one. She loved to read and she missed it. She looked through the titles. They were the dime-store novel types. As she read over the titles she came to *Melaeska, Indian wife of the White Hunter* by Ann S. Stephens. Oh, she had to check this one out! But after scanning a few pages, she shoved the book back where she found it. Reading how Native Americans were thought of in such inconsequential way was not her idea of entertainment. If that was representative of the rest of the books, she would pass.

She had a couple of hours to kill before her things would be ready, so she wandered around Las Vegas, New Mexico, of the nineteenth century.

After viewing the entire town, she figured it was time to gather up her purchases. Doing so, she walked back to the hotel, with her new, larger suitcase Clara provided as a thank you for her business and a paper parcel that held her boots.

Having placed her purchases on her bed, she had dinner in the dining room that evening. On her way upstairs for the night, she asked the clerk for a wake-up knock at 6:00 a.m.

Arianna set everything out for the morning and packed the rest in the suitcase; the entire time, she ruminated over her doomed love for Hashké.

She woke to a knock at her door announcing that it was 6:00. She got up and quickly dressed. Her shoes were snug but wearable. When she put the dress on, she felt as if she should walk and hold herself differently, more feminine, more austere. It was weird how clothing could propel you into a certain attitude. She preferred her leggings, of course, but she might be able to find some enjoyment playing dress-up for a few days with attire that was so beautiful. But there was no way she would be in the dresses for much longer than the time required.

She brought her bag down, paid her hotel bill, and ate a quick breakfast; she did not want to miss her ride. It left from a different hotel, so she sat in the lobby there and people watched. In just under a half hour, the stagecoach drove up with half the street's dirt following, then blowing onward as the coach stopped. They unceremoniously loaded her and her luggage along with the other passengers and were off in a jerky rumble.

19

They arrived at their destination at around 9 o'clock that evening. Due to the late hour, she decided to get a room at the hotel the stagecoach stopped in front of. While in her room, she pulled out the other dress, shook it out and hung it up. The dust and dirt of the road made the dress she was wearing filthy. She, herself, was just as filthy, so she ordered and took a bath, then finally climbed into bed. She was exhausted but apparently not too exhausted to keep her mind from thinking about him: his body, his face, his hands, his lips; oh how she missed him!

She had a big day ahead of her, huge, actually. She tried to school herself into sleeping but it wasn't happening. Could she really leave him after this was all over? She should, she really should, but what would life be like without Hashké? A big bunch of yuck. It would be like the Wizard of Oz in reverse, life going from brilliant, vibrant color to bland, endless greys. There would be no joy, no excitement. She would get through it, she always did, but all the good from life would be gone for a long time, maybe forever. If she didn't leave him, he would be saddled with her; a burdensome damaged mouth to feed, when he should be with someone who could be an aid to him in nineteenth century life. She fell asleep spiraling in the midst of all of the anguish ricocheting around in her head.

Arianna awoke to the sounds of daily life on the street below her window. There was an empty abyss in her chest from the contemplations of the night before. She forced herself to get up, even though she would have liked to just stay in bed for the entire day, wallowing in the unpleasant future prospects of her life without the man she loved. Her appetite was nowhere to be found, so she skipped breakfast and headed in the direction of the boarding house. She had a mission to accomplish and she would do it no matter how she felt. She put on her hospital-mask smile, the one she perfected when her dad was sick, and started down the street, nodding benign greetings to those she passed.

It wasn't long before she was at the front of Ruth's Boarding House, as is stated on a wood board swiveling in the wind from a post. Federal colonial in style, the white house with blue trim was unconventional for the area, with its strict ninety-degree angles and unembellished trim. It totally disregarded the picturesque land that surrounded the area.

She knocked on the door and was greeted by a beautiful young Native American woman. She was stunning, actually. She had no resemblance to Hashké or his brothers, so she figured she was yet another person who was enslaved by the owner. She was dressed in a clean, neatly pressed, simple blue cotton dress with a white apron tied over the top. Her hair was that wonderful, shiny black straight hair of her ancestors, parted down the middle and severely pulled back into a sculpted bun at the base of her head. She had expressive dark eyes that looked down often, as if trying to place humility at the forefront. She had a petite body, no doubt perfectly flawless. Her skin was incredibly smooth. Her nose was thin and straight. She was the perfect model for a doll. This was the kind of woman Hashké should have. A beautiful young Native American who would live to please him, not a white woman, arduous and needy.

"How may I help you?" she asked in perfect English.

Pulling up the persona required for her mission, Arianna cleared her throat and began, "Hello, I'm interested in renting a room until I find a house to purchase in the area. Do you have any rooms available?"

"Yes, we do. I am Rachel, please come in and I will get Miss Ruth for you." She guided Arianna to a lovely sitting room. There was a small floral settee to the side of the fireplace. Opposite it, were two high winged-backed leather chairs with a side table in between. A coffee table sat in the center. All of which rested on a beautiful oriental rug. The room would probably be exactly what someone would find in an upper middle-class house back east.

Miss Ruth walked into the room and Arianna stood to greet her. She was well into her middle age. She had dyed brown hair in the style of the time. She had a pinched expression as if she had just drunk lemonade that was far too tart. But it looked at home on her face, so Arianna figured it was a normal look for her. "Pristine" came to mind when describing her dress. It was made from fine silk fabric that was sorely out of place in the unruly southwest. Instantly, Arianna had a dislike for the woman.

"Hello, I am Miss Ruth. How can I help you?"

"Hello, Miss Ruth, I am Arianna Galloway. I am an artist and have decided to move to Santa Fe after seeing this beautiful land. I was hoping you had a room available while I looked for my own house to purchase or construct."

"Yes, I do have a room available; please tell me more about yourself, I do not rent to just anyone."

Arianna twirled her earing as she said in the most pretentious voice she could muster, "I should hope not. As I said, I am an artist, my parents passed away recently and being an only child, I had nothing left holding me to Pennsylvania, so I decided to see the country. As I was passing through New Mexico on my way west, I fell in love with the colors of this beautiful land." Privately thinking of Hashké, she was telling the truth. "Being of some wealth, I would prefer not staying in a hotel where my room could be next to just anyone. I'm sure you understand."

"Oh, yes. I understand completely. By the way those are lovely earrings." Miss Ruth continued, "and, yes, I have just the room for you. It runs $20 a week in advance. I also have two house servants to cater to your needs. You will be well cared for here, I assure you."

To put her guise of wealth more in Miss Ruth's face, she said, "Thank you for the compliment but before I agree to stay here, I will need to see the room to make sure it is up to my standards, you understand."

"Of course, right this way," Miss Ruth said ushering her up the stairs, opening a door to a room in front of the house with plenty of light coming in from the windows on the south and east walls. The bed was full-sized and had a tall scrolled iron headboard and mattress height footboard. There was a washstand and dresser as well as an armoire for her clothing.

"I guess this will do," she said, giving it no praise to keep this owner of slaves on the defensive. "You say you have two servants to help with my needs? I could not talk any of our staff to go on this trip with me. You would think that after all those years of my family paying their way, that they would have some loyalty, but alas, no. Good riddance, I say. I figured I would just hire someone, once I found the location I wanted to settle in."

"Yes, you will be pleased to know," the proprietor continued, under her breath, "that these girls will be happy to do just as you ask without any thought otherwise. They must." She winked as if sharing a secret.

"I sure would like to know how you have accomplished this, I have had the hardest time keeping servants loyal without the attitude," Arianna said conspiratorially.

"Well, here in New Mexico we have our own solutions for such issues, even if the rest of the country is still battling." She motioned to Arianna to come closer and she bent her head and continued, "You can just purchase one." she said.

"Actually?" Arianna asked, smiling as if she had discovered something deliciously wicked.

"Yes. It is the perfect solution. Getting serving people out here is next to impossible and they won't stay even if you do, so we simply took advantage of the natural order of things out here. They have been doing it for hundreds of years to each other, we just entered the game, so to say."

"Lovely." Arianna said, channeling Cruella De Vil. "I believe I will fit in here just fine. I will be back this afternoon if that is all right."

"Oh, yes, I will enjoy having another woman here who sees things as I do." Miss Ruth said.

"Indeed, you will." Arianna rummaged through her purse pulling out the wad of money Hashké had given her. She yanked free a 20-dollar bill and handed it to Miss Ruth. She then turned and said as she left, "See you shortly."

Outside the House of Horrors, the new nickname she had given to Miss Ruth's Boarding House, she shivered, trying to shake off the negative feelings she had clinging to her like spider webs after spending just a few minutes in there. She dreaded how she would feel after five days.

She headed back the way she had come and felt satisfied with how her plans were going. As she walked, her stomach reminded her that she skipped breakfast, so she decided that after she settled her bill at the hotel, she would eat at the café she had passed earlier.

She entered the hotel and walked toward the front desk where she waited until the man in front of her was finished. Her feet were killing her; couldn't this guy hurry up? He finally finished, turned, and seeing her, tipped his hat. His eyes lingered a bit too long for her liking as a sense of his entitlement wisped around her. She scowled in response then faced the clerk. She noticed the man stood a few feet to the side and acted as if he were reading the papers in his hands, but she could feel his focus on her.

She had just finished asking for her things to be delivered to the boarding house when the man began to approach her. He appeared to be in his mid to late 20s, just over six feet, with blond hair dented from his hat. He had attractive deep-blue eyes. He was good looking in a very opposite way from Hashké. He wore old-fashioned denim jeans with a thick leather belt and a beige cotton shirt over which he wore a dark brown-leather vest. His gun hung low on his right hip. He held his tan felt cowboy hat in his clean but masculine hands.

"Hello, I'm Daniel Reeves. I'm a local rancher, are you visiting someone in town?"

"That's awful nosey of you," she said as she tried to walk off, out of the hotel.

"I guess I am, ma'am, but you have to understand," he said as he quickened his pace to catch up to her on the wooden sidewalk. "You're the prettiest thing to enter this town since I can remember."

She snorted and said, "Is that your best line?"

He stumbled a bit at her straight-forward attitude, then recovered and caught back up to her and answered by saying, "Yes, I mean, no. I guess I don't know what you mean."

She crossed the street, lengthening her steps trying to distance herself from him. He followed. She hurried into the café and sat at an open table. He came in right after her. As the waitress greeted her with a menu, the waitress looked toward the door and smiled big at the cowboy who followed her and said, "Hi, Daniel. Have a seat, I'll be right with you." She motioned to one far from Arianna.

He ignored her suggestion and walked up to Arianna's table and asked, "May I?"

"No." Arianna said curtly, trying to clue him in that she was not interested.

"Okay." He said as he sat at the table next to hers, choosing a chair that faced her.

The waitress sat a glass of water down at his table first, along with a menu. She sat Arianna's water down with much less care. "What can I get you?" the waitress asked Arianna with a bit of malice.

"I'll have the special," she said, smiling up at her, trying to offer up the information that she was not competition.

"Get that for me, too, will ya Annie?" the cowboy called from his table.

Arianna did her best to ignore the man, but he would have none of it.

"Let's start over, I'm Daniel Reeves, and you are?" he asked.

"Not interested," she answered, trying to end the conversation not even looking at him as she said it.

He chuckled and said, "Come on, ask anyone in town, I'm a nice guy. Well respected even. What's it going to hurt, telling me your name?"

"If I tell you, will you leave me alone and let me eat in peace?"

"Yes," he said but thought, *for now.*

"I'm Arianna Galloway."

The rancher did as he promised and let her eat without bothering her.

After paying her tab, she got up and started for the door. Daniel quickly dropped his money on the table and rushed to open the door for her. The pain in her feet from the too-tight shoes prevented her from getting to the exit before he did. He smiled as he opened it. She went through and briskly nodded her thanks so she wouldn't have to say anything. She continued on her way toward Miss Ruth's. He jogged up beside her. She furrowed her brow and said, "Stalker much?" and continued walking.

"What's a stalker?" he asked.

"Never mind," she said trying to just get him to go away. "Excuse me," she said trying to step up the stairs to the boarding house.

"Are you staying here?" he asked as she shut the door in his face.

She just stood there, her back leaning against the door. *How much more blunt can I be?* she thought. "Hello?" She called out, announcing her presence.

Rachel quickly walked down the stairs and said, "I'm so sorry, I did not hear your knock."

"Not to worry. Is Miss Ruth in?"

"No. She left to go visiting," Rachel answered.

"Good," Arianna said.

Rachel looked puzzled.

Arianna continued, "Did my things arrive?"

"Yes, they are up in your room. I was just starting to put them away for you."

"Good, but is there another girl who works here with you?"

"Yes." She said, still puzzled.

"Can you get her and both of you come to my room?" she requested as she went up the stairs.

"Of course," Rachel said, then called out toward the back of the house, "Sarah."

Soon a second beautiful Native American young lady entered the room.

Arianna asked, "Please tell me one of you is Shándíín?"

The newcomer gasped at the sound of her name and nodded, tears cascading down her cheeks.

"You can understand me then, good." Arianna then asked, "can she be trusted?" pointing to Rachel. She nodded.

"Great. We have to hurry, before Ruth gets back. Sit." She motioned to them both to sit on the bed as she pulled the chair by the window around to face them. She sat and tried to explain. "I am a friend of your brother, Hashké. He has sent me to bring you back home. I am going to attempt to purchase you from Ruth so your brothers' lives won't be at risk from trying to steal you away." Even saying such a thing was hard to do. "Once I have completed your purchase, we will leave under the cover of night. Your brothers are hiding out of sight and waiting for a signal from me that I have succeeded, and we are ready to go. Do you understand?"

Grasping Rachel's hand, Shándíín said, "Yes, I have learned much English from Rachel. She is a good friend and has helped me since Miss Ruth bought me and brought me here." She smiled at her friend. "What will happen to her? Do you have enough money for both of us?"

"I don't know, is she a slave, too?"

Nodding, she said, "She was taken from her family as a babe."

"That's awful. I will do what I can, but I may not have enough."

Rachel piped up saying, "Do not concern yourself with me, I am fine. I am not like you, Sarah. I do not even remember my people at all. I am fine here. It is more important that you get back to your family. I do not have one to return to."

"I'll do what I can, I promise." Arianna was touched by Rachel's selflessness in putting her friend's needs ahead of her own. "What I have to do is act like I am best friends with Ruth and try to get her to soften toward my cause, so please understand when I am mean and treat you like she does; it is for this purpose; it is not how I really feel. I am simply trying to get her to think we are of the same nature, to get her on my side. Do you understand?"

They both nodded.

"Okay, I don't know how many days it will take me, but I will try to get her sympathies as quickly as possible. The less money I have to spend on the room, the more I will have to spend for you both."

The front door opened and closed, and a conversation could be heard downstairs.

"Go, go about your business, we will talk when we can," Arianna told the girls. They scampered off and tried to act like business as usual.

Arianna heard Ruth ordering Rachel to do something. In a matter of seconds, Rachel was back at her door knocking. "Miss Ruth has asked if you wouldn't mind coming down to meet someone."

"I'll come down shortly," She said, winking at Rachel to remind her of their secret.

Rachel smiled back and left.

A few minutes later, Arianna walked down the stairs and entered the parlor only to find Ruth and Daniel conversing jovially. "Crap," Arianna said under her breath. She plastered on her hospital-mask smile and walked in.

They both turned and seeing Arianna enter, Daniel stood.

"Arianna, I would like you to meet my dear friend, Mr. Daniel Reeves. He is a very successful local rancher. I dare say, he is the town's most eligible bachelor."

"Thank you, we've met." Arianna said.

Daniel reached his hand out in greeting. "Yes. It was at the hotel, wasn't it?" Turning to Miss Ruth he said, "You are such a sweet talker Ruth."

Arianna reluctantly took the hand offered to her. Being rude would not further her cause. She was wondering what game he was playing when he interrupted her thoughts by saying, "I was just telling Miss Ruth here, when I saw her walking up the street, that I would love to know more about her new guest. She graciously invited me over for dinner tonight. I hope you don't mind."

"No, of course not." What else could Arianna say?

"Ruth was just telling me you are an artist." He said. "I would love to see what you have painted."

"All of my supplies and work are back in Pennsylvania waiting for me to send for them when I settle."

"I'm so happy you have chosen our beautiful Santa Fe," he said.

Feeling a little hemmed in, she stood and said, "Yes, well if you'll excuse me, I'm still tired from my trip and would like to rest before dinner."

He stood and said, "Of course."

She nodded to him and Ruth, and headed up to her room. She had not planned for this. What was she going to do with the unwanted attention from Daniel? She collapsed on her bed and her mind started spinning trying to figure it all out. She knew if Hashké found out, he would not continue with their plan to wait patiently for her signal. *Well, he isn't here is he?* She just wouldn't tell him. She would go along with all of this to further their cause to retrieve the girl . . . now the girls.

As she thought more about it, it occurred to her that a rancher with resources and knowledge of the area may be helpful. After she delivered Shándíín and hopefully Rachel to the brothers, she could use the assistance of a wealthy cowboy. Maybe she could talk him into taking her back to that stupid pile of rocks, the butte that got her here in the first place so she could get back to her time, where she belonged. She understood the 21st century, but here, she was ill-suited. Hashké was the only good thing about this time and he didn't deserve to be saddled with her ineptitude of this century.

Now that her plan was taking shape, Rachel would be the perfect replacement of herself for Hashké. She knew she wouldn't be able to take watching the ideal nineteenth century woman warming up close to him, but she wouldn't be there to see it. She would leave the night of the delivery, if possible.

Dang, what a mess. Hashké would not be happy at first, but it was for the best; after all her very presence by his side put his life in danger. She didn't belong here. He would eventually see what she already understood, that she was not what he should have. Tears trickled silently down the sides of her face as her mind kept churning.

She must have fallen asleep, for she woke to a knock at her door with Rachel saying, "Dinner is ready, Miss Galloway."

"Okay. I'll be down shortly," she said, trying to clear out the fog in her brain. A lock of her hair fell out of its place into her eyes. "Oh, shoot, wait." She cracked open her door and asked, "Can you help me with my hair? I can't get it right."

"Yes, I would be happy to." Once in the room Rachel saw the evidence of Arianna's tears and asked, "Are you not feeling well?"

Seeing the concern on Rachel's face, she thought about how she must look. Arianna walked to the washstand and splashed water on her face and rubbed it briskly with the towel that lay to the side. "I'm fine."

Not buying her statement, Rachel respectfully expressed doubts.

"Really, I'm fine. It's just complicated," Arianna said, brushing off her concern.

It wasn't long and Arianna was on her way down to dinner, looking the best she had looked in days, thanks to Rachel. Before she reached the dining room, she once again plastered on her hospital smile and took in a deep breath. As she let it out, she walked in and greeted her new acquaintances with an appropriate attitude.

Daniel stood and pulled out her chair; she sat, thanking him. "Did you rest well?" he asked as he sat back down in his chair.

"Yes, I'm back to rights, now. Thanks for asking. How was your afternoon?"

"Very pleasant, Ruth and I caught up and then I conducted the business I had originally come into town for." He said.

Ruth spoke up then, "You look lovely this evening, and those earrings, I do love the way they sparkle in the candlelight. I hope you enjoy the meal I have planned for us," she said as the first course, a tomato soup, was set before them.

"Thank you, I'm sure it will be delicious." She continued, "Miss Ruth, how long have you been out here in Santa Fe?" she asked as she silently sipped at the bisque.

"I was a teacher in Albuquerque for many years before I tired of it and moved up here. The climate is much more to my liking, I had this boarding house constructed and have been here ever since."

"You must have been a babe when you taught, there is no way you are old enough to have done so much," Arianna said, hoping it would begin to soften her up.

"Oh, you are such a dear, I had a feeling we would get along famously," Miss Ruth said and continued, "Mr. Reeves has been here much longer than I have."

"Really, is this your birth place?" Arianna inquired.

"Yes, Ma'am, my parents came out here looking to start a ranch and I was born soon after."

"Do you have any siblings?"

"Why, yes, I have a younger brother and a baby sister. Well I guess she is not a baby any longer, she turned 15 this year."

"She is a lovely young lady." Ruth added while the soup plates were removed, and the main course served.

"Thank you, she is something all right," he said, "it is all any of us can do to keep her out of trouble. She can be a little headstrong. I'm not sure we will ever be able to marry her off. It is going to take someone special to be able to put up with her."

"She sounds wonderful. I would love to meet her," Arianna said, off-handedly.

"I will arrange it, then. Would you be free to come to the ranch tomorrow?"

Too late, Arianna realized the open position that her last statement left her in and had to say, "Sure, I guess, but I really do have to start looking for a house of my own soon."

"There's plenty of time for that," Ruth interjected.

"Great, I will pick you up at 10 o'clock tomorrow morning. It's settled."

"Oh, that sounds lovely," Ruth exclaimed.

Dinner was over before she had to make any more commitments and she was soon in her bed feeling like she just kicked a puppy. *How could I pretend interest in another man, even if it's merely for subterfuge?* It made her feel sick inside. She had to shove that down deep and carry on. She might need Daniel's help to get her back to the cave. Deal with it, she told herself.

She cried herself to sleep thinking of the pain she would cause both Hashké and herself.

She woke the next morning to the delicious smell of bacon. She did miss bacon. She dressed and called for Rachel to do her hair again. All set to start her day, she entered the dining room, ready to nibble on the delicious meat.

"Good morning," she called to Ruth.

"Good morning to you, my dear. Do sit and have some breakfast."

"Thank you. I will."

"Would you like coffee or tea?"

"Coffee, please."

"Did you sleep well?"

"Yes, thank you. It is so quiet here. It was easy to sleep through the night."

"Good, I would have it no other way."

"What would you like to eat: eggs, bacon, pancakes?"

"Just some bacon, if you please."

"Sarah, bring in some bacon for Miss Galloway," she said in a louder voice.

"Yes, Ma'am," came a voice from the kitchen.

Sarah arrived with a plate piled high with the smoked meat. She held the plate with the tong handle pointed perfectly so Arianna could serve herself.

Arianna placed a few pieces on her plate but then purposely fumbled the tongs so they would fall to the floor, taking with it several slices of bacon. "You clumsy girl, you should be better trained," Arianna admonished.

Ruth immediately rose and said, "I apologize," trying to placate Arianna. She continued. "I guarantee she will be harshly dealt with and I will have Rachel work with her some more."

"I should hope so." Arianna said again trying to channel Cruella. "Maybe you should look for another girl for the inside. This one may not be cut out for it. I hope you did not pay too much for her. If you did, you should talk to the person you bought her from and get some of your money back."

"Oh, no, she was very cheap and now I know why. I will follow your advice and say something to that wretched man. He made too much on our deal, to be sure." Ruth said, mortified.

"No. I'm sorry. Really, I'm just out of sorts, traveling so much. You see, I am just under so much pressure, buying a home and setting it all up on my own. I just get overwhelmed sometimes. I do apologize for speaking so harshly. Please, forgive me?"

"Think nothing of it, my dear, please." Ruth said.

"I tell you what, if you are truly unhappy with her, and the price is right, do keep me in mind. My budget will be small for house staff due to the fact that it will only be one of the many purchases I will have to make, but I will need someone who speaks English and can be somewhat proficient in the kitchen. You see, I have never cooked a thing and I fear I will starve to death if I do not have someone to do it."

"Of course, I will keep you in mind, but are you sure you would be able to put up with her?"

"Well, she will probably try my Christian patience, but I will need someone. I fear I will be desperate, my good friend. Please think about coming to my rescue."

"Of course. Yes, I will give it some thought. Don't you worry, I'm sure we can come up with something. Don't give it a second thought. Just enjoy your outing with Mr. Reeves today. We will come up with a solution for your situation. It will all work out."

"Thank you, Ruth. You don't mind if I speak in such a familiar manor? I feel so close to you, like the big sister I never had. You are so dear to me already."

"Please do, and I shall call you, Arianna. I do feel as though we are long-lost sisters. We shall be thick as thieves, I believe. Now worry not and eat, you will need your strength. There is much to do, and we will take care of it one step at a time."

Breakfast continued without further incident and soon it was time for Daniel to arrive. She waited alone in the parlor, trying not to think about Hashké. *Daniel may be her only way home.*

20

Daniel knocked on the door at Miss Ruth's house precisely at 10 o'clock. He was excited for the first time since, well, he didn't know how long. Arianna was a breath of fresh air. She was beautiful, but that wasn't all. She had spunk. He smiled as he thought of how she treated him on their first meeting. A spirited woman would be exciting in bed but he would have to make her rein it in around his family and others. An undisciplined woman would get the town folk talking. He couldn't have that.

Rachel opened the door and he was shown into the parlor where Arianna was waiting. She turned to greet him, and his breath caught. Yes, she is as beautiful as he remembered. He thought that maybe his mind glorified her over the last several hours he thought about her, but nope, she is truly gorgeous. He couldn't believe his luck; that she walked into his town.

"Hi, Daniel," she said, interrupting his thoughts.

"Good morning, Arianna. I trust you slept well?"

"Yes, like a rock."

"Great to hear it. Shall we go?"

"Sure," she said softly, still not feeling comfortable about this excursion.

They walked out the front door and waiting for them in the street was a small, two-seater carriage. It was pulled by a majestic, dapple-grey stallion that was impatiently standing at the ready, stomping at the ground. Daniel snapped his fingers and the horse stopped.

"He's gorgeous," she said

"Sterling?" he responded, not believing he would be jealous of one of his horses, but he was. "Yes ma'am, and he knows it. Do you like horses?"

"Yes, I love to ride, jumping especially," she said as he helped her into the carriage.

Again, he couldn't believe his luck, a beautiful unattached woman who likes horses. She surely must have been made in heaven just for him. As he got in next to her, he said, "Great, I'll have to show you our operation." He gathered the reins, clicked Sterling forward, and let him stretch into an extended trot. He continued, "Our spread is mostly a cattle ranch, but my passion is the horses."

"His movement is divine," she said, motioning to Sterling.

"Thank you, he epitomizes what I'm striving for in my breeding program; a horse full of pride in carriage and movement. The downside is, that a horse so full of himself requires an advanced handler. Being so high-strung, he can go south on you fast, even if you know what you are doing. My goal is to get all the fancy but with less drama, although, a little drama makes it all a lot more interesting."

"I would love to ride him! Is he broken to ride?" she asked, caught up in the excitement of being around such an elegant horse.

"Yes, I can make that happen. How about tomorrow afternoon? We could go out for a ride around town." His thoughts were that his offer would accomplish two things at the same time: first, seeing her again and second, showing everyone in town Arianna is with him.

"Maybe. I do have to spend some time looking for a house, you know," she said as they rolled out of town.

Daniel clicked Sterling into a canter to let him have a little fun. After a few minutes of Sterling stretching out his stride, Daniel's deft hands eased him back to a trot. *What would such skilled hands do on me?* she thought, but then of course, her brain answered with, *nothing like Hashké's level of expertise in making her body sing.* Arianna snapped her mind back in line. She couldn't believe her thoughts went there. Daniel is not the life she wants, she belongs in the 21st century, nowhere else.

~ ~ ~

Just behind the ridge of hills that surround Santa Fe, Hashké watched as another man touched Arianna, lifting her into a carriage and then driving off. He was going to kill a white man. He handed the spyglass to his older brother and started to rise to jump on his stallion. His brother saw the look in Hashké's eyes and tackled him. Adika'í joined their eldest brother in restraining Hashké.

Bidzii told Hashké, "No. You cannot go after her. She is doing what we asked of her. You must trust her. I have seen love in her eyes for you. He must be involved in the plan somehow. You must wait and trust her."

After a few more minutes of vigorous struggling, Hashké succumbed. "I will not go after her now, but I will soon, even if I do not see the cloth in the window. I will give her a few more days then, we will go and bring both women back."

~ ~ ~

Arianna and Daniel continued chatting about this and that for about 15 more minutes, when they arrived at a set of large ornate iron gates that were swung wide. They drove up the Aspen tree-lined path that opened up to a huge, rambling, single-story ranch house painted a soft yellow. A covered porch surrounded most of the building and was trimmed in white.

"What a lovely home," Arianna said as she looked around.

"I'm pleased you like it," he said as he pulled Sterling up at the front door. A younger man came from around the house and took Sterling's reins as Daniel got out and came around to her side. She stood and he placed his hands around her small waist and easily lifted her down, holding her too close and too long for her comfort. "Yes, well…" she said as she stepped back, putting distance between them.

He had coveted touching her ever since he first set eyes on her in the hotel. It didn't disappoint. He could feel the small curves of her body and wanted more, a lot more. As he slowly placed her on the ground, he drank in every second of their closeness, his mind filled with what he would do with her if they were alone, without prying eyes. He shivered slightly as she stepped back, feeling the loss of her heat. *Damn*, he confirmed, *I have to have her.*

Just then a very young lady, burst out from the front door. "Daniel!" she shouted as she ran toward him. She hugged him exuberantly. He chuckled, and pulling her arms from around him said, "Camille, I have someone I would like you to meet." He turned her to face Arianna and said, "Arianna, this is Camille; Camille, Arianna."

Arianna reached out her hand and Camille limply shook it, saying, "Hi" with as much enthusiasm as someone headed toward the gallows.

"Hello, nice to meet you," Arianna said with just a hint of humor.

Daniel's mother made her appearance next and held out a hand in warm greeting. "Hello, Arianna, I'm Corina, Daniel's and Camille's Mother. It is so nice to meet you. We have heard so much about you. Please, do come in, so we can sit down to lunch."

Arianna graciously took the hand offered to her and walked into the house. She had no idea she was to have a formal meal with his entire family. Looking back over her shoulder at Daniel with surprise, she was led into a graciously appointed room. It was the type of dining room in which families gathered nightly to discuss what happened that day and the possibilities the future might hold. She was guided to a chair to the left of Daniel's Mother, with Daniel to be seated next to her. The men stood until she sat, and she was introduced to his Father, Mitchell; and his brother, Benjamin. "Ben," he corrected.

"Hello, Mr. Reeves and *Ben,*" emphasizing his name for his sake. The men resumed their seats and the first course was served. As lunch continued, she thought, *this is no way a casual drive through the countryside to meet his sister and have lunch. I've been set up.* She stiffened and emotionally distanced herself as these thoughts resonated within her.

Daniel could sense Arianna's retreat. He scrambled to think of what to say, or what to do to bring her back. *Horses, she loves horses. As soon as lunch was over, I'll escort her out to the stables and show her around.*

Thankfully for both of them, the lunch soon came to an end. As he pulled her chair out for her to rise, she thanked his parents and told all of them how nice it was meeting them.

His Mother said, "You must come back soon, my dear. You are always welcome. We do hope to see more of you."

"Thank you," Arianna said with a tinge of regret she hoped no one else noticed.

Daniel placed a hand at the small of her back and ushered her out the back door into a pretty flower and shrub garden that buffered the house from the working part of the ranch. "My Mother's passion," he explained as they walked through it. He closed the garden's gate and placed her arm in the crook of his as they continued a couple hundred yards to the barns.

Arianna felt a little uncomfortable, arm-in-arm with Daniel but was unsure if she should say anything. For all she knew, this was how these things were done in this time.

They entered a big, beautiful barn and she inhaled deeply, taking in the much-loved smell of a stable. She exhaled slowly, releasing all of the tension that had been building up in her that day. She walked down the shed-row and looked into every stall that had a nose sticking out of it. She was like a kid on Christmas morning, surveying all the gifts under the tree.

He delighted in her joy. He told her about every horse. She smiled brighter at the horses than he had seen her smile at anything or anyone else. Jealousy once again rose up in him. But if horses were what it took, he would use them.

"As I told you yesterday, Sterling is the stallion at the heart of my program. It is matching the right mares to him that is the challenge. The next is keeping the offspring safe and unharmed until they mature. Breeding such high-strung horses is a definite challenge. We have a vet that is pretty much a staff member."

"I bet, but who cares when you end up with such exquisite animals? Every dollar spent is worth it for such wonderful horse flesh."

And with that statement she lodged herself permanently in his heart. He knew she was the one. Now, to convince her.

"Yes, well, thanks to the cattle we have the money to put into the horses. Soon I think they will start to hold their own in bringing money into the ranch. At least that's my goal. This ranch started with my father and the cattle. The next phase I planned is the horses."

He went for the clincher and led her into the pasture where this year's foals and mamas were held. They were greeted by delicate whinnies.

"Oh, Daniel," she exclaimed as he opened the gate and she slowly walked toward them with her hand held out. A couple of the bolder ones came over to investigate her.

"Be careful, we do start working with them the moment they hit the ground, but they are unpredictable," he cautioned.

She looked at him like he was an idiot.

He smiled to himself at her forthrightness.

"They're so wonderful. I could spend every minute of the day with them."

If I had my way, she would, Daniel thought.

Remembering what she was supposed to be doing, she said briskly, "I should get back."

His plan of softening her up worked for a little while, but he wanted her to be able to let go of what was holding her back and just be with him, nothing between them. He resolved to continue to work on that.

"Okay, I'll have Sterling brought around to the front of the house."

"Oh, can't we just leave from here. Wouldn't that save time?" she asked.

"Um, sure" he said, puzzled by why she wouldn't want to tell his family good-bye. As they walked back through the barn, he asked one of the ranch hands to get his carriage and have it brought to the front of the barn. As the young man hurried off, Daniel couldn't stop himself, he turned her toward him and bent his head down and kissed her. His goal was to knock down the wall she kept putting up between them.

She responded by kissing him back for a second, it not really sinking in what they were doing until Hashké burst to the forefront of her mind. She pushed Daniel away and said cold as ice, "You shouldn't have done that. I did not give you permission for such a thing. If I gave you that impression, I did not mean to."

"No, I apologize. I just wanted … I just wanted to get closer to you, be closer to you. I am sorry. I was out of place. I will not do it again unless you ask me to, I promise. I will be the perfect gentleman."

"I think it's time I got back," she said sternly.

"Sure," he said as he led her to the barn entrance,

Stepping out into the sun's full glare, it burned through the fog she subconsciously tried to generate to dim all thoughts Hashké. They came flooding in, as if a dam had burst. What was she doing? She was in no position to kiss another man. Her heart raked her over the coals. Did the temperature jump? Perspiration threatened. What she wouldn't give to be alone so she could give into the urge to double over, and purge everything she ate today onto the dry, dusty ground.

Mindlessly, she sat on the carriage seat, her head swallowed by guilt. They started off back to town.

Not one word was spoken by either of them on the drive back. Daniel had pushed too hard too fast. He was used to the town's women who threw themselves at him, so when the one he finally wanted wasn't falling all over him, he thought he could just force it. He should have guessed she wouldn't have gone along with it. She was a confident person. He knew she would not be bullied into anything. After all, that was what he liked about her. He was an idiot. He would just have to give her some room and let her come back around, even if it killed him. He wouldn't give her too much room though; he instinctually knew she could so easily slip through his fingers. He couldn't let that happen. He would plan outings with her, to be around her but not pressure her.

He knew she would use the excuse of finding a house to evade spending time with him, but she really needn't bother. She could just move into his family's house if he had anything to say about it. He would ask her to marry him tomorrow if he thought she would agree. Now he understood the stories his Mother read in which the men would kidnap reluctant ladies and carry them off to Scotland to marry them. He would do that in a heartbeat if he thought she would stay after the fact, but she would probably board the next train out of town just to spite him. *His Arianna would never stand for such a thing*, he thought as he smiled. No, it will take a lot of patience and a whole lot of cunning to snag her. She would be tough, but he didn't think the task impossible.

All too soon, they had made it back to the front of the boarding house. He got out and went to assist her, but she had already jumped down. She walked to the door and started to open it and said, "Thank you for a nice time."

He quickly asked before she shut the door on him, "What time should I bring Sterling around for you to ride tomorrow?" *That's right, I'm throwing down my best card, my ace*, he thought.

She hesitated, the pull of riding such a fine horse was too strong and said, "Two o'clock" and shut the door.

Daniel smiled as he left. He must not have messed things up beyond salvation if she agreed to see him again.

Happy with that, he jogged down the stairs, hopped into the carriage, and trotted Sterling off, back to the ranch.

Arianna closed the door and headed straight up the stairs to her room. She entered it and found Sarah there putting up her second dress. "Oh, hi, Sarah. Thank you for cleaning that. It looks great. I don't know how you do it." She saw the sadness in Sarah's eyes and went to hug her saying, "What's wrong?" When Sarah winced and pulled back. Arianna demanded, "No really, what's wrong? Are you hurt?" Sarah glanced at the open door. Arianna took the cue and had her sit on the bed as she closed the door. "Now tell me everything."

A single tear rolled down her face and said, "She punished me. But I'm fine; it just hurt when you hugged me. Don't trouble yourself with it."

"Who beat you?" Arianna asked.

"Miss Ruth, but it is fine. Do not worry; it's the way of things here. I'm used to it. Just tell me we will be leaving soon," Sarah said.

"Hell, yes we are going to leave. I will approach her tonight about the purchase. I'm so sorry she did that. I had no idea she would do such a thing. I did that stunt just to try to open up talks about me taking you off her hands, not to get you physically hurt. You know that, right? Please tell me you know I would never have put you at risk for violence."

"Yes, I do know that. It is fine. It would take a lot more than a few whippings to break me. I am Navajo," Sarah said proudly.

"Yes, you are. I love your people. Your brother Hashké saved my life. Did I tell you that? I owe him everything. I will do whatever it takes to get you back to your family. You have my pledge."

Sarah nodded and said, "I better go before she notices I've been gone too long."

"Okay, be strong. I will try to get this done as quickly as I can."

Sarah closed the door behind her as Arianna's head was whirling. *What was I thinking? An innocent young woman was being beaten while I was trotting around the countryside. I have to focus and get this done.* She had an hour or so before dinner and needed to firm up a plan of action.

Rachel, knocking softly on her door announcing dinner, brought her out of her deep thoughts and contemplation. She still didn't have a clear-cut plan in place. She hoped a path would open up in the conversation that she could use to bring up the subject. She walked down the stairs and sat at the table trying to look as if she hadn't a care in the world.

"Good evening, Miss Ruth. How was your day?" Arianna inquired with false interest.

"Good evening, just fine, just fine. And yours? How was your outing with Mr. Reeves?"

"Lovely, he has a very nice family." Arianna said.

"Indeed, he does. Mrs. Reeves doesn't make it into town often enough, but when she does, we do enjoy her company."

"Yes, and Daniel showed me the horse program he has been working on. It looks promising." Arianna added.

"Oh, I wouldn't know a thing about those smelly creatures."

Yet another reason I do not like you, Ruth, Arianna thought. "Well, he has a plan for expanding their farm and I believe it will be successful."

"Good, good. On another note, I was in the café for lunch today and I ran into old Mr. Henderson, he was recently widowed last year. His son has insisted he come and live with him and his wife. Mr. Henderson is getting on in years and without sweet Beatrice to care for him, I'm sure it wouldn't be long, and he would follow her. Anyway, his house is now on the market. Would you like to see it?"

"Of course. How fortunate for me," Arianna said.

"Yes, well he is leaving early tomorrow but we can see it anytime. It is available for immediate occupancy. Mr. Henry, the banker, is handling things for him. So, if you do like it, we can go to the bank afterward and make the arrangements. I would hate to lose you as a tenant, but I do expect we can continue our friendship, just from different houses. I hope I am correct in assuming so."

"Oh, of course, my dear Ruth, of course we would continue our friendship. I would have it no other way." As dinner was served, Arianna continued, "By the way, have you had a chance to think about my offer for the Indian girl. If I can move in to the house by the week's end, then I shall surely need the help immediately."

"Are you sure you want her? She is not the best domestic. She is willful and obstinate," Ruth complained.

"Well, I do see your point, but I believe anyone is much better than no one at all. Plus, as I view it, taking her off your hands might be a small repayment for your kindness. You have helped me so much since I stepped off that stagecoach. I tell you I wouldn't know where I would be without you," Arianna lied.

"Well, if you are sure?"

"Oh, quite. Does it take you long to replace one?"

"No, they are readily available. All I have to do is send word and the next day, I have one delivered."

"I am so glad. I did not want to put you out in any way." As they finished the meal, Arianna tried to introduce the most delicate part of the exchange, the price. "By the way, how much will I owe you for Sarah?"

"Well, let me see, I have put so much training into that one. Three-hundred dollars would probably cover it."

That witch! Arianna thought. *Looking out for my interests, my heinie.* Schooling her expressions, she said, "That much?"

"Yes. They don't grow on trees, after all," Ruth said.

I really do not like this woman, Arianna thought while twirling her earring. "I can see that price for a large male who would work the fields, but not for a house girl."

"Well, they usually don't bring that price fresh from the trackers, but I have put so much time and work into her, she didn't even know one word of English," Ruth said.

How to make this work? Arianna thought, *I can't have come this far to not succeed. I don't have the $300 for one, much less* *the $600 for both. And I have to bring Rachel for Hashké.* She twisted her earring some more, trying to think.

"I do love those earrings; they sparkle so especially when you twirl them like you do," Ruth hinted.

That's it, the earrings! Their huge sentimental value had nothing on freeing two human lives. Her heart was pounding with excitement. She may have just solved all of her problems.

After schooling herself, she said, "I tell you what, how about a trade, one of my earrings for Sarah?" Arianna saw a glint in Ruth's eyes so she continued, "No, that wouldn't work, these diamonds are far more valuable than an Indian girl, plus you would have to have the pair. I guess I could trade both earrings for both girls, but you would come out way ahead, they are a family heirloom after all."

"Well, I have helped you out so much, plus I did find you a house. I even introduced you to the most eligible bachelor in town," Ruth insisted.

"Yes, you did, didn't you? I guess I could. Have we come to a deal then?" Arianna asked.

"Yes, I believe we have. Shall we shake on it like the men do?"

Trying to think of a way to prove proper ownership if caught, Arianna said "Actually, my father was such a stickler for paperwork, he made me promise to always have proper documentation in every transaction I undertook. It drove me batty, I tell you. But still, I just wouldn't feel right without it. Would you mind, terribly?"

"No, not at all, my dear," Ruth concurred.

"Great. Shall we just stroll into your office?" Arianna asked, the dinner finished.

They got up and Arianna followed her. Ruth took out a sheet of paper and started writing. When she was finished, she showed it to Arianna. It read that the two Indian girls known as Rachel and Sarah are given in exchange for two diamond earrings by Arianna Galloway. They both signed and Arianna took out her earrings and without even the slightest bit of reservation, handed them over to Ruth who said, "Pleasure doing business with you."

"And you," Arianna said as she rolled up the paper.

"You don't mind that the girls still work for me until I get replacements, do you?" Ruth asked.

"Heavens, no. What would we eat?" Arianna giggled as if that were the funniest thing ever, playing her part flawlessly. "As long as their replacements get here before I move into my house, that is just fine with me." Turning to leave the office, she said, "Well, I'm heading for bed. Business just wears me out."

"Good night, my dear." Ruth said in a patronizing tone.

"You, too. See you in the morning for breakfast," Arianna said and turned to walk up the stairs. She glanced back and said, "Oh, can you send one of the girls up here to help me get ready for bed?"

"I sure will." Ruth said as she left for the kitchen.

The knock came and Arianna ushered Sarah inside and shut the door. "Okay, it's all been arranged. I have officially purchased both you and Rachel," Arianna explained with a huge smile and went to hug Sarah but stopped herself, remembering Sarah's battered body. "Anyway, tomorrow I will signal your brothers and we will leave that night after everyone is asleep. Do you guys have anything else to wear? We are going to have to ride horses out of here."

"No, Rachel and I only have what we are wearing. But, we may have a problem." Arianna looked at her questioningly. Sarah explained, "Rachel does not know how to ride. She was taken as a babe and has never been on a horse."

"That's okay, she can ride with Hashké. Do you think that will work?"

"Yes, I'm sure she will do anything to leave this place and Ruth."

"Great. It's all set, then. We leave tomorrow night. I know it will be difficult but, try to act like business as usual, Okay?"

"Of course."

Arianna gently hugged Sarah. "Until tomorrow night, then." She opened the door and closed it behind her. She was sure none of them were going to get any sleep tonight. She took her dress off, laid it over the chair, and slipped on her nightgown. With a sigh of relief, she took the pins out of her hair and rubbed her scalp where the pins had forced it in unnatural directions. She ran her fingers through the long strands as she got in bed. She turned out the lamp and tried to force herself to close her eyes and sleep. She must have been successful because the next thing she knew, a hand covering her mouth startled her into wakefulness. She began to struggle until she heard Hashké's voice saying, "Silence, it is me."

"What are you doing here? Do you want to blow everything?" Arianna said in an angry whisper.

"I think you need to be reminded that you are mine," Hashké said in no uncertain terms.

"You are willing to ruin everything because you are jealous? Unbelievable." She was saying when his mouth came down on hers.

He kissed her hard as if trying to brand himself permanently on her lips.

He pulled her nightgown over her head and untied her under garment. He had her completely naked in mere seconds. He pushed his breechcloth to the side and climbed over her. He grabbed both her hands in one of his and held them over her head. Posed at her entrance, she was at his mercy when he demanded in a hushed stern voice, "Who's are you, who do you belong to?"

She bristled at his domineering behavior, but she knew in her heart he wasn't doing it to be abusive, he was merely a nineteenth-century man from a culture very different from hers, feeling threatened by another. Reminding herself of this, she acquiesced and admitted, "You. Always you. Only you."

As soon as he heard the words he craved to hear, he entered her, resulting in an unexpected, irksome sound from the antiquated bedsprings. He immediately stopped his movement, and while still inside her, lifted her up off the bed, and knelt down, placing her on the carpet. He moved her hands back over her head and drove into her to complete his possession of her. Her orgasm struck with the intensity and speed of lightning as he kept driving into her with determination tainted by anger. His relentlessness pursuit drove her to a second release. In utter satiation, her muscles uncoiled, and her body lay serene. It was then that he let his climax overtake him. His body, though still being held up on his elbows, relaxed. He bent his head down and kissed her completely. When he finally pulled back, his mind was left muddled and free-floating.

He slowly released her arms and she wrapped them around his neck, not wanting him to move off of her. *Dang, what he did to me!*

He rolled them both over, putting her on his chest. She lay there, breathing in deep and exhaling out all the angst and worries plaguing her since she left his side. With his arms around her, grounding her to him, she acknowledged, "I missed you."

After a few minutes, she quietly guessed, "You saw me today, with Daniel, didn't you?"

His answer was short but heavy with gravity when he said, "Yes."

She let a few more minutes pass before she said, "I have done it. I have purchased your sister."

He looked up at her. She lifted her head up off his chest and looked back at him and continued, "It happened during dinner tonight. I have to do some things tomorrow to wrap it up but, it is basically done."

He hugged her and said, "Let's go now."

"No, I have set it all up for tomorrow night. It is only one more day. We have to do this right. I do not want the soldiers after us and if I can do this the way I have it planned, they won't be. Trust me."

He reluctantly agreed.

She continued, "So tomorrow when you see me with him again, you cannot freak."

"Freak? I will kill him."

"No, Hashké, you have to keep yourself under control. What you will see is just a front for getting us all out of town without any issues." *And a way for me to have help to get back to the butte, to where I belong, to my century,* she thought. "Promise you will leave it alone. I must do this my way, when we are back at the cabin it will be all about your way. But for one more day, it has to be mine. Please, just give me one more day. Okay?"

Disinclined, he gave in anyway. It was only one more day and if it ensured his sister's and Arianna's safe return, he would do it. "Yes."

"Great. Also, we will have a third person to bring with us. She is your sister's friend. I have purchased her, too. She does not know how to ride; she was taken as a baby from her tribe and was brought up in the kitchen and not around horses. You can just put her in front of you and keep her from falling off, right?"

He looked at her with skepticism but agreed. He would agree to anything to end this separation from her and get her back to the cabin.

Her mind drifted while being held in his arms, "I can't believe you got in here without detection. You are crazy. You have to trust me now, okay?" He gave one quick, short nod. She wasn't completely convinced; she knew he had a short fuse, but she had to finish this right, to set it up for her future plans. "It is getting late, you better go. We will be together tomorrow night with your sister back safe, with you and your brothers."

He agreed and lifting her, placed her back in bed softly. He covered her with the bedding and kissed her thoroughly one last time. Reluctantly, he extracted himself from her, righted himself in his clothing and drifted back into the shadows, disappearing as quietly as he came.

ANYTIME, ANYWHERE

She lay there, replete, all the stress having been driven out of her body.

21

The next morning occurred the same as all the previous ones had here in Santa Fe, with false niceties and bacon. During breakfast, Arianna and Ruth agreed to go look at the Henderson house later that morning. When it was time, she met Ruth and they walked out the door, as Ruth was telling her how excited she was for her to see the house. They walked with their arms linked as if they were the best of friends. Little did Ruth know that it was all Arianna could do to go along with the ruse; it turned her stomach when she thought about what Ruth did to Sarah.

After a short walk, they arrived at the modest house opposite in style to Ruth's. This one was made of adobe and quite a bit smaller.

The door was unlocked, of course, and they walked in. "It isn't much but with a fresh coat of paint and better furniture, you will make it lovely, I'm sure." Ruth said. They looked into every room and in, keeping up her guise, Arianna talked of her plans for each one.

"Well, sounds like you will be staying in my establishment a little while longer with all the renovations you want to do," Ruth recommended.

"You are probably right, would you mind?"

"Not at all. Stay as long as you like, my dear. Shall we go to the bank and finalize it?"

"Actually, I'm famished and then I have to get ready for my riding date with Daniel, so I'm afraid I will have to put it off until tomorrow."

"However you insist," Ruth said as she shut the door behind them. As they walked back to the boarding house, Ruth once more had a one-sided conversation about ordering this and that for Arianna's new house.

When they arrived back, Ruth yelled for Sarah and Rachel to be quick about getting lunch ready. Gosh, Arianna hated this woman. She couldn't wait to be gone from her company.

Lunch was prepared quickly and having to back up her claim that she was hungry, she ate plenty. She made her excuses and headed up the stairs to her room. She flopped onto her bed. She would just close her eyes for a second, the previous night's turmoil and activities had kept her from getting enough sleep.

The next thing she knew, soft knocking persisted at her door. Sitting up and shaking her head to clear it, she said, "Yes?"

"Mr. Reeves is downstairs in the parlor, Ma'am." Rachel said.

She never took naps. *Stress sure drains the energy right out of you*, she thought. Hurriedly she set herself to rights, proceeded down the stairs and into the parlor. "Mr. Reeves, so sorry to keep you waiting," she said, trying to cover up her grogginess.

"Think nothing of it. And it's Daniel to you, Arianna." He said stepping closer to her. He placed her hand in the crook of his elbow and led her out the door.

Sterling stood outside in all his stud-liness, tied to the rail along with another big, grey horse but darker in color. "This is Triumph, he is Sterling's first son."

"Well, he is a stunner, too. Aren't you?" she said turning to the new horse, petting his nose.

"Shall we?" Daniel asked.

Sterling was saddled with a sidesaddle. She had never ridden in one but how hard could it be? Daniel easily lifted her onto the big horse. He handed her the reins along with a long crop like the dressage ones she used in her time. She worked the reins through her fingers to get a light feel of Sterling's mouth. He rounded nicely for her and she complimented him.

Daniel mounted his ride and they started off in a brisk walk. "So how do you cue a horse in a sidesaddle? I always ride astride." At the look on his face she covered her tracks by continuing, "much to my Father's chagrin."

His expression of relief told her she covered pretty well. "I mean I know it isn't done but it just feels more balanced when you take fences astride. It is much more dangerous to jump in a sidesaddle, with all the weight purchased atop the horse instead of around it, don't you think?"

"Well, I wouldn't know but I suppose you are right." Then he went on to answer her first question, "You use the whip to cue as the second leg. But that won't be necessary on Sterling; he will just follow my lead. Also, you can just use voice commands. He is very smart and responsive."

"Great." They picked up the trot and Arianna found her balance quickly in the new position. She was enjoying how supple the big grey horse was in the bridle as they left the town.

After several minutes of riding, he asked, "How was the Henderson house?"

"How did you know about that?" she countered.

"Nothing happens in this town without everyone else knowing."

"Oh. It was fine; a bit small, but it will do for now."

"Good," he said.

She wasn't sure if he meant good, it's too small or good, it's fine. But she didn't really care either way.

They picked up a canter and rode toward a stream. As they got close, they slowed their horses and he walked them into it to allow them to drink. "You are a good rider," Daniel said.

"You doubted me?" she asked.

"No, it's just people always think they are better than they actually are. But not you, you ride exceptionally well."

"Thanks, I love riding. I would do it every day, all day, if I could."

Taking that opening, Daniel said, "You could if you wanted to. I could make that happen for you." Not wanting to push too far he stopped the conversation there, much sooner than he really wanted.

"Daniel, things are just so complicated right now. I have so much to do and it's just not a good time for me to start a relationship."

"Just know I will be here waiting for you. Take whatever time you need, but please let me be a part of your life when you are ready."

She looked at him and saw the sincerity in his eyes. "Thank you. I appreciate your and your patience. I do want to ask you something, even if I can't explain everything right now but . . ." she took a deep breath and continued, "if I need your help, can I come to you?"

Not knowing what she could possibly be talking about and not really caring about the particulars, he said, "Of course. I would do anything for you. You have to know that."

"I presumed so, but I just wanted to make sure."

"All you have to do is ask. Are you in some kind of trouble? How can I help?"

"Oh, no, I'm fine." Seeing the doubt in his expression, she continued, "Really, I'm good. I was just asking if something in the future happens. You know that I have no family. I am alone and thought I could ask you if something did come up. It's not about anything right now." She was muddling this all up, she knew, but she just wanted some reassurance.

"Tell me," he demanded.

"Daniel, please let it go. Everything's fine, I promise. Forget about it. It's something I may need help with in the future. That's all. Promise me you won't give it another thought."

"I promise. If you need anything, all you have to do is just let me know."

"I sincerely appreciate that. Being able to count on you means a lot. It's getting late; we should head back."

As they rode toward town, Daniel's mind was hung up on her request. What could she possibly be alluding to? He couldn't miss the gravity of her words. He would do anything for her. He would scoop her up right now and take her to his ranch, protect her, keep her from whatever was troubling her, if he thought he could get away with it.

Too quickly, they were back in front of Ruth's. He dismounted and tied Triumph to the rail. He stepped over and helped her down, again, holding her close for far too long. Oh, how he wanted to embrace and kiss her again.

She took a step back, breaking the spell. "Thank you for letting me ride Sterling. He is truly wonderful."

"Any time, and I mean that. Can I see you tomorrow?"

"No. I'm afraid tomorrow is going to be a full day. I will let you know when things ease up." She turned and walked up the stairs, placed her hand on the doorknob and turned back to him and said, "Really, I appreciate all you have done for me." She opened the door and closed it behind her before he could say anything more.

She entered her room and shut the door. Her bed looked so inviting; living a double life wore her out. She pulled out her luggage and removed her backpack. Reassuring herself that her favorite pieces of clothing were there, waiting for her, she placed them on top of her bag for quick retrieval later. She zipped the bill of sale securely in one of the backpack pockets, then pushed all of it back under her bed.

As she lay there, she mentally scanned the diagram of her plans. Rachel will ride with Hashké and that should be the start of things with them. Two days in Hashké's arms would do that for any woman. Her jealousy sparked when she thought about someone else where she had belonged, but she buried it down deep. It was for the best.

On the ride to the cabin, she would periodically check her compass so she could find her way back to Santa Fe. And when she could, she would slip away, leaving Rachel to take her place with Hashké. He would fall for her, who wouldn't? She was beautiful and sweet; Arianna couldn't have picked a better choice even if she had 20 women to choose from. It was meant to be.

Rachel knocked lightly at Arianna's door; breaking the tunneling mess her mind was in, letting her know that dinner was ready. Arianna pulled Rachel into her room and closed the door. "Are you and Sarah ready for tonight?"

"Yes. We will wait for you inside our room off of the kitchen."

"And are you okay with riding on Hashké's horse in front of him? I promise he will keep you from falling off."

She nodded and smiled.

"Great. I am very ready to leave this place, too!" She opened the door and let Rachel go down first, then hung the signal cloth out the window by closing it on a corner, confirming things were still on for tonight.

Dinner dragged on for what seemed like hours. The torture of disingenuous, back-and-forth chatter finally ended, and she politely left the table for her room. She had several hours to kill; she knew her mind would spend them thinking about how empty life will be without her love in it. Even if she did let another man in at some point, she knew deep down in her soul that it would never be like it is with Hashké.

Several hours passed since darkness fell on the streets of Santa Fe. Arianna had been counting the chimes every hour on the big clock in the entry. After allowing several minutes to pass after the latest quarter-hour chime, she crept down the stairs and spied the clock to make sure she was correct. It was 11:23, perfect. She quietly went back up the stairs and changed into her beloved leggings and leather top Hashké made for her. She shoved the dresses and her too-tight shoes into her luggage bag. The comb that he made her, the coin purse with most of the brother's money still in it, and the bill of sale were in her backpack. She tucked away $40.00 of the unspent money into a zipper pocket on the side. After slinging it onto her shoulders, she grabbed the bag and silently crept down the servant stairs. She slowly opened the back door and nodded to Hashké, who was holding the reins of three horses. She went to the room where the women were waiting and motioned them out. The three women left the house of horrors for the last time, noiselessly shutting the back door behind them. Hashké embraced his sister, then lifted her onto the paint. He walked to Arianna, kissed her senseless, then put her up on her mare, tying her luggage behind her saddle. She patted her old friend. He walked back to Rachel, set her in place, then swung up behind her. As they walked out of town, they did so in single file, disguising their number. The eerie silence struck Arianna; even the horses weren't making any of the usual sounds of clopping down a hard-packed road. She looked down at the horse in front of her and saw leather boots fashioned around each hoof. She marveled at Native American ingenuity.

As soon as they had reached the tree line with his brothers concealed in its shadows, Hashké dismounted and one by one, slipped off every boot from the horse's hooves and tucked them into a pack.

Bidzii looked toward the young woman on Hashké's horse and his chest tightened, the hairs on his arm standing on end. He was sure his heart stopped beating as well. She must have sensed him staring because she turned to look at him and smiled. He looked away, taken aback by his reaction to her and unprepared to deal with the completely foreign feelings welling up from uncharted depths.

Hashké jumped back up on his horse and they cantered off, continuing in single file, still wanting to conceal their number.

22

Daniel rode into town and got a rude surprise when he went to Ruth's to ask Arianna out for dinner later that night. He knocked on the door and when no one answered he opened it and stepped inside, calling for Rachel, then Ruth. No one answered. He searched the house, but it was completely empty.

He walked back out the front door, closing it behind him and went down the street trying to get some answers. He peered into the café window and spied Ruth eating lunch. He walked in.

Seeing him, Ruth called out, "Oh, Daniel, the worst thing has happened. My dear friend and yours has disappeared!"

"Arianna is gone? What do you mean?" he asked, alarmed.

"Yes, this morning I called for the girls, wondering why breakfast wasn't ready, and they were nowhere to be found so I went upstairs to see if Arianna knew what had happened to them. Her room was empty."

"Did she mention she was going to go anywhere?"

"No, not at all. As a matter of fact, we had planned to go to the bank today to finalize the Henderson house purchase."

"That is peculiar. But why is Rachel or Sarah not around, either?"

"Well, that's just the thing, I sold them to Arianna the night before last so she would have domestic help in her new house. And now everyone is gone. I didn't have anyone to even cook my breakfast. It is just awful. I had to put my order into Jake for two more girls, but I don't have Rachel to train them anymore. However will I manage?"

Not a believer in slavery of any kind, Daniel said rather curtly, "I'm sure you will survive." He asked one more question, sure he knew the answer, but still it needed asking. "Did she owe you any money? Did she pay her bill?"

"Yes, of course. As per my policies, she paid me the week in advance, but I think I will keep her refund, she gave me no notice of her leaving and the girls were supposed to stay until I had replacements. I am truly disappointed in Arianna, she did not go along with the plan we had agreed on."

"I thought so, I just had to ask."

He got up and walked back to the boarding house to see if he could find any evidence of wrongdoing. What else could explain her sudden disappearance? His mind, again, reminded him that yesterday she asked him if she could come to him for help. This whole thing wasn't setting well with him. She must have been in trouble and wasn't able to get word to him. He walked all around the house but found no evidence of wrongdoing, nothing out of place.

Convinced she needed him, he bounded onto Sterling's saddle and rode off toward Fort Marcy. He would scour the entire state looking for her. Hell, he would scour the entire nation to find her. He rode Sterling hard to the fort to gather some troops to help him in his search.

~ ~ ~

It wasn't until noon on the second day when the small gang of liberators and liberated reached the secret cabin. They dismounted and released the horses who trotted off to graze.

Hashké stalked toward Arianna and gave out a loud, boisterous war cry befitting those old western movies. When he reached her, he bent down and slung her over his shoulder. He carried her off into the woods without a word to those around.

She laughed but complained, "Hashké put me down! We have company. We can't just go off and leave Rachel and your sister."

As they disappeared, the rest of their party looked on smiling, shaking their heads.

Shándíín asked her other two brothers what was going on.

"He's full of love for her," Bidzii told her.

"How did this happen?" she asked.

"It is a very long story. I will let her tell you tonight at the meal. Adika'í and I will go and hunt now. What is she called?" He nodded toward her friend.

"The white people call her Rachel. She was taken as a babe and does not remember her name or her people."

"She looks Ute." He said with a hint of disdain for that tribe.

"She may be, but she was a good friend to me. You will be nice no matter what tribe she is from," his sister insisted.

He nodded and the brothers left to find their meal.

Rachel and Shándíín gathered wood and started a fire. They sat down and Rachel let out the breath she had been holding for two days. Shándíín hugged her. Their nightmare was over, they were finally free.

Hashké put Arianna down beside the hot spring. He roughly pulled her clothes off and then undressed himself. He picked her back up and carried her into the water.

Arianna let him have his way.

They sank into the warm water and she immediately relaxed. It felt so good to be home. Home? Yes, this did feel like home. She tried not to think about all that implied, it helped when Hashké started kissing and stroking her. *God, I love this man.*

He placed her on his lap as he lowered himself onto their favorite rock that sat a couple of feet underwater.

She should name it The Sex Rock or maybe The Rock of Love, Rock of Seduction? But all her thoughts scattered when his fingers entered her. She caught her breath and melted onto his shoulder.

He stroked her woman's mound and plunged his digits in and out until he could sense her getting close. He turned her around, so her back was to his front, her legs on either side of his. He guided himself into her and she gasped. She was so tight. He took his time to fully seat inside her. He pulsed a few times in her and she moaned. He grasped her hips and lifted her and then pulled her back down on him. She felt him differently in this position. She arched her back and he lost control. He quickened his pace, splashing water everywhere. He grabbed her breasts as he started to come. She came apart just as he shot deep inside her. After a few more jerks, his muscles loosened and she slumped back against his chest, his arms around her, holding her securely to him.

She could have fallen asleep right there and then, in her love's arms. She didn't know how much time had passed when she heard Bidzii yelling something in Navajo to Hashké. He answered and then kissed her neck as he reluctantly got up and out of the warm water. They dressed and he held her close as they walked back to the camp. His brothers were preparing some meat for the flame and the women were sitting close to one another talking.

As they walked up, Shándíín called to Hashké, "So, you want to tell me what is going on, you having love for a bilagáana?" She smiled, teasing him. He sheepishly nodded and picked Arianna up again and kissed her while she was in his arms to demonstrate just how he did feel. "Okay, okay, we get it. I hear there is quite a story to you two and this unusual pairing."

Hashké sat Arianna down so she faced the women and then sat next to her. "You will not believe it if we told you," he said.

"Try us. We want to hear."

He looked to Arianna asking her if she wanted to tell the story. "Should I tell them everything?" she asked. He nodded. She took a deep breath and told how she was from a different century and how she got here. Then she told of the wolf attack and Hashké's care. By the time she ended, the meat was ready and her audience was stunned.

She finished by saying, "That's why I went to get you both, I owe your brother my life. It was the least I could do." Hashké and Adika'í served everyone the meat, with Bidzii making sure Rachel was given the first piece.

It was just then that Arianna remembered the business part of the ordeal. She got up and went into the cabin, retrieved the money that was still left, along with the distasteful purchase agreement paper, and came back to the fire and handed all of it to Hashké. He looked at her questioningly and she told him it was the money left over and bill of sale. He smiled then set it aside without looking at it, keeping her from having to explain the amount remaining.

As Arianna spoke, Bidzii's eyes kept drifting to Rachel. She shyly returned his glance, but not right away. He was still surprised by his feelings toward her. Earlier, he had to restrain himself from yanking her off Hashké's horse. He wanted to lash out at his brother for holding her while they rode. Their lives were in danger and that was what he focused on? He needed to get himself back under control. She had just been freed from a life of slavery; she didn't need any other complications. But his body and mind were not so willing to comply.

As they ate, they peppered Arianna and Hashké with several questions. The conversation then turned to what is to be done now. It was decided that another cabin needed to be built for Shándíín and Rachel. But until it could be constructed, the women would sleep in the cabin with Arianna. Hashké disagreed. He did not want to sleep without his love by his side, but after some serious ribbing from his siblings, he relinquished.

Arianna was grateful. As much as she loved sleeping with Hashké, she would never be able to sneak off if she did. She figured she would wait another day or two, letting everyone begin to relax into daily life, then try. That would give her time to sneak some jerky into her backpack and fill her water bottles without being seen.

The next two days came and went without Hashké giving a second thought to Rachel, but Arianna supposed it was due to her still being in the picture. As soon as she wasn't around, she was sure nature would take its course and her plan would be fulfilled.

She planned to leave that night. The mare has had plenty of time to rest and she had all of the supplies she needed, plus she had her compass to guide her way. She should be fine. She would not go straight into Santa Fe but to the outskirts, to Reeves' Ranch and wait until she saw Daniel ride out. She would catch up with him and explain as best she could what she did and why.

After the meal, she announced she was turning in early because she was tired. She was, in fact, exhausted, and she didn't know why; the big pressure was over, no one's life was relying on her to save them, and really, all that was left was to just sneak out of Hashké's world. Maybe she was getting ready to start her period. That would be just perfect. How long had it been anyway? She completely lost track, it should be soon. But with all of the pressure and stress, her body may just skip this one, she thought as she entered the cabin. She looked through the packs to find the dress Hashké bought at the trading post, it would be perfect for any interactions she may have during her travels to her butte. Once she shoved it into her backpack, she laid down and closed her eyes for just a little bit.

Thank God, she woke in the middle of the night having to go to the bathroom, or she would have slept the entire night away, she thought.

She carefully slunk out from the bedroll and as quietly as she could, made her way outside with her backpack secured on her shoulders. She crept to where she had hidden the mare's bridle at the edge of the woods behind the big tree to the north. Her heart was pounding but she still needed to empty her bladder, so she did her business, then gathered the bridle and walked to the mare. She didn't bother saddling her;

it would make too much commotion plus a missing saddle last night would have drawn unwanted attention to her plan. She easily slipped the bridle onto the mare and led her to her mounting rock. Once seated, she squeezed her into a quiet walk until they were far enough away for the mare to be able to pick up a canter without being heard. She didn't know what time it was, but she knew it was later than she had planned on leaving. She really wanted more than just a couple of hours' head start before day break. It was still dark and hard for her to see the compass clearly so she had to guess at her direction for a little while longer, then she would set her course and strictly follow it.

She rode on until the sun's morning light started chasing the darkness across the horizon. Looking down at her compass, she found she was off the mark. She turned the mare to correct their direction and continued on.

Rachel woke just before dawn. It was her body's normal rhythm, after years of captivity. She walked outside and saw the men were up as well. They were going to start on the new cabin today. She nodded to them and went to do her business. When she returned, the place was in an uproar. Hashké called out to her as she came back, "Have you seen Arianna?"

"No, not since I went to bed last night. Is she missing?"

He nodded and sprinted to get his horse's bridle and his weapons. He grabbed a couple of handfuls of jerky as well and shoved it into his pouch. His brothers were walking the perimeter of the pasture, looking for her trail. Bidzii found something and signaled Hashké. He whistled for his horse, who galloped toward him. Hashké deftly slipped the bridle on. He swung up and galloped to where his brother was. He spotted the trail and raced after his woman.

One thought ran through his mind; he was going to seriously punish her. She promised she would stay. *Why would she go? Did she not want him anymore?* He thought she did, her passion was as bright as his when they made love. Could she be going back to that white man? Her direction did not indicate that but maybe she planned to meet him elsewhere to try to throw him off their tracks.

He couldn't, wouldn't live without her. He would run her down and tie her to him. He would make her sleep outside with him on his pallet from now on, until they finished the second cabin.

About an hour into his gallop, her tracks changed direction back toward Santa Fe. He would kill that white man, then she would have no reason to leave again. He would enjoy doing it, too.

It wasn't quite another hour when he found her.

She heard the pounding of a horse's hooves and could feel it was Hashké even before turning to look which she did anyway. He was bent low on his horse, in a flat-out run toward her.

Her heart started pounding from knowing she had been found out; in an unconscious flight response, she squeezed the mare into a run. The mare did so but traitorously whinnied to the stallion in a friendly greeting. It felt like her heart was going to leap right out of her chest as she flew across the grassy terrain. The pounding hooves were getting closer. She looked back and saw the fierce, determined expression on his face and knew there was nothing to do, so she pulled up and slowed the mare.

Hashké slowed his stallion but didn't stop. Instead, he rode alongside her and bent toward the mare's reins, yanking them out of Arianna's hands, yelling to her to hold on.

Arianna did not understand why they didn't just stop and talk about it, but did as he demanded and grabbed the mare's mane. As they galloped into a dense tree line Arianna looked back and could see a far-off cloud of dust in the direction they had come from. They plunged down into a gully carved steep from rain runoff. Once they were deep enough that they couldn't see out onto the flat plain they had come from, Hashké slowed them to a stop.

He was enraged.

She braced for his wrath, but it didn't come.

He placed his finger over his mouth signaling her to be silent. He cocked his head as if he were trying to listen for something. He dismounted and crawled up to the crest and spied ten soldiers and that man Arianna had the carriage ride with. He looked back at her with a dangerous glare. She flinched in response and just sat there waiting for his fury. They stayed there, not moving or saying a word for a good 30 minutes, she guessed.

Once he was sure the soldiers were far enough away, he started into her at a whispered yell. "Do you want to be with him, that yellow-haired Daniel? Is that what you want? They are looking for you." Before she could answer he continued. "If you do, I will kill him, and put an end to that."

"No, you can't. I don't want him. I was just going to get his help to get back to my butte so I could leave you in peace, with a pretty Indian woman for you to love."

"What are you speaking of?"

"Rachel. I brought Rachel back for you. She is beautiful and sweet. She knows how to cook and can actually help you and not be completely dependent on you, like I am. I am no good for you. She is." Tears started cascading as she finally confessed what she had been holding inside for so long.

"You are not right here," He said, pointing to her head.

"But don't you think Rachel is beautiful?"

"No, I do not look at her in such a way. Bidzii does, but I do not."

"Your brother likes her?" Arianna asked in between sniffles.

"Yes, he has not said as much but I have seen the way he looks at her."

"That can't be; I brought her back for you."

"I do not want her. I want only you!"

"Oh, Hashké, I had all of this planned out so you could have someone you deserve, not some scarred, disfigured person who is nothing but trouble for you."

He plucked her off her horse, pulled her to a fallen tree trunk, sat and bent her over his knees and paddled her. And not the fun way, either.

"Hashké, stop. Please stop. I'm sorry. Please, Hashké!" She exclaimed through her sobs.

When he felt she had the punishment deserving such statements, he ceased. "You will never say such things ever again. Do you understand?"

"Yes, Hashké," she said.

He started removing her clothes. She let him. She knew she was never going to be allowed out of his sight or touch ever again. But truly, she didn't mind. She didn't want to be away from him either, if he didn't want anyone else. She tried to give him what he should have; he refused it. Now she can be at peace.

She gave herself up to him and they made love right there, in the dry bed of the gully, full of passion and tenderness.

They slowly dressed and he put her back on her mare but didn't give her the reins. He mounted the stallion and led her back. She knew why he took her reins, but it didn't make it any easier to swallow the obeisant state it implied.

They made it back to the cabin by the evening meal. Over dinner, Hashké told his brothers of the soldiers and that they were looking for Arianna. With their grim expressions, she guessed this would mean a great deal of trouble for them.

"What if I go and tell him that I do not wish to be found," she offered.

Hashké looked at her as if she committed a heinous crime. "You will not ever go again."

"Okay, I won't, I promise, but what if I write him a letter or something."

"You will have nothing to do with him or I will kill him and end this once and for all."

Arianna knew he was serious, deadly serious.

She wanted to make this better but didn't know how. They finished dinner and bedded down for the night. Arianna, of course was sleeping outside, next to Hashké. He pulled her close to him and put an arm and a leg over her securing her to him. She knew it would be like this for a while to come. But truly, she didn't mind; she loved having him wrapped around her. She slept soundly for the first time in days.

At breakfast Hashké studied her for a long time.

"What?" she asked.

"Where are your earrings?"

"Oh, that. I traded them for Shándíín and Rachel."

"Why would you do such a thing? They were a gift from your parents."

"Ruth wouldn't sell the women for a reasonable amount, but she liked my earrings, they were an easy trade. Really, it was the least I could do. Did you know your sister was beaten? I could not let that happen again for either of them. I had something Ruth wanted so I traded them. Not a big deal."

He held her, thanking her for her sacrifice. He would endeavor to replace them somehow.

She smiled up at him shrugging her shoulders. They were nothing compared to the lives of two women.

23

The next few weeks were spent building the new cabin and enjoying each other's company. Rachel was even teaching Bidzii some English, the language he vowed never to speak. He was falling hard. With the extra money they now had, they were able to purchase supplies that were a luxury: flour, butter, jam, and some vegetables. They even purchased seeds to plant in a garden.

Life was good. The only cloud was that she knew Daniel was continuing his search for her. She wished he would just give up, already. She secretly thought that he just needed to get laid and focus his attention on the next woman.

Arianna still had not seen the slightest hint of her period. Deep in her gut she knew why but hadn't said anything yet. Frankly, she was a little scared. What would it mean to be pregnant and give birth in the nineteenth century? She needed to tell Hashké but telling him would make it real. She was at the most, two months pregnant; she thought she could wait a little longer before she had to say anything. She was going to make sure the pregnancy was well seated before bringing it up. Hashké would be thrilled, she knew. She didn't want to get his hopes up until she was sure and out here that meant time.

Meanwhile, rumors were beginning to make their way north of the terrible conditions the Navajo were forced to endure at the Indian internment camp, Bosque Redondo, near Ft.

Sumner. She knew it wouldn't be too much longer and the brothers would be off to do something about it. They were not the sort to stand by and watch if they could help.

With the second cabin finished, it was decided that Adika'í would slip down from the mountains to gather information. He would leave the next morning.

That night, the meal was unusually quiet.

Adika'í was very comfortable with his mission. He was used to living on the outskirts. He told jokes, trying to break the somber atmosphere. Getting away was actually a relief for him. Staying in one place for so long was making his skin crawl. He needed action. This domestic tranquility with all its trappings was getting on his nerves.

He left at daybreak.

Arianna was working in the garden when she got light-headed. She bent over to try to settle her brain. Hashké saw and rushed over to her.

"Are you ill?" he asked.

"No, I'm fine. My head just swam for a moment. I guess I didn't eat enough or something."

He looked at her like she wasn't telling him the truth, then asked "Why have you not told me yet?"

"What are you talking about? You don't know everything," she insisted. He looked at her with that astute visage he wore, probably since childhood. It really annoyed her. In response, she blurted out, "I think I'm pregnant. There, I said it; are you happy now?"

Hashké whisked her up and twirled her around, kissing her.

She yelled, "Hashké, put me down. I'm going to be sick."

He immediately set her down gently and looked deeply into her eyes and said, "Thank you. Yes, I am very happy." Full of awe, he kissed her deeply.

Shándíín and Rachel, who had just returned from the stream, asked if everything was all right. Full of pride, Hashké announced, beaming, "Arianna is with child." High-pitched shrieks erupted from the girls as they rushed over to Arianna.

GINA HOFFMAN

Hearing the commotion, Bidzii walked toward them with a puzzled look on his face. Hashké gladly explained. His brother clapped him on the shoulder, congratulating him on his prowess.

There was a sense of elation in the camp, but Arianna was not swayed by the euphoria. A considerable part of her was actually frightened and unsure. A hospital, complete with modern medication and sterility, would be what she would prefer, thank you very much.

Hashké, sensing her reticence, took her on a walk to her favorite place, the hot spring. He lovingly removed her clothing and followed her in. She breathed deeply, calmly, allowing the stress to wash away from her.

Hashké moved behind her, his front to her back and sat on the Rock of Love with her. He reverently placed his hand on her stomach. She leaned her head back on his shoulder. He took advantage of her exposed neck and kissed her there, softly, intensely. He whispered in her ear, "I love you and our baby."

She turned to face him and looked at him, amazed how this warrior who could kill in seconds was now taken down, bowing in adoration at her feet by the idea of the tiny being growing inside her. She felt so empowered at that moment, like the queen of the world. She straddle Hashké, the feeling of sovereignty flowing around her like the warm water of the spring. In that moment of awareness, she made love to him with the utmost solemnity. He sat there on the rock in the pool beneath her accepting her position of supremacy. They came in sync with an intoxicating orgasm that left them both satiated in each other's arms.

The walk back to the camp was slow, with their fingers tangled in each other's. But the reality of daily life had Hashké and his brother leaving to hunt not long after. Later, dinner was consumed with looks of intensity not just between Hashké and her but also between Bidzii and Rachel.

ANYTIME, ANYWHERE

It was only a matter of time, Hashké thought. And as it turned out, that time was only minutes. As Arianna got into bed, Hashké saw his brother leading Rachel into the woods.

24

dika'í returned 10 days later. Over dinner he explained the situation. He told them that the food being given to their people was more often than not spoiled and tainted with worms and vermin, and many were dying from stomach sickness. No steps were being taken to correct this by the army. They did not care if the Navajo die.

Adika'í went on to explain further that the army's attempt to house the Navajo was woefully inadequate. They tried to get them to live in barrack-type housing where many of the previous occupants had died. This goes directly against Navajo ways. If a person dies in their hogan, that hogan is sealed and a new one is built. This is to prevent any evil left from attaching itself to an unwitting occupant. So, many of the Navajo were sleeping out in the open or in ditches, with only a single blanket for warmth and many not even that, because there weren't enough blankets to go around.

Wood for warmth and cooking was scarce. Many were walking up to 20 miles and back to find wood for their fires; all trees that were closer had been chopped down. They had to do this every day because they were not given a horse or cart to carry the wood, they could only bring back that which they could carry on their backs and in their arms.

Their people were wasting away, and the situation was dire. All of the promises made by Carleton to feed and clothe and protect those who surrendered were not being kept. Bosque Redondo was even raided by other tribes like the Comanche, the Ute, and by Mexicans who stole away unguarded women and children for slavery. The army did nothing to stop them.

As Adika'í gave his report, the atmosphere turned to ever-increasing outrage. They had heard things were bad but could never have imagined such atrocities.

"We have to do something!" Shándíín declared. They all agreed.

"We must get messages into the camp and tell them that it is possible to live in hiding and that there is plenty of game in the northern foothills and mountains," Adika'í suggested.

"Yes, and that we will guide them to the safer areas," Hashké offered.

"We will need to prepare; hunt many animals to dry the meat into jerky for them to eat on the journey back," Bidzii said.

"Yes, that is good planning. Will we leave the women here?" Adika'í asked.

"No," Shàndíín demanded, continuing, "since the soldiers are already looking for you, my brothers, I should go into the camp. They will not be expecting a woman to bring a message to get the people to leave."

"She has a point," Arianna interjected.

"Then she should go but Arianna and Rachel should stay," Hashké decided.

"But what about Reeves and the soldiers from Fort Marcy, they are still searching for Arianna. They might stumble upon our cabin. With no men here to protect them, they could easily be taken," Bidzii added.

Hashké cursed. "We cannot leave them unprotected."

Rachel said in her shy voice, "Then we all go."

"I think that is the only way we can ensure the women are safe, but Arianna will have to travel more slowly due to her being with child," Hashké said.

Adika'í asked, "What is this?"

Hashké grinned broadly and proudly proclaimed, "Arianna and I are expecting a babe!"

"Blessings are on you and your mate, my brother! That will not be a problem. We will go ahead, get things started. Your delay won't impede our plan," Adika'í said.

"I can ride without causing stress to my pregnancy. In my time it has been shown that a woman can continue to exercise as long as her body was used to doing it before becoming pregnant. I will be just fine," Arianna claimed.

Hashké wasn't convinced. "We will take our time," he said while giving her his 'behave' signal.

Arianna threw up her hands in a gesture of exasperation.

Shándíín added, "It is settled then, we will ride out as soon as we are able to dry enough meat; what do you think, three or four mature bucks?"

"Four. We should also make some dried cakes. Hashkè can go and purchase the flour and corn we need from the trading post," Bidzii agreed.

"That gives us a week, no, two, before we go." Adika'í said.

"It is decided," Bidzii declared and got up to check on the horses for the night. Rachel followed him.

Arianna was helped up by Handsome and they went into their cabin.

"Hashké, I will be fine. I am in good shape. The baby will be okay," Arianna tried to explain.

"I will not discuss this with you."

She knew it was a doomed cause from the start, but she had to try to argue her case. She decided to pick her battles and curled up in Hashké's arms for the night.

~ ~ ~

By the end of the second week, they had enough meat drying and cakes made for their plans. The first group started off, taking some of the jerky and cakes with them, but the bulk would be coming on pack horses led by Arianna and Hashké.

The journey was about 250 miles. They had agreed to meet at the south side of the lake located about 12 miles to the northwest of the fort.

Arianna wanted to go much faster but since she didn't know the way, she had no choice but to follow Hashké's pace. It took them three days longer to meet up with his siblings on the banks of the lake. Over the evening meal, they caught up on all that had happened.

Shándíín explained, "I have been able to establish contact with two clan leaders who are open to leaving the fort, Barboncito and Ganado Blanco. They have been living peacefully as they promised but Carleton has not kept his word. They are tired of the white man's lies. They think that life outside the fort could not be any worse than it is in. They are going to spread the word quietly among those they trust and see how many want to leave. I am to give them two days and then return for the count. I will come back here with the information and we will make the plan for the return journey. Right now, the soldiers are not guarding our people very closely. I think they realize that the Navajo need to find food and gather wood for their fires to survive so they are often outside the encampment. It is a good time for a number to leave. But I am afraid that the number will not be large; our people are very weary. They have no fight left in them. They are weakened. It is very sad to see."

"We will bring any and all we can, even if it is not much. You have done well, Shándíín," Hashké complimented her. "We will wait for the numbers then."

That night Arianna and Hashkè shared a pallet as they always did. The only difference was that Hashké now held her slight baby bump instead of her breast all night. She was very contented no matter where they were.

The next day came and went slowly. On the day that followed, Shándíín left after breakfast. When she returned, all activity stopped awaiting her news.

"We will have around four hundred Navajo coming with us. Do we have them all leave at once or over several days?" Shándíín asked.

As the eldest, Bidzii decided: "A hundred and fifty should come in the morning, a hundred more staggered throughout the day, but the bulk following at dark. Once all are at the lake they will be fed and then rest for a few hours overnight. We start the journey early the next morning. I would like to head out that night, but I fear they will not be in any condition for that. Best to feed them and let them regain strength, then set out."

Everyone agreed.

Shándíín and Adika'í headed back to the camp to relay the news to Barboncito and Ganado Blanco. She would lead those in the morning group. Adika'í would wait and bring the midday group. Barboncito and Ganado Blanco would lead the third group under the cover of darkness since they were too recognizable to slip out unnoticed during the day.

Late morning, the first group reached the camp and was fed. Mid-afternoon, the second group started filtering in but with disturbing news. Adika'í gathered his brothers and told them, "I was recognized by a Ute that I gambled with and won a lot of money from a couple of years ago and who might still hold a grudge. I don't know why he was in the camp, but he could be trouble."

"Well, we will deal with it if something comes of it," Bidzii told his youngest brother.

When the third group arrived, the women fed the last of the refugees and helped them bed down for the night as the brothers met with the clan leaders. They explained the situation and Barboncito offered to send one of his trusted men back to the fort to monitor the situation. If there was a problem, he was to steal a horse and ride to alert them. If all was well, he was to follow at his own pace after making sure no alert was sounded. The directions to the secret cabin were given to the man and he left to go back to the fort.

They all rested except for the few who were stationed as guards. When dawn broke, the people were fed, and the camp dismantled. Every trace of them having been there was erased. They walked in two columns to hide their numbers.

25

On the third day of their journey, the exodus halted as a rider rode up fast from behind, yelling to them. The rider dismounted as the horse was still moving and called to the leaders as he tried to catch his breath. Someone handed him a skin with water in it. He took a big swallow and started telling them what happened.

When Arianna heard the rider approach, her stomach dropped to the ground, knowing it could only be bad news.

In Navajo, the man explained in between gasping breaths, "Word made it from the Apache to the guards that something was afoot. An Apache saw Shándíín talking to Barboncito and Ganado Blanco several times earlier in the week. He was interested in her and asked about her. Others who knew of her explained who her tribe was. Then when he saw Adika'í the day everyone left, he put it together that your family was responsible for talking the Navajo into leaving. Now they want to make an example of you and what you have done. To discourage any more Navajo from leaving, they have set up a forty-mile perimeter around Bosque Redondo. They had orders to shoot any Indian leaving the camp without a pass. They have also sent out many soldiers to find and kill all who were responsible for leaving."

As he gulped in air, continuing to try to catch his breath, the brothers looked at each other. Bidzii said, "We must leave these people and draw the soldiers away from them. It is clear they do not care about these Navajo, only about us and our insubordination. We knew this was a risk."

Hashké translated for Arianna and Rachel.

As the clan leaders and the brothers talked, Arianna pulled Hashké aside and asked, "What about my butte? What if we went back there and tried to go to my time? I don't want to die, and I know you don't either, and I think the soldiers will not stop until they find us and end us. I think it is our only option." She stopped and thought for a moment, then continued, "I do know I was brought here for a reason and I don't think that it is so I could die here. Whether or not it will work is another thing, but we should try. Do you know how to get us back there?"

"I do not want to lose what I have finally found." He said as he put his hand on her belly. He continued, "So I think you are correct, and we should try."

He turned to his brothers and pulled them aside to tell them what Arianna and he were thinking. They too, agreed it was worth the attempt. If nothing else, it would be in a different direction from the people they freed, who were headed north toward Canyon de Chelly.

They gave Barboncito and Ganado Blanco the packhorses and all the food except for what the small band needed while they tried to make a run for it. Soon they took off, leaving the escaped Navajo with hopes of living a free, peaceful, and plentiful life.

Galloping the horses toward the northwest, the small band no longer had the luxury to take the journey at an easy pace. Arianna tried to appease Hashké's concerns. She could see his worry. She did feel fine. The mare had a wonderfully smooth canter. She couldn't have picked out a better mount for a journey in her condition.

It took them three days to find her butte, on the horizon. Luckily, they had been able to stay a day ahead of the cavalry that were indeed, hunting them. If the entrance to the cave was not open, they might still have time to get out of sight near their first camp by the stream. From there, they could hide their trail by walking up the stream a good way and then to California, perhaps. She always loved California.

26

A s Hashké got to the base of the butte, he pulled up his stallion, dismounted, and went to help Arianna down from her mare.

After setting her feet back on the dry desert ground, Arianna heard that wonderful, awful noise, of a small dog barking. She shouted, "Hallelujah! Yep, that blessed Shih Tzu! Do you hear it?!"

Hashké held her as he strained to listen. Then he heard it, too. "Yes!" he exclaimed, picking her up and twirling her. He sat her back down as she reminded everyone that the dog barking was what got her to climb the rocks the first time.

"We have to get to that cliff up there," she said pointing at it. "It isn't a difficult climb, but you do have to plan your foot and hand placements carefully. I will go first since I have been up there many times already and have the way memorized."

Arianna's mind was going this way and that trying to think about what was about to happen, hopefully. She pondered on all of the possible ramifications and outcomes. "We have to free the horses. If this doesn't work and we are stuck in this time, Hashké, you can whistle for your horse, right, and we can use him to round up the others? But if it does work and we do time travel, we will need resources to help us settle in my time, so bring all the blankets; they are worth a fortune in the twenty-first century. Oh heck, bring everything else you think we might need or could use."

They gathered their resources in bundles the men would carry on their backs up the cliff.

Arianna turned to her new family and asked them, "Are you sure you all want to come to my time? It is very different and will take some getting used to, but I think you will like it. I will help you adjust. White people and Indians are free to be with anyone they want. The old prejudices are mostly gone. You can do whatever you want as long as it does no harm to anyone else. The world will be open to you. The Navajo live in peace. They are no longer hunted and persecuted. They are free to go anywhere, live anywhere, do anything they want. What do you say?"

They unanimously agreed that the future sounded a whole lot better than their present situation.

Arianna turned to start climbing. Hashké followed her. He wanted to be there if she slipped. Next, Bidzii sent up Shándíín and Adika'í. As they reached the top, he sent Rachel up and then followed her.

As Arianna reached the cliff, she saw the little dog. There he was, in all of his red-bowed glory. She crouched down and patted her thighs trying to get him to come to her, feeling a one-sided kinship with him, but he still wouldn't draw near, that little Shih Tzu! She turned to focus her attention on those coming up behind. Hashké pulled himself onto the landing and then saw the dog. He started laughing. It really was a little dog with a red bow on his head.

Arianna said, "See, I wasn't just telling stories; there he is." Hashké smiled at her and gave her a big hug.

"Are you feeling okay? he asked as he put his hand on her tummy.

"Yes, we are fine. Now help your sister."

He obeyed and turned to assist Shándíín. He pulled her up and then next, offered his hand to Adika'í.

Arianna turned her attention to the rock wall; then she saw it, the entrance to the cave was wide open! She turned to the ones who were already up on the cliff and shouted, "It's open, it's open!" She followed the dog into the cave and Hashké trailed after. She had forgotten how dark it was in the interior. She let her eyes adjust and could now make out the carvings. Hashké studied the depictions as she went outside to see if everyone made it up; she directed them inside.

Once all were in the cave she explained, "The first time, I chased the dog in here and saw all of the carvings. Then my attention went to this middle pillar. The dog tripped me, and I put my hand down on here to steady myself and stop my fall," she said as she pointed to the spiral carving with a hand in the center.

"Should I put my hand down now? Is everyone ready?"

"Yes," Bidzii commanded.

She held her breath and reverently placed her hand in the center of the carving. Nothing happened.

"Dang!" she said as she removed her hand. She took a minute to relive everything that had occurred that day and then excitedly said, "Blood! My hand was bloody that day. I need a knife."

Hashké unsheathed his knife and held it out to her. She could feel the skepticism around her, but she knew that it really had happened. She just had to remember every piece of the puzzle.

She sliced her scarred hand and gave the knife back to him. She held his hand with her left one as she placed her bloody hand back on the center of the carving and.... the sound of rocks rumbling could be heard.

EPILOGUE

NEW MEXICO 2013

Hashké stepped outside his home where Arianna and his children slept without worry. As he quietly shut the door behind him, he walked the few steps to the railing that ran the length of their wrap-around porch and leaned down, grasping the hand-hewn, lacquered wood and closed his eyes thanking Mother Earth and the holy people for his blessed life of peace and prosperity. He opened his eyes and scanned the hundreds of acres he and his family had purchased just a few miles outside the Navajo reservation. The sun was peeking over the horizon, decorating the sky with tones of blushing pink, cadmium orange, and butter yellow. The rays pushed their way around the barns but ran into the mountains to the north. The brisk morning would warm with the rise of the flaming star. Life was good.

Waking into the cave after they ventured across time, Hashké and his family gathered their possessions, walked out onto the cliff and saw the future world with hope in their hearts for a life filled with acceptance and possibility. They would not be disappointed.

Arianna pointed out the immediate visual differences between the two worlds by drawing their attention to the endless ribbon of road and the telephone cable and poles stitched alongside it. There was her lonely car, patiently waiting for her return. She explained what each of those visuals were and what they meant for their life in the twenty-first century. The rest would wait for the evening meal to expand on the advances the world made since their birth. For now they knew that when they scaled back down the butte, the cavalry would not be there to harass and incarcerate or kill them.

On the ground, Arianna and Hashké led the survivors to the stream where they met. It would be the perfect place to camp away from modern civilization while they slowly acclimated to the present time. There would be plenty of wild game and fresh clean water to hold them over until Arianna could arrange for permanent housing with money from the sale of their nineteenth-century goods.

Hashké's first ride in her car still made her giggle in delight and probably always would. His smile grew as their speed increased, cresting in a warrior's cry his ancestors would be very proud of as they reached highway speeds. After finding the work order under the windshield wiper, Arianna was thrilled that, indeed, her tire had been fixed. She had forgotten all about the reason she went hiking in the first place, her mind instead consumed by all the steps needed to get her new family settled in her time. She gave thanks for the thoughtful person who fixed her car even though she wasn't there. Arianna and Hashké timed their trip back to the city so that they would arrive at Arianna's apartment after dark, allowing Hashké to enter unnoticed, due to his ancient attire.

Arianna led him around her space, pointing out the modern conveniences, ending in the hot shower, which they both enjoyed together, intimately. He finally was able to understand what she was trying to describe by the creek so long ago.

Afterward, she ordered a meat-lovers pizza, which he did absolutely love, and consumed it together in front of the TV as Arianna taught him about the evils of a man-monopolized remote.

Arianna slept that night like the dead in her warm, comfy, soft bed. Hashké did not. Unfamiliar noises had him in a continuously alert state. She woke fully rested to find Hashké already awake, eyes darting this way and that with every sound. She realized too late that of course he wouldn't be able to rest in a modern city with all of its modern noises. Luckily, she would be the only one to leave the apartment today. Arianna had planned to go to the store to buy him a pair of Levi's and a couple of t-shirts with money she would get after selling one of the smaller knives they had brought back with them. She knew of an antique store that specialized in Native American antiquities. It was a business that stood out on her daily commute to the diner due to all of the colorful items displayed in the windows. But first, she would stop in the diner and quit her job. There would be no time for shifts, given all that needed to happen as quickly as possible. While her friends there were sad to see her go, they were thrilled for her newly found love, which was the reason she told them she was moving. A quick stop at the grocery store was all that was left to her errands.

Arianna returned to the apartment to find a normal twenty-first century event, a man, asleep on the couch while the TV softly droned on. She smiled as she tried to enter without waking him. He, of course, sat up, alerted to her entrance, then grinned mischievously. The dream he woke from must have been good. He crouched down and stalked toward her as she shut the door behind her. He wrapped her in his arms and began ravishing her as he carried her off to the bedroom.

~ ~ ~

It didn't take very long to sell, at premium prices, a few blankets along with some other artifacts they had brought with them. Collectors eagerly snatched up the pieces. They soon had enough to pay for the large piece of land they wanted in cash. They waited to sell the rest to pay for the five houses and two barns that currently sit on the property. The horse ranch they had envisioned was now a successful operation, employing each of the time travelers in one way or another, according to their interest.

Hashké and his brothers and sister regularly traveled to the Navajo Reservation to teach the young about the old ways, reinvigorating pride in their culture. While the true reason they had this highly prized knowledge was still a secret, nonetheless, one could see the effects of the growing pride in their culture; the young stood taller, more confident of their place in the world. Politics of the Navajo council were injected with vigor not seen in a long time.

REALM OF THE HOLY PEOPLE

The Navajo goddess, Changing Woman, felt the pull of thankfulness from one of her favorite children. She looked down on him and smiled. She knew the passion that he had before Arianna came into his life would be what would bind the pair together through the difficult road they had to travel to save the Navajos' light as well as their own. Arianna's ethnicity, tender heart and strong will as well as her deep desire to do the right thing, would help drive them to accomplish all she and the Holy People had hoped for. Although . . . Arianna's self-doubt of her own worth could have doomed the entire endeavor.

The course of action the gods conspired to bring about the current state of affairs was a complex one that all started during a simple conversation in the spiritual realm between herself and Arianna's father. They happened upon each other while watching the physical world with uneasiness, her for her people whose illumination was dimming, him for his daughter, whose own soul's luster had started to wane. They found a common desire to aid their children's circumstances and endeavored to work together to bring about the possibility for the changes needed for all concerned. The challenge was how to get Arianna to the place where the divide between the two realms was the thinnest. When Arianna's father shared her love of animals, Changing Woman brought in the trickster Coyote and the plan took shape. They agreed that he would go to the physical realm as a modern helpless, small breed of dog, and lure Arianna to the zone of subtlety, where time is more easily manipulated. This place is sacred to her children, the Navajo, and remains shrouded in secrecy.

Word soon spread throughout the spiritual planes and interest as well as suggestions poured in, helping to refine the plan into a fine jewel. Changing Woman could not be more pleased with the outcome. Hashké and his family are flourishing, and her people's light has brightened drastically. There continues to be work ahead but now the path is incandescent.

The End

ABOUT THE AUTHOR

Gina Hoffman started riding at the age of two when she refused to get off the pony ride at the state fair. Serious about her new passion, she started competing with her horses a short couple of years later, sparking a life-long love affair with the equestrian world.

She believes her greatest accomplishment is the raising of two fascinating young men. Luke, the oldest, is her well of encouragement. And Cameron, her first editor, always insisting she could do better.

While she continues to ride, she does so more for pleasure rather than competition. In this chapter of her life, she finds the most joy in writing stories and creating art.

www.authorginahoffman.com

CPSIA information can be obtained
at www.ICGtesting.com
Printed in the USA
FFHW020716290120
58084206-63169FF